LAURA THALASSA

D1707681

the Forsaken

BURNING EMBER PRESS

A Burning Ember Book
Published in the United States by Burning Ember Press, an imprint of Lavabrook Publishing Group.

Chapter 1

I PLUMMETED FROM the sky like a fallen angel. Except for maybe the fact that I was screaming like a banshee. Doubt any celestials fell with as little grace as I did. The wind snatched my shrieks away and shoved air down my throat.

I cannot believe this is happening.

I gripped Andre's hand tightly in my own. We hadn't let go of one another since we jumped from the jet. Already our plane was a small bead of light moving farther away from us with every passing second. It would land, and the House of Keys, the supernatural world's governing body, would descend on it like carrion to a kill. It would only take minutes more for them to realize we were not onboard.

We'd bought ourselves hours at most before the hunt resumed. And this time the monster that the Politia hunted was me.

Because they thought I was the Anti-Christ.

Needless to say, I wasn't having the best day.

Even with the light of the moon and my night vision, it was difficult to make out the geography beneath us. The land below glowed enough to alert me that Andre and I wouldn't be touching down in a body of water—thank God. Other than that, it was a crapshoot where we ended up—it could be anywhere between Romania, where we left from, and the Isle of Man.

Andre drifted closer to me and wrapped a hand around my parachute's cord. For a second we stared at each other, long enough for me to read Andre's intention from his face. With the wind howling in my ears, this was the closest we came to speaking. He gave the cord a yank, and my hand was savagely ripped from his as my parachute unfurled.

My hand didn't like that. It wanted him as close as possible.

I drifted down, the night air freezing against my face. God, I'd been so cold since Andre revived me from Bran Castle. At least, worst-case scenario, hell would be a nice vacation from this God-awful chill that had set in my bones.

I saw Andre's parachute open beneath me, and some part of me relaxed, until I realized that I was drifting away from him. There must be a way to navigate this parachute, but fuck it if I knew how to do it. So I let the wind carry me where it might.

A tree broke my fall. I smashed into its branches and

jerked to a stop, my body dangling nearly ten feet above the ground.

My breath came out in sharp pants. The only other noise was the groan of my straps and the tree limbs holding me up.

With shaky hands I unsnapped myself, and my freed body plummeted once more.

I hit the ground in a crouch. All around me, as far as I could see, trees stood like dark sentinels.

Another fucking forest.

Seemed I'd only just extricated myself from the one in Romania. I straightened and rubbed my numb hands together, my breath misting in front of me. Stretching my hearing out, I listened for signs of Andre.

Instead my skin prickled. Something out there in the darkness watched me.

"*Consort.*"

My shoulders tensed as the voice whispered in my ear. Something *did* watch me. The very something I ran from.

The devil—Pluto—stepped out from the darkness. He looked like a dark prince in this place, the shadows curling and clinging to the edges of him. It might just be my imagination, but they seemed to wrap around his head like a wicked corona. For all his evil, his otherworldliness was breathtaking.

The entire supernatural world was after me—the good guys, the bad guys, and those with ambiguous motives—and they all wanted me dead thanks to the being in front of me.

"I have nothing to say to you."

3

After I'd gone back on my deal, he'd released every secret and dark deed of mine to the news. Every. Single. One. The supernatural community now knew I'd led to the extermination of vampires, and more importantly, they knew I was destined to join the devil.

The devil's unholy presence seemed to slither up my legs, through my hair, and into my mouth, like it was a living, breathing thing. Like it craved my company.

His eyes glittered. "A woman of few words. You're rarer than the white whale. I truly have been fated to a covetous thing."

"We are not fated."

"Come, consort," said Pluto. "I've laid you in my bed, touched your bare skin with my fingers, spoke of eternity with you. Enough with the lies. We are beyond that with one another, are we not?"

"*Gabrielle!*" Andre's voice trickled in from far away.

I opened my mouth to call back to him. As soon as I did so, my lungs constricted. I reached for my throat choking on words I couldn't force out. My eyes moved to the devil.

He tilted his head, studying me like I was fascinating. When I glared at him accusingly, a corner of his mouth curled up.

Stop it, I mouthed, because I couldn't seem to actually voice the words.

Now both corners of the devil's mouth lifted, and his eyes glittered. "What makes you think I'm the one doing this to you? I can't kill you in this form," he said, running his hands down the fine fabric of his suit.

My sight dimmed at the lack of oxygen even as my skin flared up. I guess the siren in me thought she had a better chance of getting us out of this situation than I did.

I blinked several times. The last thing I wanted was to be blind in the devil's presence. Through my hazy vision I thought I saw him frown. He flicked a hand and released me.

My lungs expanded, and I fell to my knees, gasping for air.

He crouched by my side. "It's going to be like this until you're mine."

"And then it will be worse," I said, my voice raspy.

"*Gabrielle!*" Andre's voice was much closer.

The devil swiveled his head at the sound, his expression inscrutable. "Come with me," he said, returning his attention to me. "Tonight. Right now."

He leaned towards me, far too close. Close enough to know that he smelled of burnt souls, that his skin had no pores, that his eyes moved and shifted as though firelight lit them from behind. They did so even now.

"*Soulmate!*" Andre called.

Spell broken.

I scrambled away from the devil. "No."

He stood and extended a hand towards me. "I can take you from this place. It doesn't have to be painful." Because pain was what everything boiled down to in the devil's eyes.

I stared at his hand like it was an asp poised to strike. "You've never extended me that courtesy in the past," I said, "so why should I believe you now?"

5

"I want you with me. It is as simple as that."

"I will *never* go with you willingly."

Slowly the devil retracted his hand. He stared at me for a long moment. Long enough for me to feel awed—if not frightened—by his presence. Long enough to feel that inexplicable pull towards him once again.

Finally he inclined his head. "So be it. I'll be seeing you soon, consort."

A powerful gust of wind shook the trees and blew away the devil's form.

The last thing I saw were his almond-shaped eyes, and then they too dissolved into the night.

I WAS STILL catching my breath when Andre found me.

"*Soulmate.*" He was at my side in an instant. He ran his hands over me, I'm sure to see if I'd hurt myself from the fall. "What's wrong?"

I swallowed down my renewed fear. "The devil found me." Yet again. At this point he and I were practically biffles. Now all we needed to do was braid each other's hair and make friendship bracelets.

Andre's brows furrowed. He leaned in and ran his knuckles down my cheek. "Are you okay?" He watched me with such unbearable sadness.

I leaned into his touch and closed my eyes. With him so close, it was easy to pretend the nightmares away. I nodded, opening my eyes. "Now I am."

Perhaps it was the way I said the words or the way I looked at him when I spoke.

The reserve in Andre's eyes dropped away, and something too big for words replaced it. Desire. Love. Compassion. None came close to everything I saw in those eyes. He looked as though he wanted to devour me with his touch alone.

A distant howl shattered the moment. Andre's head snapped to the sound. His nostril's flared, and I could see his pupils dilate.

"Where are we?"

His mouth was a grim line as he glanced around. "An enchanted forest. Germany, if I had to guess." He held his hand to me. "We need to move."

My sluggish pulse picked up. "Enchanted?" I took his hand.

Before he could reply, another howl broke through the silence of the night, this one closer.

"Time to run, love." He gave my hand a nice tug, and then we were off, running through the trees.

My heartbeat sped up at both the exertion and the endearment.

Another howl joined the first.

"Please tell me that was just your normal, furry wolf," I said.

Andre shook his head.

Damn.

"Where are we going?" I asked, jumping over a fallen log.

"Away."

Not going to lie, that sounded like a decent game plan to me.

As we ran, I took in the subtle glow of the forest. I'd gotten used to my night vision, but after Andre brought me back from the edge of death by feeding me his blood, my own transformation into a vampire had sped up. And right now it made the night dance with all sorts of light.

It barely made up for the bitch of a headache bright light now gave me.

"How can they possibly know we're here already?" I asked.

"Those that pursue us might not know that we, specifically, are here. Just that there's an interloper on their land. Werewolves are territorial."

Behind us, more howls had joined in. They appeared to be moving in our direction.

"Are they gaining on us?" I asked. It sure sounded like it.

"Some are closer than others."

He hadn't answered my question. I'd thought that we were heads faster than other beings, but his evasive response made me wonder.

My breath came out in ragged puffs and my heart staggered out an ill-timed beat.

I caught movement from the corner of my eyes and swiveled my head to the left. I barely had time to say, "Werewolf," before the massive hellbeast pounced on me.

My fist came up, and I socked the giant wolf in the temple as my skin flared. It barely slowed the creature down.

Andre grabbed the wolf by the back of its neck and threw it against a nearby tree. I heard the sickening thud its head made when it slammed into the trunk.

It collapsed at the foot of the tree, and for one second I thought the creature was dead. It looked too still. Then I heard it snuffle.

The siren pushed her way to the surface. Not for the first time I found it ironic that she, the cursed part of me that feasted on danger and lust, always came to my rescue.

Andre stalked over to the creature just as the werewolf shook its head, like it was trying to clear its mind. He used the creature's confusion to grab its head. I could already tell by Andre's coiled muscles and his well-placed grip that he intended to kill it. The wolf began growling and snapping again, as if aware of how close to death it was.

The siren in me schemed; the human in me recoiled from the needless bloodshed. Neither wanted the werewolf to die.

"*Wait,*" I said, glamour weaving into my voice.

Instantly Andre's movements halted, and the werewolf chuffed, its lips curling back and then relaxing, like it couldn't decide what it wanted to do. I didn't know how much of its mind was human and how much was beast, but I needed it to listen to me.

"*Change back into your human form,*" the siren in my voice commanded.

The wolf whimpered, its body shaking. I could feel Andre's eyes on me, and slowly he relinquished his hold on the wolf.

"*Change back into your human form,*" I repeated.

Andre came to stand next to me. "Reversing the transformation might not be possible this close to the full moon."

At the sound of my soulmate's voice, my fangs descended. I turned to him, my eyes locking on his neck. No pulse thudded there, but I could practically taste his blood already. And if he bit me ...

"Focus, soulmate," Andre said.

I blinked, pushing away the lusty haze of my thoughts. I noticed he wore a sly smirk, like he knew exactly where my thoughts had been a moment before. Only he would feel smug that his girlfriend was fantasizing about biting him.

God we're freaks.

Dragging my attention away from Andre, I focused on the werewolf, who was slowly morphing back into a human. His face looked agonized, and a twinge of remorse pulled at my heartstrings. The siren stamped that emotion out, instead choosing to revel in the power of conquering another's freewill.

Nearly a minute later, a shivering man replaced the wolf.

"*We were never here,*" I said. "*You will let us go and call off the rest of the wolves.*"

The man nodded, his eyes glazing over.

Their howls were closing in on us.

"*You will do everything in your power to call them off the chase. Only then can you change back into a wolf.*"

The man shuddered but nodded. Despite his human form, he let out a series of yips and howls. Instantly the forest fell silent.

Andre took my hand. "Let's not stick around to see what happens."

I stared down at our entwined fingers, struggling to

rein in my lust. I didn't dare speak for fear that the siren would continue to seep into my voice.

Again we began to run. This time the chorus of howls didn't follow us, but that didn't slow either Andre or me down. Now that the fight was over, the siren slipped away, sliding back down to the depths of my soul. Thank goodness. I had enough to deal with at the moment.

Eventually we caught sight of a dirt path, and we followed it until it turned into a road. I seriously considered kissing the ground at the sight. My body ached from the distance we'd covered, and emotionally, I was barely hanging in there.

The first signs of civilization showed up less than a mile later. We slowed to a walk as we entered a small town. Most lights were completely out. This late in the evening, no one but vampires and werewolves were awake.

I glanced over my shoulder at the thought. "Think we lost them?" I asked Andre.

"Depends on whether or not they live here." He frowned. "Werewolves aside, I think we have other things to worry about," he said, his eyes roving over the houses in front of us.

"Like what?"

"Your face."

My eyebrows shot up. "You think anyone's going to recognize me here?"

"Recognition doesn't matter. You are a siren, one of the most beautiful creatures to exist. People remember that kind of unnatural loveliness. They talk, and those who look for you will listen. Your face will be a trail of breadcrumbs leading your enemies to our doorstep."

I swallowed. I'd escaped the devil not two days ago. I couldn't go back. But a quiet, calm part of me whispered the sad truth: It didn't matter what I wanted. I was already as good as dead.

Chapter 2

WE STOOD ON the front porch of a weathered bed and breakfast. Inside I could hear two heartbeats. Unlike our surroundings, a lamplight glowed in the window.

I twisted the ruby ring Andre gave me around my finger. "Think this is a good idea?" I said.

"Given our circumstances, we don't have much of a choice," Andre said, glowering at the door.

I took a deep breath and nodded. I couldn't shake the feeling that I had a huge target on my back.

I cracked my knuckles then rang the bell. In the silent night, I clearly heard someone wake up and their shuffled steps down the stairs.

A moment later the door opened, and an old man in pajamas answered. "*Guten Aben–*" His voice cut off as soon as he got a good look at me. He stared for longer than was comfortable, until Andre cleared his throat. "*Guten Abend, meine Frau und ich fuhren ...*"

My head snapped to Andre as he spoke in rapid-fire German. How many freaking languages did this man know?

He placed an arm around me then touched my stomach. I gave my soulmate a sidelong look. He was spinning some tale that obviously involved my belly.

The old man's eyes returned first to my stomach, then almost against his will, they drifted up to my face, drawn like a moth to flame.

I gave him a tight smile just as Andre laid his hand protectively over my stomach once more. He continued to chat amicably with the owner, and by the end of the conversation the man was chuckling and ushering us in.

"What did you tell him?" I whispered to Andre as we were led to a room.

His lips curved. "I told him that my pregnant wife and I were driving through the area when our car broke down, and we needed a place to stay."

My cheeks should've flushed—a day ago they would've—but it was just one more part of me that had changed since Andre's emergency blood transfusion.

"Did he believe it?"

"Hardly. But I told him I'd pay him twice his going rate for the last minute accommodations."

The man led us to our room and bid us goodnight. As soon as the door clicked shut, Andre crossed the room and closed the blinds.

"Will that be enough to protect you from the sun?" I

asked.

"It'll have to do." Andre turned from the window. "And I no longer believe I'm the only one that needs protection from the sun." His eyes fell meaningfully on my pale skin.

He was probably right. I'd been sleeping through most of the day, so I hadn't really had the chance to test his theory, but I wasn't really clamoring to. Aside from the pain it was likely to cause, I think it would just be one more frightening reminder that time was running out.

"The Politia are likely already scouring the area around where we landed. I think we'll be okay for the night, but we'll have to leave tomorrow at sundown to stay one step ahead of them."

Imbeciles. Didn't the morally righteous supernaturals find it even slightly strange that evil beings also wanted me dead? Had it even crossed their minds that killing me might be a bad idea? The devil, after all, couldn't truly lay any claim to me while I still breathed. But once I died, heaven knew what horrors awaited.

Andre's brow furrowed. "Soulmate, are you feeling okay?"

I refocused my attention on the man in front of me. "What do you mean?"

"You smell ... imbalanced."

Now that he mentioned it, my body felt off. My stomach churned and a pressurized headache was forming behind one of my eyes.

I wrapped my arms around myself and sat down on the edge of the bed. "I think everything's just catching up with me." The entire supernatural world wanted my head.

The entire world. No one had those shitty odds save for me.

Andre sat down and pulled me onto his lap. He pressed my body into his chest, his arms enveloping me. "I've got you, soulmate."

He ran his hand over my hair. "What we need is—what's that term ... ?" He stared off into space for a moment. His face lit up as it came to him, and he snapped his fingers. "Ah. A *game plan*. We need one of those."

Against my will, my lips quirked. He was endearing when he acted like this. Judging from the way laughter danced in his dark eyes, he knew it too.

"Agreed."

He stood, picking me up with him, and I just sort of let him. It was so unlike me.

My head tucked into the crook of his neck as he led me over to a small table set to the side of the bed. I could almost feel his reluctance to let me go when he set me down in my own chair. I'd bet money he'd considered keeping me on his lap. Because that was where my thoughts were.

Business was *definitely* getting in the way of pleasure.

Andre slid into the seat across from me. "Let's assess what we brought along and go from there."

He reached into his pocket and set a wallet and a cellphone down on the table. I followed his lead and emptied my own pockets. Like him I carried my wallet and phone. I glanced at my device. "No reception."

"Mine has no reception either. It's for the best," Andre said, flipping over the phone. "These things can be traced. We'll have to dump them before we leave."

Leaving my phone meant I'd lose my friends' numbers.

It felt like I was shedding the last of my former life.

I set the cell aside and checked the rest of my pockets. From one of them I pulled out a slip of paper. It was the note Cecilia had tucked away inside my birthday card. Originally it had a riddle scribed across it. Last time I checked, the riddle had changed subtly.

I laid it flat on the table.

Find me back where it all began.
C

For a moment I stared in wonder at the note. It had changed again. In place of the cryptic poem was a cryptic sentence.

I exhaled. Really, it'd be nice to receive straightforward message from Cecilia every once in a while.

"Andre, do you have any idea what this means?" I tapped on the slip of paper.

He slid the card over to him and read the message. Picking it up, he flipped the card over. "Is this from Nona?"

I nodded, though I knew the woman as Cecilia. She had raised me for the first several years of my life and saved me from an early death. Only later had I learned that she was a fate. Specifically, *Nona*, the fate that wove the thread of life.

I rubbed my temple. "Where *did* this all begin?"

"The Isle of Man." Andre didn't even hesitate before he spoke.

"How do you know?"

Andre flipped the note and presented the backside to

me.

(Hint: It's an island you've lived on.)
P.S. This is as straightforward as I get.

I sputtered out a laugh. "Ouch." I just got burned by my godmother. "So we head back to the Isle of Man, just like we had been?" Wiser strategies should exist. We'd be walking right into the lion's den. The Isle of Man was the epicenter of the supernatural world. I might as well waltz into the Politia's headquarters while I was at it and turn myself in.

Andre ruminated on my words, staring at the note again. "If the fate that raised you thinks we should go to the Isle of Man, I'm willing to trust her instincts."

"But ... how?" There were hundreds of miles between here and there, and so far we had ... one ally. Cecilia.

Andre ran a hand through his hair, tousling his dark locks. "We'll want to be as unpredictable as possible. Right now the Politia likely knows we landed somewhere in Germany. They will have plotted out a region where we might be located, and they will have their people on the lookout for evidence of our presence."

My eyes met his. "The parachutes."

A muscle in Andre's jaw jumped. "It couldn't be helped, soulmate. We were being chased."

"How long before the Politia finds them?"

Andre rubbed his jaw, a mannerism I always found in-credibly sexy. His hand paused as his nostrils flared. He focused his attention on me, his eyes dilated. For all my changes, he could still smell my attraction to him. Figures I'd retain that embarrassing trait. At least the blushing had disappeared.

He looked halfway ready to toss me onto the bed and forget planning for the evening.

I cleared my throat. "I mean, do you think they'll find us before sundown tomorrow?"

Andre's fingers dropped from his jaw and tapped along the table, his eyes lingering on my neck. "If we are very unlucky, then perhaps."

Well, that answered that.

Noticing my expression, Andre reached over and took my hand. "Soulmate, I've faced worse odds. So have you. You may be cursed, but in some ways you have the best luck I know."

His thumb rubbed my knuckles. "The devil doesn't get outmaneuvered. It's not in his nature, nor is it in ours to beat him at his own game. That you have is proof that the impossible is now possible."

He gave my hand a squeeze then released it. He leaned back in the chair, his body dwarfing the thing. It groaned as he crossed his ankle over his other leg. "Today is not the day we die. And so help the world if I'm wrong, because I will overturn both earth and hell to reunite with you."

BY THE TIME the sun was about to rise, we had a loose game plan in place. An exceedingly stupid one, but at least it was something. Andre owned a couple properties here in Germany, and we were going to visit at least one of them.

That meant a chance confrontation with any vampires that happened to be there. Vampires that now knew I was fated to kill them. That was the second, more obscure prophecy that I starred in, the one that drove Andre's right-hand man, Theodore, to try to kill me several months ago.

They know everything.

My head rested against Andre's chest as he held me tightly to him in the room's bed. His hand traced shapes into my back. Back when winter break had begun, I had imagined long days with Oliver and even longer nights with Andre. I'd been concerned with the Politia's opinion of me and plotting how I was going to deepen my relationship with Andre.

Never had I imagined jetting out to Romania to solve a string of murders, nor had I imagined that the devil would make another play for my soul, or that I'd be on the run.

And definitely not this—this intimacy borne from survival and struggle. It was deepening our relationship even now. How could it not? My soulmate gave up everything the instant he chose to jump out of a jet with me rather than handing me over.

Andre was right. In some ways I did have the best luck. I'd landed myself him as a mate. Even if he could be scary as shit at times.

I shifted, causing him to pull me tighter to his body. He pressed a kiss to my forehead and peered down at me, his lips curving up. "My little mate is in my arms. All is well in the world."

Yep. I had the best luck.

Andre rearranged us so that I was as close to him as I would ever be, save for sex. He'd only just closed his eyes when his body stilled in the most unnatural way.

"Andre?"

Nothing. I reached out from where I laid next to him and touched his skin. It felt cold and lifeless. The last couple of times we'd slept together, I'd fallen asleep with him. I hadn't noticed just how horrible it would be to see him like this. Lifeless. He'd wake up once the sun dipped below the horizon. But for the duration of the day, he was *gone*.

Even as sleep tugged at my eyes, my body felt jittery. It still didn't demand sleep the same way Andre's did. And right now my mind was too noisy to let me rest.

Pushing away from the bed, I wandered to the window. I fingered the edge of the curtain. Now would've been the time to test whether or not the sun could burn me. I glanced back at Andre's still form, sleeping the sleep of the dead. I wouldn't risk frying him to test a stupid theory.

Bzzzzz.

...

Bzzzzz.

I turned away from the window. On the table, my phone vibrated, the white of its screen lighting up the dark room. It shouldn't be ringing. I'd seen for myself that the device had no reception.

I approached the cell, almost afraid to see who was calling me. Air rushed out of me when I read the caller ID.

Caleb.

I couldn't answer it. Every crime show I'd ever seen recorded and traced calls this way, and chances were high that they'd put him up to this. But crap, it was Caleb.

What must he think of the articles written on me? What must he think *of* me? My hand twitched, eager to ask him. Instead I shoved my thumbnail between my teeth and paced, impatient for the buzzing to cease.

An eternity later it did. I sank into the chair in front of the phone and gingerly picked the device up.

No reception.

My scalp prickled. Caleb had placed a call that never should've gone through. Could magic have been used? If so, had the Politia arranged this, or was it possible that Caleb had gone around them?

I pinched the bridge of my nose. Of course he hadn't gone around them. They were the Politia, and he was their star pupil. No amount of wishing could change that.

I jumped when the phone buzzed again.

1 new voicemail

My hands felt sticky with sweat and my heart seemed to have lodged itself in my throat when I saw the message. Did I want to hear whatever Caleb had to say?

No, I really didn't.

I was, however, a glutton for punishment. So I picked up the phone, tapped on the screen, and pressed play.

I brought the phone to my ear just as the message began.

"Gabrielle." Caleb's voice was thick with emotion,

and after saying my name, a long pause drew out. "I've seen the news." Another pause. "They want your head." I heard him swallow. "The Politia is looking for you, but shit, so is every other creature out there."

My hand shook as I listened.

"And ... I heard about you and Andre. That he's your *soulmate*." He said it like it was a bad word. "Four months we've been friends. Worked together. You knew that entire time, didn't you?" I could hear the betrayal and the hurt in his words. Perhaps Leanne wasn't the only one with foresight because I knew this was coming.

He let out a hollow laugh. "Can't say you didn't warn me. I just ... I feel like a fucking idiot ..."

He cleared his throat. "I'm sorry. That's not why I'm calling. Just ... I hope you're far away from the Politia and those that can hurt you. Don't trust anyone." He hesitated, then sighed. "Not even me."

Chapter 3

I WOKE UP to the sensation of fingers running through my hair.

"Mmm." I stretched out lazily.

Rumbling laughter vibrated beneath me, and I opened my eyes.

Andre smiled from where he lay beneath me, and it crinkled the skin around his eyes. The hand that wasn't playing with my hair encircled my waist.

Sometime while I'd been asleep, one of my own legs had slipped between his, and one of my arms was splayed possessively over his stomach.

... And judging from the damp spot on his chest, I might've been drooling on him.

Oh God, if the devil weren't after me, I'd have gladly died from embarrassment.

I wiped my mouth—yep, I'd definitely slobbered on him—and began to push myself up.

Andre's arm tightened. "Mmm, not so fast, soulmate." His eyes closed. "Let me enjoy this for just a few moments more."

Warmth pooled low in my stomach at his tone, reminding me of all those times we'd come so very close to getting intimate.

I lay back down against him, aware of the way our bodies lined up. He was all hard muscle against me, the body of a man raised on physical exertion.

Resting my chin on one of his pecs, I gazed up at his face, struck by the masculine beauty of his face. His strong, square jaw, high cheekbones, and those soft, sensual lips ...

Andre's eyes opened, and they had a mischievous twinkle in them.

"Penny for your thoughts," I said.

He chuckled. "My thoughts aren't nearly so cheap." His thumb brushed against my lower lip. "I will, however, give one up for a kiss."

My eyes moved to his mouth. Before I'd fully registered what I was doing, I'd already slid up his torso. Easiest tithe I'd ever paid.

I leaned down until my lips brushed his. The earth could've quaked and I wouldn't have felt it over the electricity that passed through me where our mouths met. Never would I get over this. How a simple kiss could awaken me completely. It made me crave more.

His arms came up, encircling my waist. At first, he

smiled into the kiss, smug that he got exactly what he'd wanted with so little persuasion. The smile soon fell away, however, and he groaned as my tongue teased his mouth, then found its way in.

Andre and I had been hurtling towards something for months, and lying in this bed, pressed so closely together and tasting one another, it seemed like it would happen today. This very moment.

Which is why I wrenched myself away from him. His arms released me reluctantly. Both of our fangs were out, and we were breathing hard—laughable when you really thought about it. Andre didn't need air.

Andre's eyes hungered for more, and I could almost see him considering dragging me back down into bed and resuming where we left off.

I stood, noticing how my skin glowed lightly, and walked to the window just to avoid looking at him. Otherwise I might just throw all care to the wind and resume our former activities.

A second later, Andre joined me. "It's a rare and humbling moment when a teenage siren exerts more self-restraint than me."

I smiled at that, though a bigger part of me regretted fleeing that bed.

He pulled back the curtain back so that we could stare out into the evening. Rain came down in torrents. Despite the storm, townspeople milled about, going about their normal lives. Right then I resented them for it. While they wondered what they'd eat for dinner, I was wondering if today would be the day I died.

"They haven't found us yet." I stated the obvious.

Andre dropped the curtain. All the affection he'd shared with me was now reined in. In it's place, his eyes glittered with purpose ... and a little malice.

"Let's get going before we push our luck any more."

Packing consisted of me shoving Cecilia's note back into my pants and disabling our phones. I tried not to think of Caleb's message as I did so. He'd warned me not trust him. I'd replayed the message over and over again, hearing every broken note to his voice, every poignant pause. And I'd relived his embarrassment over finding out that Andre and I were soulmates.

That particular vampire now studied me as I brushed my hands off and headed to the door.

"Penny for your thoughts?" Andre asked, throwing my earlier words back at me. I knew for a fact that if he could, he'd barge into my mind and pillage all my thoughts until he'd obtained every single one.

The punk.

"They'd cost you more than a penny—and more than a kiss."

He raised a sculpted eyebrow at that and looked as though he didn't mind paying whatever tithe I had in mind.

I snapped my fingers and pointed at him. "By the way, you never paid up."

"Hmm?" he said, holding the door open for me.

I walked out into the hall. "This morning when you stared at me, what were you thinking about?"

"I stare at you a lot, love. You're going to have to be

more specific than that."

I rolled my eyes. "I kissed you in return for your thoughts. What were they?"

"Ah." Andre smirked like he was remembering something amusing. "Just how badly I wanted your lips on mine."

And he'd gotten exactly that. Scoundrel.

BEFORE WE LEFT I had to glamour the innkeeper to forget about us. For once I deeply appreciated the siren in me; her inclinations might fall on the wrong side of the law, but damn if she wasn't helpful for getting out of a bind. She made being lawless easy.

Icy rain drizzled down on us as we left the small town on foot. I was chilled to the bone, and by the time we'd crossed the town, I was pretty sure I looked like Samara from *The Ring*.

So far no one had stopped us, which probably meant no one had figured out where we were. I shivered, and Andre tucked me against him. Unlike me, he didn't seem cold. And rain soaked he looked like he could walk onto the cover of GQ or Men's Health.

No fair.

Ahead of us a taxi that Andre had called for back at the B&B waited for us. Just as I stared at it, a shadow moved from my peripheral vision. My head snapped to the movement, but I saw nothing. Just rain and darkness and streetlights spilling what little light they gave off onto the street.

"What is it?" Andre asked, looking over my shoulder.

I'd forgotten he was there, and I'd also forgotten just how observant he was. He hadn't lived and ruled for seven centuries due to his looks alone.

I shook my head. "Just shadows," I said, brushing it off.

Andre's arm tightened around me, and he hustled me the rest of the way to the car. He knew better than me. In the supernatural world, shadows were never just shadows.

The taxi drove for over two hours, only stopping once we hit Munich, where phase one of our craptastic, we-will-surely-die plan would begin.

When it pulled up in front of a coffee shop, I raised my eyebrows. "A ... coffee house? You live above a coffee house?" It seemed so not Andre.

He winked. "I'm full of surprises."

It says a lot about Andre that he was able to pay the driver most of the fare in cash. I had to use a bit of my magic to persuade him that he wasn't getting partially stiffed when he so obviously was.

Andre took my hand. "Come, soulmate."

He led us past the coffee shop, down a narrow alley. Here flakes of snow lightly drifted down. We hooked a left at the end of it and turned onto a small road. Businesses butted up against it, and we eventually stopped in front of a door that seemed as though it, like the others, led to some shop.

Andre yanked on the knob, breaking the lock, and ushered me inside. The first thing I noticed was the motorcycle off to the right of the door. The bike had been parked in front of a garage door that rested next to our entrance.

"Where are we?" I asked, looking beyond it. A long hallway extended away from us.

"A persecution tunnel of mine." Andre flicked on the lights just as the door closed behind us. I heard metal scrape and turned in time to see Andre using a steel beam to barricade the door.

Who in the hell leaves steel beams just lying around?

Andre caught my eye. "You're better off not asking, soulmate," he said, hearing my unspoken question.

Above the door a grainy screen embedded into the wall showed us footage of the alleyway. I glanced from it, to the beam, and back to the motorcycle.

I really didn't want to know.

As far as persecution tunnels go, this one had been *nicely* outfitted. It made me wonder just what sort of unsavory events Andre had been up to here in recent years.

He has a criminal record a mile long, Leanne had once said.

Hello criminal record.

Andre came up from behind me and placed a hand on the small of my back, urging me forward. Together the two of us headed down the hall until we hit another door, this one equipped with a thumb scanner.

Jesus.

Andre pressed his thumb to the pad, and a moment later, the door swung open. A room waited for us on the other side, and beyond it, another hall stretched out.

"Do I even want to know why you need all the security?"

"No."

Fair enough.

We continued on for what felt like forever, but was

probably only another minute or so, when we came up to a normal door.

"No retinal scanner?" I asked. "And here I was hoping."

Almost against his will, a grin broke out along Andre's face.

"Are you sure this is a good idea?" I asked. Andre's coven had a habit of coming and going to his estates; surely one or two would be here.

I guess it didn't matter, regardless. It was too late now for regrets.

"If anyone tries to harm you, they will rue it. That I promise you." Andre's eyes flashed as he looked at me. My mind went to the bloody bodies scattered around an altar beneath Bran Castle, all cut down by this man.

Yes, I believed with absolute certainty that my soulmate would make good on his promise.

I cracked my knuckles. "Let's do this."

ON THE OTHER side of the door was a small study. I made a note that if I ever returned to Bishopcourt, I would see if the study there had any secret passageways. We exited the room and entered a large entryway.

As soon as Andre's house staff caught sight of Andre and me, they scrambled to accommodate us. Apparently their loyalties still lay with the king of vampires, news or not. When their eyes landed on me, and they stared—not with fear or hatred, but with rapt attention—I realized it might even be simpler than that. They were human. Mortal. Normal. And they'd never seen a siren before. I'd never been so relieved to be gawked at.

"Andre?" A male voice called out.

I swiveled to see a man with blond hair stroll from another room.

"My God man, you should not be here—" His eyes moved to me. It took less than a second for his shock to appear then vanish from his face. Drawing his lips back, he hissed. "What is that godforsaken creature doing here?"

Ah, there was the angry vampire. Just when I thought I might actually get a little respite from the fighting and fleeing.

"She's with me, Tybalt," Andre said, stepping forward. Every line of Andre's body promised aggression, "and she has my protection."

Tybalt's muscles tensed, and I fell into a fighting stance. Words were pretty and all, but this dude was beyond them.

Andre must've thought so too. His body blurred, and he rushed the blond vampire just as Tybalt began to lunge. Grabbing the man's neck, Andre slammed him into the ground. The marble floor cracked at the force of impact.

"You will not harm your queen."

My skin tingled at his aggression, my siren chomping at the bit to get out.

The man hissed again. "Andre, this is madness. She's wanted by the devil. You've let the enemy into your home. She'll kill us all."

Andre didn't like the sound of that. His fist came down hard on Tybalt's face. I heard things crack, smelled the vampire's stolen blood as it dripped out of his crushed nose, and heard his whimper.

"You think I don't know?" Andre roared. He slammed his fist down again.

Ho boy, someone had been hankering for a fight, and now he'd found one.

"For Christ's sake, Andre," Tybalt said, his words somewhat garbled from the hits, "you killed Theodore on her behalf. She needs to die."

Andre hissed back at the man, his fangs fully descended. As I watched, he applied pressure to Blondie's neck.

I glanced around. Andre's human servants had made themselves scarce. I wondered if they were used to seeing unnatural things here or if they'd been hired for their discretion. Or perhaps they fell into the third category: clueless and scared shitless.

When I swiveled back around, the man's eyelids were fluttering and he made slight choking noises.

"You think this is some sick game to me?" Andre's voice echoed off the walls. "The devil wants *my soulmate.*"

He pulled his fist back, but it wavered. "The devil wants her," he repeated. This time grief and not anger ruled his voice. "And you wish me to deliver her to him."

Nope, I was wrong. Anger was back. Still, that fist hesitated.

"I could not devise another betrayal so great as that," Andre said. "She is my soulmate, and while she lives, you and every other vampire will afford her the respect she is due."

The man's eyes flicked to me and his upper lip twitched, like he wanted to snarl again but only just held himself back. Finally he nodded.

Andre didn't relinquish his hold.

Right now I needed allies, and these were my people—our people. Maybe, if given a chance, I could convince them.

Just like you convinced the Politia, a bitter voice inside me said. I swallowed. My life might come down to the associations I made.

I stepped up behind the two and placed a hand on Andre's shoulder. Blondie's gaze darted to the touch.

"Andre, please."

I thought he wasn't going to listen, but after several seconds he slowly released his grip on the vampire. The blond man stayed on the ground and rubbed his neck. His facial wounds had already healed.

I reached out a hand to help him up, but Andre pushed it down and stepped in front of me.

"I will die before harm comes to my mate," he said. The three of us knew the weight of that statement. If Andre died, every vampire descended from him—essentially the entire coven—would die with him. "You'd be wise to consider her prophecy through that filter."

Tybalt's eyes widened. When his gaze traveled to me, it was as though he was seeing me in a new light. "I had never considered that interpretation."

Holy shit. *I'd* never considered the prophecy in those terms either, but it made a sick sort of sense. As far as I was aware, the prophecy hadn't said that I would personally kill off every vampire; it had said that I'd lead to their extermination. Perhaps my involvement was indirect. But that interpretation meant Andre died. I almost choked on the idea of him dead and gone.

Andre held an arm out to Tybalt as though he hadn't been wailing on the dude a moment before. I guess it was a peace offering. The vampire took it, and Andre hauled him to his feet. "Unfortunately," Andre said, "considering the bounty out on my mate, that might be the only interpretation left."

Now when Tybalt met my gaze, something like pity clouded his features. "I see." He inclined his head, first to Andre, then to me, looking sheepish. "Apologies for the hostility. As always, Sire, I am at your service."

"Good, because I need you to pass along a message to the coven," Andre said, stepping away from him to return to my side. "For now, let it be known that unless all vampires want to wipe themselves from existence, they should do everything in their power to keep my mate alive."

Tybalt's face grew grim, but he gave a jerky nod.

"Alert the coven that I'm calling for a meeting at Bishopcourt. Tell them to make their own accommodations on the Isle of Man. No one is to set foot on my property until I give the order to do so. Once I'm in town, I will give the details of the meeting and explain more fully my and Gabrielle's circumstances.

"Let it be known that the estate is to be neutral territory. If anyone betrays our meeting to those outside the coven or thinks to attack, they will be bled, gutted, and burned at first light."

Holy shitballs, that was intense. I kept my mouth clamped shut.

"Consider it done," Tybalt said. With another bow of

his head, he left us.

Andre turned to face me, his eyes daring me to challenge his orders. He knew I hated violence. But hey, threats never hurt anyone.

Until they did.

Andre reached out a hand to me. Another peace offering. I stared at it; Tybalt's blood still stained it.

"Are you going to take my hand?"

"Would you really do it?" I asked, my gaze flicking up to him.

"Without hesitation, love." My heart sputtered at the endearment, even as another part of me recoiled at his statement.

"And would you enjoy it?" I don't know why I asked. Maybe because I had never really considered the dark part of Andre.

He didn't answer immediately. I could tell he was wary of what my reaction would be. "Normally—no," he finally said. "But if it endangered you, I would relish every second of it."

I believed him. So help me, I did.

His eyes glittered as he watched me. "Does that scare you, soulmate?"

"What do you think?"

"I think that if roles were reversed, you'd be shocked by what you wouldn't do to save me."

He loved me something fierce and dreadful, and I knew in my heart of hearts everything he said was true—even the last part.

Especially the last part.

I took his outstretched hand. He gave me a small smile. "Now," he said, forcing some cheerfulness into his voice, "my soulmate must be hungry."

And just like that, things were normal once more.

Andre brought me to the kitchen and asked one of the servants to whip up something for me to eat.

"Which would you prefer—" Andre said, placing his hands on my hips and maneuvering me next to the counter, "to drink blood straight from the source or from a bag?"

I cringed, but even as I did so, my canines descended. Seemed like I no longer craved just food.

Ew.

I mulled his request over. The thought of tapping into a live vein seriously turned me on, and that seemed wrong.

"Um, blood bag." I'd save nipping someone's neck for later.

Andre called one of his servants back over to prepare us both a glass of blood as well as a plate of pasta for me.

"What about you?" I asked once the servant left. "What's your preference?" I hadn't fully thought through that question until I asked it.

Visions of Andre pulling some scantily clad woman onto his lap and tapping into her jugular filled my mind. I remembered how good it felt to drink from another—and how good it felt to get bitten. Surely something like that would lead to other, more carnal acts. The possibility killed me.

"I've always preferred my meals living," he said, only confirming my fears.

I glanced away. How would I come to terms with this aspect of ourselves?

Two of Andre's fingers touched my chin. "But," he said, tipping my head back to face him, "I will relinquish live feedings for as long as it makes you uncomfortable."

My gaze darted back to Andre. "What if I'm never comfortable with it?"

"Then I will come to enjoy the taste of packaged blood."

I furrowed my brow. "You'd do that?"

"For you, anything." He smiled. It faded a second later. "There is, however, a chance that in the upcoming days neither of us will get a choice in the matter."

If we were hunted. I desperately hoped I wouldn't need blood that badly. As it was, I was barely coming to terms with the fact that I needed to drink it at all.

"We will prevent that the best we can." A statement Andre emphasized by calling over yet another servant.

"Sir?"

"Bring me an enchantment bag and pack it with the necessities—including blood bags, human food, and spare clothes for Gabrielle."

The servant bowed his head and disappeared out the room. He, like the others, had smelled human. "He knows what an enchantment bag is?" Even I didn't know what that was, though I'd wager I would very soon.

"You of all people, Gabrielle, should know that all is not as it appears. My servants—even the human ones—must know a thing or two about the supernatural world and about me before I'll hire them."

I stared at the door the servant had left through. "If

they know so much about our world, then what's to stop them from squealing on us the first chance they get?"

"It's easy to enchant humans."

Oh. Well, that sounded unpleasant.

Another servant chose that moment to enter the room carrying a tray with two glasses of blood and a plate of pasta on it. I couldn't keep the twisted smirk off my face when my eyes landed on the sight. It shouldn't look so normal.

"Thank you," Andre said, nodding to the man as he set the blood and food in front of us.

I stared at the steaming plate of pasta. It looked delicious, but I found I had no appetite for it.

Andre took one of the wine glasses and leaned against the counter, his eyes narrowed as he assessed me.

He notices everything.

I gingerly picked up my fork and speared the noodles, shoving the pasta into my mouth. It tasted like chalk, and my throat closed up at the intrusion of food. I could barely eat my favorite meal. Instead my eyes kept returning to the blood.

Andre took a sip of his drink, then leaned forward to push my glass towards me. "It's okay to crave it, soulmate." He had been watching, and now he was trying to make me feel better about my new, freakish craving.

I grabbed the glass and took a sip. I practically moaned at the taste. I took another gulp, and then another. I paused only to take several more bites of pasta. It tasted a little better now, but nowhere near as good as the blood.

Guess I was a little too ... *bloodthirsty.*

After I finished eating, Andre led me upstairs, holding open a door to what looked like the master suite. "Soulmate, relax and freshen up. I will take care of the details of our parting from this place."

I stepped inside and turned back to face him. "You're not going to join me?"

Immediately heat seeped into his gaze. "I would like nothing more, soulmate."

I hadn't meant the question as a sexual offer *per se*, but now that he was looking at me like that, my mind couldn't help drifting to all the ways one could relax together. My skin glimmered. I was pretty sure I would also like nothing more.

He ran a hand through his hair. "I must get our plans in order." Reluctantly he pushed away from the wall. The look he gave me promised to resume this discussion.

Eep.

"I'll be back to collect you inside an hour. Until then," he raised an eyebrow, "enjoy yourself enough for the both us."

IN THE BATHROOM, I splashed cool water onto my face, telling myself to get a grip. People were after me; the last thing I should be thinking about was getting physical with Andre. I grabbed a nearby hand towel and dried my face off.

How *was* this all going to work? Him and I living on the run? How far would we get? And how long would I survive? I didn't doubt that Andre had the resources to keep me alive, but what kind of existence was that?

"Not a good one."

I dropped the towel as my head snapped up to the mirror. Just behind my reflection stood the devil.

I swiveled around to face him, my hands gripping the edge of the counter, but on my side of the mirror no one was there. When I faced my reflection once more, the devil was still there. The bathroom he resided in was dimmer; he brought a bit of darkness with him.

Because he was perverse, he slung an arm over my reflection's shoulders and glanced down her shirt. "Not a bad rack, consort." The devil was being playful. That was so, so wrong.

"Why are you here?"

He gave me a look that said, *Really?* "Can I not visit my future wife? She is quite lovely." He leaned into my reflection, breathed in her smell. I suppressed a shiver at the sight and rubbed my neck where the skin chilled.

"It's good sport, you know," he said. "Watching you flee from the entire world. How will you die? Who will be the one to do it?"

"Amusing," I agreed.

I heard a faint series of cracks and I glanced up at the source of the noise. A fine sheen of ice formed at the corner of the mirror. Slowly it spread.

Perhaps even stranger than the ice was that the devil's presence should've chilled me more than it did.

His arm dropped from my reflection's shoulders only to wrap around her stomach. Her eyes widened, and I couldn't be sure if my reflection was acting independently from me.

His thumb nudged my shirt up and rubbed the skin of my midsection. I'd never considered the stomach to be a taboo area, but the way he stroked my reflection ... it seemed way too intimate.

"You act as though this disgusts you, but I know you are curious," the devil said, using his other hand to brush along my cheek. "You wonder what being with me will be like."

"I don't."

"Oh really?" He pressed a kiss to my reflection's cheek. A phantom breath brushed against my own, drawing out my gooseflesh.

The devil ran his hand down my arm. "Your body says differently."

"I could never be with someone like you."

A wicked smile pulled at his lips. "I assure you, you could. Logistically, it's really quite easy."

Thank God I could no longer blush.

He turned to my reflection. "You haven't accepted your dark nature, but it stirs in you. I can coax it forth. I *will* coax it forth. Then, I think you will find you could be with no other save for me."

If he could do what he claimed, I was so screwed.

He let go of my reflection and backed up. "The powers that be have forsaken you."

I shuddered because no matter the lies he might spew, in this he spoke the truth.

"Just remember—they might've forsaken you, consort, but I haven't."

Those words echoed long after he disappeared.

I haven't.

Chapter 4

I SHOWERED AND padded out into the bedroom, towel wrapped around me.

I my eyes landed on the bed, where an outfit had been laid out. I paused. Black leather pants and a skintight black shirt waited for me.

Even more mortifying, someone had placed a lacey thong and bra next to the clothing. Out of curiosity I walked up and checked out the tags.

Well they'd at least got my size right.

I sighed. I was going to look like Lara Croft: Slut Slayer.

By the time I slipped on the pair of boots that rested next to the bed, someone knocked on the door.

"Come in!" I shouted.

Andre sauntered in, his hair wet from the shower he must've fit in between planning the next phase of our escape. The moment he caught sight of my outfit, air seemed to hiss out of him.

"I think I need another shower," he said. "A cold one."

Okay, not helping. It felt like my ass was eating my underwear *and* my pants. Guess more than my teeth wanted a bite out of something.

"Leather, Andre? Really?" I asked.

"Blame my servants," he said, but his eyes shined with mischief. I could practically see him making a mental note to give them a raise.

Andre strode forward, and his eyes already undressing me.

My body squeaked under his gaze—though that might've just been the straining leather—and my skin flared up. That was all it took.

I backed up, grabbing the bedpost I bumped into. We both heard my slow heartbeat pick up. "People are after us; we have to—"

"The world can wait," Andre said. "My soulmate has needs that I only I can satisfy."

My hand slipped from the bedpost. Andre came up to me and cupped my face. His thumbs stroked my features. I saw his desire-laden gaze flick to the bed, and my skin brightened further.

My hands floated to his waist. Chiseled muscle rippled beneath the fabric of his shirt. "Cotton, Andre?" I said, rubbing the material. "Why do I have to wear some poor cow when you don't?" That was real fair.

"The lady doth protest too much." He took my wrists and moved my touch down a few inches to the supple leather of his pants. "See? Leather."

All rational thought fled me. My hands were dangerously close to things I wanted to get familiar with. I fought with the siren rising in me. If she took over, the deed was as good as done. Which I wasn't actually against, except that she was capable of taking away Andre's free will.

Unaware of my thoughts, Andre leaned in and brushed a kiss across my lips. "Soulmate, I love it that I can affect you this way."

"Mmm." I was afraid to speak. Afraid of the glamour that would ease into my voice.

Sensing the battle within me, he pulled away. He stroked the side of my face. "I'm not afraid of her, soulmate—she's a part of you."

When I wrested control of my voice I said, "She'll take things way too far."

He raised an eyebrow. "You say that like I have a problem with it." Andre's fangs had descended, and he was making no attempt to mask their presence.

Heat flooded me as I processed his words, and now I struggled in earnest with the siren. My control over her was getting better with each passing day, but she was also getting stronger.

Someone shouted downstairs about company, pulling us both from the moment.

Andre prowled over to the room's window and glanced out before coming back to me and taking my hand. "You were right, soulmate."

"About what?"

"We need to move. Now."

I glanced back at the window as he led me out of the room. "What did you see?"

"Our enemies encroach." Andre strode down the hall, and I had to lengthen my stride to keep up.

"What's the game plan from here?" I asked instead.

"There is none."

I gave him a sharp look, which he ignored. "None?"

Now the corner of his mouth tilted up, albeit a little grimly. "Nothing official, anyway. The moment our plans solidify, seers everywhere will be able to pinpoint our location."

Crap, he had a point.

"Wouldn't they then foresee us arriving in the Isle of Man?" I asked. Those plans had solidified.

He led me through the mansion back to his study. "Probably."

We were so doomed.

Andre stopped me in front of the door to kiss my forehead. "Trust me in this, soulmate: all is well. I'll curb my words to protect your mind from seers, but we are not traveling blindly into the unknown."

Funny, it sounded like that was *exactly* what we were doing.

Tybalt hurried over to us. "Sire," he inclined his head, "your orders have been carried out. We will meet again at week's end."

Andre slapped him on the shoulder. "You are a good man."

Tybalt's eyes flicked to mine. I could see his uncertainty; he still didn't fully trust me. "One of your servants waits in the tunnel with those items you requested. Is there anything else you need?"

"None."

"Then keep yourself and the queen alive. Until then." He bowed and stepped aside.

The queen ... not going to lie, I could get used to a title like that.

Andre held open the door to the study. Once I'd entered, he followed in behind me. He rounded his desk and crouched behind it.

"Andre ... ?"

A moment later he reappeared, holding several holstered knives. He set them on the desk before ducking below again.

Whoa. "Please tell me I won't need to use that."

"I promise nothing," he said, placing another two knives on his desk. He bent down once more, and when he stood he pulled out ...

"A sword?" Seriously? Images of Andre gutting members of the Elysium Order danced before my eyes. "Wait, why do you even *have* an armory beneath your desk?"

Andre strode over to me and began strapping the knives to my legs. "Being the king of vampires is a dangerous position. One can never be too prepared."

Clearly.

Andre slung the sword over his shoulder and strapped the remaining knives to himself. He knelt at my side, checking my weapons to make sure they were secure on my body.

"If the situation arises, swear to me that you won't hesitate to use these," he said, rising to his feet. His hands gripped my arms tightly and his eyes bored into mine.

I tried to speak, then cleared my throat. "I swear it," I whispered, though I had no idea if I could actually hold up my end of the bargain. Killing bad guys was one thing, but if the Politia came at me, I wasn't sure I had it in me to put my life above theirs.

Andre scrutinized me for a moment, then nodded, seeming satisfied. He grabbed my hand and opened the door that led to the persecution tunnel.

We worked our way back through the hallway we came in through. Waiting by the next door was the servant Tybalt spoke of. He held what I presumed was our enchantment bag, though you'd never assume magic had touched it. It was made of leather and canvas and looked painfully ordinary.

This girl was not impressed.

"The bag contains all the provisions you requested," the servant said.

Andre took it from his servant and slung it over his shoulder. His eyes moved to a bank of screens I hadn't noticed during my first trip through the tunnel. They'd been set into the walls, and judging from the grainy footage, they were capturing the area surrounding the house.

"What have you seen?" Andre asked the man.

"Three separate groups watch the house. Most of them have focused their attention on the front and rear exits, but," he nodded to one of the screens, "In the last five minutes some have staked out the alley." Our exit.

"How did they know?" I asked.

"Seers," Andre said, studying the screens.

The servant didn't bat an eyelash at the explanation. Andre's employees must indeed be more than they appear.

I studied the footage. At first I saw nothing out of the ordinary, but after looking long enough, certain details popped out. A row of silver Mercedes, a group of people who glanced in a certain direction a bit too often, bulges mostly hidden by loose clothing.

"Soulmate." Andre watched me. "Ready?"

I swallowed and nodded. We left the monitors and Andre's servant. A strange thrill filled me as we crossed that final hallway once more. It was back to me and Andre against the world. If this was how I was going to spend my final days, then I couldn't complain too much. There was no other company I'd rather keep.

Rather than exiting the final door out, Andre circled the motorcycle.

I sucked in a breath. "You want us to ride the metal death beast?"

Andre slid the bag off his shoulder. From inside it, he pulled out two leather jackets. He handed one to me. "If you're referring to the motorcycle," he said, shrugging the jacket over his shoulders, "then yes." He opened a small compartment at the back of the bike and placed the bag inside it.

I slipped on the leather jacket, noting absently that it fit me like a glove. Now I knew what all the leather apparel was for.

"My mom would so not be cool with this," I said.

Andre shrugged off his sword to put on his jacket, then

fitted the weapon back over the leather. "Your mother would also not be cool with you dying," he said, zipping up the jacket. "I consider riding a motorcycle the lesser of two evils." He nodded to the helmet resting on the leather seat. "That's yours as well."

I might've drooled a little at the sight of Andre in fitted leather. When he saw my starry-eyed look, he grabbed the helmet and fit it over my head for me. Guess I wasn't moving fast enough.

He swung a leg over the bike, then patted the seat behind him. "Get on, love."

Gingerly I slid onto the bike behind him. I was so going to die. And in leather pants of all things.

Andre grabbed one of my thighs and pulled me flush against him. "You need to remain this close to me, or else you risk sliding off."

Oh, that I could do.

"Wrap your hands around my waist—beneath the leather."

Again, not a problem. I did as he said, letting my fingers run over all the hard planes of his chest. Beneath my hands, Andre's muscles clenched. He glanced over his shoulder, a sculpted eyebrow arched.

"What?" I asked, innocently.

He shook his head, a grin spreading across his face. "You're making this hard for me, soulmate. *Very* hard." Sex dripped from his words, making my own muscles tighten.

He pulled a pair of shades out of his jacket pocket and slid them on.

"You're not going to wear a helmet?"

The corner of his mouth lifted. "That's a cute thought."

"It's called safety."

He cranked on the engine and the motorcycle roared to life. "Does anything about me strike you as 'safe'?"

"You're a horrible role model," I muttered, leaning into him.

The punk chuckled at that. Chuckled.

He hit a button embedded on the wall next to the bike, and the garage door set alongside the barred door lifted.

He gunned the throttle and the engine roared as we took off, leaving the persecution tunnel. My grip clamped down on him as Andre hooked a sharp left. The tires skidded, and the vehicle leaned dangerously close to the ground. I could already tell I was going to need new underwear after this.

Andre pulled back on the throttle and tires squealed as the bike shot forward out of the turn. So much for being inconspicuous.

The motorcycle propelled us down the alley. I squeezed him tighter as the wind whistled through my helmet.

I chanced a glance behind me.

Big mistake.

Several people ran out into the alleyway behind us, pulling out phones and—

"Gun!" I shrieked. Between the engine, the wind, and my helmet, I doubted Andre had heard me, but even if he had, there was little he could do at this point.

A moment later a shot rang out. Then another. Over

the noise of the bike I could hear screaming. We hadn't been hit, but someone else might've been.

I closed my eyes, shoving down my rising sickness. They were trying to hit me. Trying to kill me. I doubted that a bullet would lay me out, but it would really, really hurt.

It would, however, piss me off something fierce.

The backs of buildings blurred as we sped by them. Another gun blast, another series of screams.

I could hear cars turning onto the ally, and I didn't have to look to know it would be those silver vehicles that had laid in wait outside Andre's home.

I swallowed back my bile at the thought of getting caught here and now. I had to trust that the man I clung to could get us out of the situation—because at the moment, I was completely useless.

Where the alley emptied onto a busy road, a cluster of individuals waited, blockading our exit. These guys didn't look quite so official as those tailing us. They were a little rangier, their faces a bit rugged and sinewy. On the good-versus-evil spectrum I'd say they canted more towards the wicked side.

Andre accelerated as we approached them. Guess we were playing chicken. I shuddered at the thought of getting upended from our vehicle. This could get dicey.

Fifty feet. Thirty. Ten.

Five.

At the last possible second, the human wall dived out of the way—though from the slight bounce of the motorcycle, someone didn't move quickly enough.

I glanced back in time to see a man clutching a foot, his mouth open in a silent wail. I stared long enough to see him and the rest of his group scatter when the line of silver cars swung out of the alley. Behind them, more individuals exited the side street, chasing after us on foot.

Good luck with that.

I faced forward once more, my limbs going boneless. That had been so close. Too close. And we still weren't out of the woods yet.

Andre weaved in and out of traffic, though that sounded so ... tame. What he did was a violent dance—using his supernaturally quick reflexes to speed up then suddenly drop us into openings between cars. Too bad that pasta still wasn't agreeing with my stomach. I might be a badass vampire chick, but I was getting green with motion sickness.

Don't barf in your helmet. Don't barf in your helmet, I chanted.

Cars honked as Andre cut them off. Belatedly I realized that he wasn't just slipping between cars. He was causing gridlock so that the Mercedes wouldn't be able to follow.

At the end of the block a green light switched to yellow. Andre laid on the throttle.

"Andre ..."

He shouted something back at me, but the wind snatched it away.

Fucking-A, I wasn't going to have to worry about our pursuers trying to kill me. Andre would do a perfectly good job of it all on his own.

The light turned red and the bike sped up.

I held my breath as we darted into the intersection. Turning my head, I stared down the car barreling towards me.

This was it.

Chapter 5

"You ... DRIVE LIKE shit," I said as Andre swung himself off the bike. We'd stopped at the edge of some farmer's field after driving out of town.

I sort of slid off the motorcycle. Andre caught me and steadied me on my feet. "You okay?"

I nodded my head, then shook it, my helmet sliding around as I did so. My stomach was roiling and my body was shaking from the last half hour's near-death experiences. All twelve of them. I'd counted.

After narrowly escaping getting hit by an oncoming car, Andre had continued to weave in and out of traffic and blow through lights, regardless of their color. I discovered tonight that a vampire's reflexes were fast enough to avoid what should've been unavoidable collisions. Fifteen minutes ago we'd managed to ditch all our stage-five clingers.

Not that it stopped Andre from driving like a crazy person.

Frowning at me, said vampire pulled my helmet off. "Are you sur—?"

I took a couple staggering steps away from him and vomited up the bloody dinner I'd just eaten. Pasta: one; Gabrielle: zero.

"*Soulmate.*" Andre knelt next to me and placed a hand on my back.

I took in a couple deep breaths and inhaled. "I'm okay."

"You are *not* okay." The back of Andre's hand went to my forehead.

I brushed it away. "I'm not ill, just carsick."

"You should eat something."

My stomach cramped up at the thought. "No!"

Andre glanced at me sharply.

I cleared my throat. "I mean, *no,*" I said, this time a bit more calmly. I stared across the field. "What are we doing here?"

Andre followed my gaze. "I wanted to check in with you before we continued."

I took in several deep breaths. "Does that mean I have to get back on that thing again?" I asked, nodding to the bike.

Andre didn't say anything. Instead he brushed my hair from my face, a small crease forming between his brows.

How gentle he was when it came to me. This same man who hadn't flinched when we'd been shot at earlier. This man who was willing to cut down every one of my enemies.

He headed for the small storage compartment at the

back of the bike. From it he pulled out a bottle of water and sauntered back over to hand it to me.

"Thanks," I said, taking the bottle from him. I took several long, deep swallows, which went a long ways towards calming my stomach. Food might not agree with me at the moment, but water still did.

"We need to find shelter," he said.

Meaning we would, in fact, have to get back on the bike. Oh joy.

I cast a hateful glance at our ride. "How long will I have to be on it?"

His lips thinned.

"That long?"

"I'm sorry, soulmate; I don't know where we'll end up or how many miles lay between here and there."

Ah. Right, I'd almost forgot about the seers we had to dodge. I could already tell it was a tricky business, getting somewhere you needed to go without really knowing how you're going to get there.

His face became grimmer. "That was the Politia earlier."

I breathed in and out through my nose. "I figured." Nothing more needed to be said. My four months spent working with them had all been for nothing.

"Caleb ..." I couldn't finish the thought.

Don't trust anyone. Not even me.

"He has his duty and we have ours."

I nodded, pressing my mouth into a tight line. I had to face the facts: my former partner and friend—the guy I'd solved a case with only last week—was likely hunting me as well.

An equally terrible thought hit me. "Do you think Oliver and Leanne hate me?" I asked.

"Soulmate, how anyone could hate you is beyond me," Andre said.

That was laughable, considering our situation.

Seeing that I needed a bit more reassurance, Andre stepped in close, and his fingers lightly touched my cheek. "No, I do not believe they hate you. They already knew your secrets. If their friendship is true, as I suspect it is, nothing between you will have changed."

It seemed so simple, so obvious when he put it that way. Too bad I still had my doubts.

"Now," he said, his thumb brushing my lower lip, "are you ready to continue?"

I sucked in a breath and nodded. I could beast this thing. I picked up my discarded helmet and followed Andre back over to the bike. Around us, the shadows rippled as wind tore through the fields. It lifted my hair, as if trying to tug me away with it.

On its own, the world was a strange place, with its own beguiling magic. And it had me bewitched completely.

IT TOOK US another hour to find shelter, but this time I actually enjoyed the trip. Andre had stopped driving like a maniac, and if anything, he was being too careful. Someone was feeling guilty.

The fields eventually gave way to woods. These were the lands that birthed many of the fairytales I knew. I eyed them warily as we passed them, waiting for something to happen. I kept envisioning monster roots shooting out and wrapping themselves around me before dragging me away.

Paranoia had obviously taken over my life.

Suddenly, Andre veered off the road.

"Whoa, what are we doing?" I asked.

If he heard me, he chose not to respond.

He wove the motorcycle between trees, some low-hanging branches snapping as they got caught on the bike.

Oh God, this was going to awaken all sorts of buried claustrophobia. I pressed my eyelids closed as we passed between them, my earlier nausea stirring once more.

We didn't drive for too much longer. As soon as we came upon a rocky outcropping, the bike slowed to a stop. Andre killed the engine, standing to flick the kickstand out.

"Why have we stopped?" I asked, still holding onto his torso.

"Because, little mate, we need to rest." Andre hopped off the bike, his feet crunching into the brittle leaves that covered the ground.

Reluctantly I slid off the bike and removed my helmet, shaking out my hair with a hand while Andre opened the trunk.

I cast a glance at our surroundings. Another bloody freaking forest. I was beginning to hate nature. Even now we could be in the same woods where Hansel and Grettle almost got eaten by the evil witch. Bet that fairytale was true.

I bet siren tasted good, too.

Andre took out our bag, and from it, he pulled out ...

"Is that a tent?"

"It is," he said.

"What are you doing with it?"

"Tonight we're camping."

"Here?" I waved at our surroundings. Things happened in forests like these. Altars grew out of the ground. People disappeared. Mythical creatures made appearances.

"Here," he confirmed. Andre was already hauling the tent makings apart.

"But ... but what about the sun?" I was officially drawing at straws—although this was a legitimate concern.

"I'm not that delicate, soulmate."

"And werewolves?"

The edges of Andre's lips curled. "I don't smell dog. I think we're safe."

I warily eyed the tree next to me, earning me a laugh from my soulmate.

"Believe it or not," Andre continued. "I've done this before. For the moment, we're safe."

I guess that was that.

I went over to try to help him put our makeshift home together, but he shooed me away. "Soulmate, let me be your champion for a while."

"Champion?"

Andre sighed as he slid poles through the material. "Your knight, your defender. No one remembers these things anymore."

"Oh," I said, then furrowed my brows. "So you're defending me from what, pitching a tent? Give me a little more credit than that."

He snapped a pole into place. "Women taking men's words the wrong way," he muttered, "now that's one thing that's remained constant over centuries."

I swatted him on the arm, causing him to grin.

"I know that you're more than capable of doing this," Andre said. "Doesn't mean I want you to."

He removed the holstered sword slung across his back then shrugged off his coat, giving me ample opportunity to gawk at his arm muscles. My skin began to glow. As he went back to putting together the tent, his nostrils flared and his lips twitched.

If I kept this up, I wouldn't be able to fit inside it between him and his ego.

I swiveled away, peering at the peculiar canvas of the tent. The material had a strange iridescent sheen. I crept closer to it and ran my fingers over the material. "What is this?"

"Refractive silk," Andre said, sliding another pole in. "It bends light and gives the illusion that we're invisible."

"Whoa." That was ... epically cool.

I sat on a nearby boulder and watched Andre's progress. But now that I finally had a moment to process the last several hours, my thoughts strayed back to our getaway.

I cocked my head. "You're a bad dude, aren't you?" Andre hadn't hesitated once during that escape, and he'd seemed more than equipped to handle both fleeing and fighting. Almost like he'd gone through the motions before.

He smirked as he slid another pole through the material, though something sad and serious lingered at the back of his eyes. "Quite."

I nodded to myself.

"I am still sorry that you got matched with me." Andre looked up from his work.

I met his gaze. "I'm not. I think you're the best thing that's ever happened to me."

His nostrils flared—probably testing the air to see whether I was lying or telling the truth. But if he was looking for deceit, he'd be sorely disappointed.

I stood up just as the tent went up. My jaw slackened when I saw just how well the thing blended in with its surroundings, especially impressive considering just how large the thing was.

"Wow."

Andre held open the flap. "Come inside, soulmate. I'll join you in a minute with our things."

Death and fighting were forgotten for a moment. I walked over to him and peered inside. Andre watched me closely, a smile dancing on his face and his eyes shining brightly.

Inside, the material was a velvety midnight blue, and a repeated pattern of fleurs-de-lis and roses had been woven into the material. I could see all this because the walls of the tent glowed dimly, as if by the light of several phantom candles. Even empty as it was, the place had a richness to it, reminding me that my soulmate was an immortal king. Sometimes I forgot.

I walked up to one of the walls and touched it. The velvet looked ... old. Not in a moth-eaten, decayed way, but in a way that spoke of long hours toiling over dyes and looms. For all I knew, Andre had owned this tent for centuries, and the magic woven into it had prevented it from aging. It seemed like something one would invest large amounts of money in once upon a time.

"What are you thinking about, soulmate?" Andre asked from behind me. I hadn't heard him enter.

I turned to see him scrutinizing me with no little amount of desire in his eyes.

"You," I said.

"Oh?" The air thickened with Andre's spicy scent. His pheromones.

I took a step back as they hit me. It reminded me that he was a predator, used to hunting down fleeing things.

We stared at each other across the expanse of the tent, neither sure what the other's next move might be.

With an effort Andre tore his gaze away. He sealed up the tent's flaps then headed to the back of the room.

Andre shrugged off the enchanted bag, letting it drop to the floor. Metal slid against leather as he then removed his sword from his shoulder and the knives strapped to his sides. He knelt and set the weapons next to the bag.

Next, he opened the sack and began pulling out furs and blankets—

Furs? My eyes darted to the fluffy white fleece.

Mary had a little lamb ... then Andre got ahold of it.

"Soulmate."

"Hmmm?" I ripped my gaze from the fur. Andre pulled out a blood bag from his belongings and tossed it to me.

I caught it. "Mmm, dinner." I tried not to think about

how blood had become more appealing than human food in the last day. I stuck the straw in my mouth and guzzled it down, watching Andre as he set up the bed.

He placed two pillows down, side by side.

A bed for *us*.

This wouldn't be the first time I slept alongside him, but something about the way those furs were piled in the corner of this richly decorated tent made me feel like a barbarian queen with barbarian needs.

My soulmate has needs that only I can satisfy.

Andre breathed in deep, then pierced me with another heated look. His muscles were tightly coiled.

I cleared my throat. "I still can't believe my *champion* is making me sleep in the woods," I said, because it seemed like the only way to put distance between this. Us.

Andre stood—the king who just spent the last twenty minutes readying our camp—and came over to me. He tilted my face to his. "How might I make things better for my sweet siren?"

Another endearment. And now he was looking at me like he could see through my weak attempts at being rude.

"A toothbrush and toothpaste."

Andre went to our bag and dug out both, presenting me with them.

I blinked. "Oh. Uh, thanks." It had been more of a pipedream than an actual request. I'd assumed I'd have to go sans toiletries while we ran. I should've known he'd include it if he managed to pack a tent and furs.

I stepped out of the tent and brushed my teeth several times to get rid of all traces of my earlier sickness. The trees rustled as a gentle breeze stirred them, and a short distance away an owl hooted. This place seemed peaceful and remote enough, but would it hide us well enough for the next day?

My fears and insecurities came rising to the surface. What if they found us during the day while we slept?

It didn't take too much imagination to figure out what would happen. A stake in my heart and Andre dragged into the sun. I might still be human enough to wake up in the middle of it, to be cognizant of the fact that I was getting killed, but Andre wouldn't. Not until he was fully in the throes of death. The images were horrifying, and I had to force them down. We could only stay the course at this point.

I headed back for the tent ... and promptly ran into it. The thing quivered, like it might go down.

"Soulmate?" Andre's disembodied head leaned out of the tent a moment later, his lips twitching like mad.

"Don't you *dare* laugh."

"Wouldn't dream of it." Andre held the flap open.

I re-entered, my eyes seeking out the bed before I averted them once more.

"So, what are our next moves?" I sat down next to it and began to remove my shoes.

Andre followed me down to the ground, and his hands covered mine as I reached for my boot. Electricity jolted through the touch and our gazes met.

Breathless, I let go of my shoe, and Andre's fingers curled over the leather. He removed it for me, his hands skimming over my calves and caressing my ankles as he pulled it off.

He moved to the other boot, his hands again gliding over my leg. Andre was making shoe removal into some erotic dance, paying homage to my legs.

My socks were quick to go next, and then Andre's hands drifted to the knives strapped against me. He unhooked the holsters with the utmost care, setting them on the edge of the bed, next to his own.

The atmosphere was changing, the air heavy with our barely-restrained desires.

My pulse tapped out some tune as his scent enveloped me once more. He picked me up and moved me onto our makeshift bed. I dug my fingers into the thick fur beneath me.

Andre's body leaned over mine. I stared up at him, feeling strangely vulnerable. This was what men and women did together, what I wanted to do with Andre. And it felt like a whole world of emotions wrapped itself into every touch and look.

He found my jacket's zipper, and he dragged it down. The sound of parting material seemed louder than a fireworks display. With his help, I shrugged the garment off.

His eyes softened as he gazed down at me. "My love, there are not words to describe all the ways you are magic."

My throat constricted. I knew the feeling. He was my deepest wish, my most coveted dream, and impossible though it seemed, he was *real*. That was the most awe-inspiring magic out there.

Andre slid a hand behind my head and leaned down until his lips pressed against mine. Almost reverently he stroked my mouth with his own, building a slow, steady fire at my core.

He tasted like home, like finally, *finally* my soul could be at ease because he was here. He nipped at my bottom lip, demanding entrance. Half of me wanted to resist, just to see what my demanding boyfriend would do, but the other, dominant half knew I didn't have that much self-restraint. My lips parted, and his tongue scoured my mouth.

His body pressed flush against mine, and his hand skimmed down my side. Stopping mid-thigh, his grip tightened as he pulled my leg closer towards him.

He broke away from the kiss, and his lips skimmed my jawline. "I want to remove every last shred of fabric from your body and mine," he whispered into my ear, pressing a kiss to the underside of my jaw while one of his hands traveled down my torso "and bury myself so deep inside you that neither of us can remember where I end and you begin."

I let out a gasp at his words, my skin brightening. His fingers trailed along the hem of my shirt before finding the edge of my pants. Deftly they flicked open the top button and delved beneath the fabric of both pants and panties.

"Andre—" I couldn't decide if I was going to ask him something, tell him something, or plead with him. In the end I decided I just wanted the sound of his name on my tongue.

His hooded eyes burned into mine as his fingers found my core, and I jolted at the sensation, even as he let out a groan. "Ah *dios mio*," he said, "you feel even better than I imagined. And how I have imagined." His fingers stroked me rhythmically, and I found myself moving against him. "I cannot wait to taste you, soulmate."

Taste?

I was panting. Oh my God, I was panting like a freaking animal.

Under his stare I felt stripped bare, and there was nowhere to hide. All my vulnerabilities were laid out for him to judge. If his face was anything to go by, I had his wild approval.

His tempo increased as he moved down my body. He used his free hand to tug my clothes farther down my legs. Then he bent his head down, and—*all that is holy*—I lost myself to sensation.

BREATHING HEAVILY, I lay boneless on the bed.

Needs met. Needs most definitely *met.*

Andre gathered me to him on the bed. Limply, I rolled onto his torso.

He chuckled and stroked my back, holding me close. "This is my heaven. Your scent on my skin, your taste in my mouth,"—I definitely managed to get a blush going at that—"your spent body draped over mine."

I buried my face into his chest, at a loss for words or action. What was the etiquette here? Did I reciprocate? Did we do more? Should I thank him? I should probably thank him.

"Thank you," I whispered.

Beneath me, Andre stilled. "'Thank you'?" he repeated.

I knew it was the wrong thing to say by the tone of his voice.

He sat up, forcing me to look at him. "Soulmate," he chastised, "that is not how this works—how *we* work. You never need to thank me for anything I give you. *Especially* not that."

I winced. Now would be a great time for a horde of angry supernaturals to strike—anything to break up this awkward-as-hell conversation that I just had to start by opening my big, fat mouth.

Seeing my expression, Andre cursed under his breath. "I did not mean to embarrass you." He ran a hand through his hair. "I forget sometimes that you have not been with me since the very beginning. That you are young and your feelings are fragile yet."

"Andre," my voice was barely a whisper, "you are killing me. Can we please change the subject?" I mumbled.

He gave me a sly smile. "Of course—though I'm afraid it will be hard for me. My mind is replaying the last twenty minutes on repeat." More quietly he added, "You cannot know how long I've craved you like that."

Andre was proving to be horrible at changing the subject.

He lay back down, and I readjusted myself so that I was half on half off of him.

"Soulmate, that is only the beginning," he whispered in my ear.

I shivered.

Not the beginning, a small voice whispered. *The end.*

Chapter 6

"WHY IS THERE a blanket over my face?"

"Hmmm?" I stirred, hearing the rustling next to me.

A moment later I was flipped onto my back. I blinked several times and stared up at Andre. He gazed down at me with amusement in his eyes. "Did you cover my face to protect me from the elements?"

I rubbed my eyes. "Blanket?" I dimly remembered Andre falling asleep. I'd been nervous that the material over our heads wouldn't be enough against the power of the sun, so I'd made sure to cover him with another layer.

"You *did*." He appeared oddly touched by the action. "I promise you I am more resilient than that."

His fingers brushed the skin of my lower belly, and my thoughts went back to the previous evening. My pulse picked up at all the things that Andre did. Judging by his smoldering expression, he wanted to resume last night's intimacy.

Andre stiffened, his eyes unfocusing. He canted his head, his hungry look changing to one of concern.

His eyes refocused. "The forest has betrayed us." He spoke so low even I had to strain to hear him.

I sat up at that. Oh, I *knew* this was going to happen. One does not fuck with forests.

"The trees must have whispered our location to the folk that live here," Andre continued.

"How do you know that?" I asked quietly, reaching for my weapons. Andre helped me strap them on before getting his on as well.

"I can hear them."

Them who?

"They haven't found us yet, and they're still some distance away. If their senses aren't too good, we might be able to slip by undetected."

"Who *are* the folk that live here?"

Andre shook his head, his eyes concerned. "We might find out soon enough."

ANDRE'S FORM BLURRED as he rapidly deconstructed the tent. I did my part by shoving our provisions back into the enchantment bag after I dressed.

I still hadn't heard any of these forest folk, and I really hoped that was because they were far away and not because they were covertly surrounding us.

"Ready, soulmate?" Andre asked, putting the last pieces

72

of the tent back into the sack.

"Where's our bike?" I asked, glancing around.

Andre sauntered towards one of the trees and reached out. His hand seemed to sweep the air, until it wasn't sweeping air. It looked like a rip in space as he pulled off the same refractive material that made up our tenth. Beneath it was the motorcycle.

I grabbed my helmet and fitted it over my head while Andre stowed away our provisions in the bike's little trunk.

"Is it safe to ride this motorcycle two days in a row?"

Andre came around to the front of the vehicle and pulled out his shades. "Of course."

"But what if they trace our plates?"

Andre smiled at that, like I was cute. "My license plates are enchanted. They rearrange themselves for each pair of eyes that read them."

I whistled. "That seems useful for breaking the law."

"It's served me well."

Yep, Andre was definitely a bad dude.

Andre patted the seat. "Ready?"

I hopped onto the back of the bike. "Let's do this bitch."

WE'D BEEN ON the bike for only a few short minutes when I began to hear what sounded like thunder. Slight tremors ran through the earth, making me think that the devil himself was about to split the ground open and crawl out from beneath.

A flash of movement blurred in my peripherals, but by the time I turned my head, it was gone. Another blur sped by on the opposite side. This time when I swiveled, I got a good look at the source.

Holy-mother-of ... *hooves*. Those were the forest folk? *Centaurs?*

I'd barely had time to process the sight when a dozen of them converged on either side of us, carrying crudely made weapons.

I let out a little squeak. I'd assumed the forest folk would be pixies or ethereal elves. Not these scary-ass beasts that seemed intent on taking us out.

Andre turned his head slightly. I couldn't be sure, but I thought I heard him say, "You good?"

No. Absolutely not. Four-legged men were chasing us. Even over the roar of the engine I could hear their pounding hooves.

I squeezed Andre tighter as he gunned the vehicle, and I swear I heard him chuckle, like this was his idea of fun.

They couldn't keep up, not really, but they seemed to be herding us towards more of their comrades who were waiting for us farther in.

A spear—no joke, a *spear*—whizzed by, narrowly missing us. Then another. Had these people never heard of gunpowder?

With alarm I realized that while these centaurs might not be able to keep up with us, they could throw these javelins faster than the speed of out motorcycle. So far, all of them had clattered innocently enough to the ground, but I could see the barbed tips of each. If one of those spears embedded itself into flesh, it would hurt like a mo-fo to get out.

74

No sooner had the thought crossed my mind than I heard the sickening thump of one lodging itself snugly between my ribs. My grip loosened and my lips parted as the pain hit me. I gasped.

Sweet baby Jesus, that burned.

Andre cut the bike sharply to the right and slammed on the brakes. I moaned as my body jerked and the spear cut deeper into flesh. He threw a hand out to help cushion me—big thanks there—and cut the engine.

I would not glance over my shoulder at my wound. I would not.

I peeked, and *oh God*, I had a pole sticking out of my side. I could feel the skin beginning to seal over it.

Just when I assumed the worst thing would be pulling out a barbed spear from one's skin, my body had to up the ante and reseal the wound with the weapon still embedded in it.

Joy.

Dozens of centaurs circled us, rallying war cries. Some held up their spears and fist pumped the air with them. Not all of those that encircled us were men. A few were women, their breasts bound with linen wrappings. They looked just as fierce as their male counterparts.

Amidst all this, Andre swung a leg off the bike and casually pulled off his shades. He nodded to our opponents, assessing them as they surrounded us.

I slid off the bike, biting back a cry when the spear handle banged against the vehicle, jostling the injury.

"Give us the girl," one of the centaurs demanded. His voice rumbled much deeper than a human voice, despite the fact that the upper half of the centaur looked identical to a man.

Andre flicked a lazy glance over his shoulder at me, his face hardening at the sight of a giant freaking weapon protruding from my body. A low growl emanated from somewhere deep in his chest.

His hair shifted and rippled. It was his calling card. The vampire king's equivalent to the flick of a cat's tail, a signal that he was getting pissed.

He swiveled back to face the centaurs. "I don't think so." His hair began to whip about him.

I had no idea what Andre was planning, but chances were, a lot of centaurs were about to die. I wasn't just going to sit here and watch.

Gritting my teeth, I grabbed the base of the spear. Using one hand, I braced the head of the thing. I wrapped the other around the shaft and yanked sharply down. Wood splintered, and I twisted it the rest of the way off.

When I glanced back up, I noticed several of the centaurs had crept unsettlingly close. Near enough to make a lunge for me while Andre was distracted.

But the ones who crept up on me were all male, and their leers did nothing to settle me.

"Whoa, back the hell up." The helmet muffled my words, earning me a few chuckles from the centaurs nearest me.

My skin flared up in irritation, and I whipped off the helmet.

Go screw yourself. The words were on the tip of my tongue before I realized that I had no idea what would result from that command when the siren was riding my voice. Curious though I was, I did not want the visual.

I glanced at Andre, who'd pulled out two daggers, leaving the sword sheathed. He casually flipped them in his hands, like he'd handled them thousands of times before. He probably had, and hot damn if that was not sexy.

His hair was still rippling, his unearthly anger only just kept in check.

One of the centaurs goaded him. "Getting a taste of that piece of ass before the devil does?"

Andre lunged, his body a blur. He drove the blade of one of his weapons into the centaur's heart. His victim didn't even have time to scream before Andre was finished with him. And then he was moving onto his next victim, a blur of anger and action.

And, cue the mayhem.

The centaurs at my back descended on me all at once. Strong hands grabbed me and dragged me with them. I was pressed against the bristly fur of one centaur's chest, the action grinding the spear deeper into me. I hissed at the sensation, the pain making me woozy.

My nostrils flared and I breathed in a lungful of horse as another centaur pressed in close, fingering my hair. "Pretty thing, this one. Perhaps we shouldn't kill her right away."

I glanced over at him, his human torso tapering away to his equine body. When he caught me staring at him, he spoke again. "If you're lucky, I'll let you ride me first."

One should not mess with a siren. We can get you to do things. Unnatural things.

I let the monster in me rise. The centaurs leaned towards me as my glowing skin beckoned them closer. "Why don't you all ride each other?" I said, my voice ringing melodically. I'd let them interpret that one however they liked.

Though it wasn't a direct order, the centaurs within hearing range all took up the suggestion. The creature pinning me to his chest now released me to grab the man who'd only seconds ago made the lewd comment. Others began to grapple with one another as each tried to mount those next to them.

Across from me, Andre paused to glance over at the commotion on my end of the circle, and he did a double take. Behind him a centaur reared up with a spear.

"Duck!" I yelled, the siren entering my voice. Immediately the entire gathering—including those centaurs still trying to ride each other—ducked. I bit the inside of my cheek to cut off the crazy laughter that I wanted to let loose.

"She's commanding people with her voice!" one of the centaurs shouted.

Before anyone could even try to cover their ears, I yelled, "Stop fighting and listen up!" Movement halted. Some paused with spears raised.

I shrugged off a hand that had grabbed at me, drawn to my glowing skin, and sauntered into the middle of the group. "Andre, I command you to ignore everything I'm about to say." He gave the barest inclination of his head before he turned away, already following my orders.

"Centaurs," I said, addressing the remaining group, "in

thirty seconds you are all going to forget that I exist. You'll never be able to recognize my name when you hear it, or my face when you see it. You're going to run back the way you came, and you're only going to stop once you're close to collapsing."

After thirty seconds ticked by, the group of centaurs kicked up dust as they retreated into the forest. A couple of them awkwardly got off each other, averting their eyes with embarrassment as they did so.

My skin dimmed. Only when the siren had descended back into me did I approach Andre. I placed a hand on his shoulder, and he blinked several times, as though waking from a stupor. He rubbed his temples and shook his head. "Remind me never to piss you off." His cheeks were flushed, and he wiped a drop of blood from the corner of his mouth. He had several holes in his attire and smears of crimson where their weapons must've pierced him.

Littered around us were the bodies of several fallen centaurs, their throats slit or, in some cases, ripped open. Looked like Andre had bummed breakfast off of the forest folk while he fought.

His eyes roved over me, stopping when he saw the broken end of the spear still sticking out of my back.

He stilled. "It didn't work its way out?"

"Was it supposed to?" I asked, peering down at it.

Andre sheathed his knives, his attention wholly focused on me. His arm brushed my side as his hand wrapped around the base of the spearhead.

"Andre—"

"Do you remember the first time we saw each other?"

he asked me, dragging my attention away from the weapon.

"What does that have to do with anything?"

His fingers were now probing the wound. "I saw you across the room. The connection for me was instant. You were the sun, and I was a moth drawn to your brightness."

I narrowed my eyes. "I swear if you yank this thing out while you're talking, I will make you hump a tree, then film it and sell it to the media."

His hand fell away from the spearhead, clearly convinced I'd make good on the threat after my little show with the centaurs. "You're wounded and in pain, soulmate. The sooner this thing is out of you, the sooner you'll feel better."

Maybe, but ...

I hugged my arms. "It's barbed," I said, like that was any type of explanation. It would reinjure me on its way out.

"You're my brave mate. This is nothing." Andre knelt, getting a better look at the entry point. I shivered as his thumb traced over the surrounding skin. He leaned in and kissed the point of entry. He was being tender with me; it was a shocking contrast to the killer I'd seen only moments before.

"We need to leave soon," he said. "If I don't take the spearhead out now, you'll have to ride with it in."

I tried to imagine riding over the bumps and dips with the weapon still lodged in me, every jostle scraping the bone of my ribs.

I put the pad of my hand to my eye. "Fine." He just had to be reasonable.

This was so going to hurt like a mo-fo.

Andre readjusted his grip, but I laid a hand over his, forcing him to pause. "Talking won't distract me."

A sculpted eyebrow rose, and an edge of Andre's mouth curved up. He stood, and his hand reached out and stroked my neck, his thumb rubbing circles around my jugular vein. "I can think of a few other things that might suffice."

He pressed a kiss to my cheek, and I turned into the touch, my mouth meeting his. I could still taste the blood on his lips. A month ago it would've made me recoil. Now my fangs dropped, and I deepened the kiss, my nature craving more. Andre's mouth eagerly responded, our tongues twining.

All the while Andre drew slow circles over my jugular vein. The sensation coaxed the siren closer and closer to the surface. She'd only just withdrawn into me, but the taste of blood and the promise of passion were too much for her to stay away.

Andre broke off the kiss, his eyes moving to my neck. He stared at my pulse, mesmerized by it.

Do it. I clamped my mouth against the command, but when his eyes met mine, I nodded in consent. I didn't mind the prospect of a spear getting yanked out if it meant I'd get to experience Andre's bite.

He hesitated, I'm sure remembering the last time when he'd drawn too deeply from me. Lust shaded his eyes. Blood-letting and sex weren't so different for vampires.

"I don't want to hurt you."

I rolled my eyes, still keeping my mouth closed. He'd

been about to yank a spear out of my side seconds ago—hell, he still was. His bite would be far less painful. But this wasn't really about hurting me. This was about Andre's self-control. Between our bond and our natures, things usually got out of hand.

I made the decision for him. Wrapping a hand around the back of his neck, I brought his face forward until his nose skimmed the skin there. His breath fanned out against me, and I drew in a heady lungful of whatever pheromones Andre was giving off.

Captivating his prey. That was what he'd called it when he first taught me about drawing blood. Back then I'd been worried that the lust it compelled in me was somehow fake. But there was nothing fake about us. This. Andre could captivate me without the aid of pheromones.

His mouth widened, and his fangs punctured my flesh. There was an initial twinge of pain, followed by the electric shock of pleasure. My skin lit up at the sensation, and a lazy smile spread across my face. I could die a happy anti-Christ this way.

Andre groaned against my neck, and he pulled me closer to him. His hands brushed over me as he drank, heightening my pleasure. It felt like I was being touched for the first time.

I didn't notice his wandering hand until it was braced against my body. Somewhere deep within me, the remnants of fear stirred. This should hurt; I should be worried. The siren, however, purred at the thought of mingling pain and pleasure, and I leaned into Andre.

He jerked the spearhead out, and my back arched. On

the wave of endorphins that I rode, I only noticed a fuzzy sensation where the wound was. Distantly, I heard him toss the spearhead aside.

Andre's fangs retracted, and he kissed the wound he'd inflicted on my neck as I came down.

My body swayed. He steadied me, his brows furrowing in concern. "Soulmate?"

"I'm fine. Just feeling ..." High. Really, *really* high.

Andre cursed, running a hand over his face. "I'm sorry, soulmate. I shouldn't have drunk from you."

Still soaring from the bite and the endorphin rush, I pressed my fingers to his lips to get him to quiet.

His eyebrows rose.

"You're prettier when you're not talking," I explained.

One second I stood in front of him, the next I was thrown over his shoulder.

"Hey!"

"I am king of vampires, soulmate. Not something mute and *pretty*." He gave my backside a pinch to emphasize his point.

I yelped. "That is *not* chill."

He lifted the edge of my torn shirt.

"Okay, Andre," I said, reaching behind me for his hands, "this crosses a line—" Now that I was really starting to come down, my awareness was returning, and finding myself thrown over Andre's shoulder like a sack of potatoes was not endearing him to me.

He touched the tender skin at my back. "It's still healing," Andre said, more to himself than to me. His voice, which had sounded playful only a moment before, now held a somber note.

"Put me down."

Making sure not to jostle my wound, Andre slid me off of his shoulder and onto the seat of the motorcycle, his eyes stormy. Again I swayed a little as blood rushed from my head.

Andre headed towards the trunk and dug out several packages of sweets. A week ago, the sight of them would have my stomach rumbling. Now, however, it twisted on itself. The thought of forcing those down my throat had my gag reflex already warming itself up.

He handed them to me. "Forgive me for taking your blood. These will help replenish what you've lost." A vertical line formed between his brows, and I realized that Andre worried that my blood was not replenishing quickly enough on its own. That was why he reacted the way he did when I swayed from the comedown. He thought I'd been faint from blood loss.

"Andre, it's alright."

He shook his head. "Not when we have enemies after you. I just didn't realize ..." His eyes dropped to where my wound had been. It was still sore, when it shouldn't be.

He tore his gaze away from my torso to the food in my hands. "I know you're probably shaken, soulmate, but please try to eat."

I stared down at the preservative-riddled cinnamon roll and the two chocolate chip cookies he'd given me. If anything, my stomach was making it clearer now more than ever that it did not want food. But I couldn't ignore the desperation in Andre's eyes, and it frightened me. If my situation scared him, then how bad off must I be?

Before I could think too much on it, I unwrapped one of the packages and shoved the cookie into my mouth. It took a painstaking minute, but finally, with a thick swallow, it slid down my throat. Only the sick taste of sugar remained.

I just force fed myself a cookie, and I didn't enjoy it. That was just wrong.

Andre's eyes fell to the remaining packages in my hand, but I shook my head. "I'm sorry, but I can't." Already, my stomach heaved. I pressed the back of my hand to my mouth in an effort to keep it down.

It didn't work.

I felt myself pale. I dropped the remaining food and ran to the nearest tree. Gripping its trunk, my stomach convulsed until I puked. Even then, it kept spasming until I retched up everything.

I shook from the aftereffects, feeling faint. Ugh, I was *never* eating another cookie.

I didn't hear Andre approach me, but I felt his hand fall to my back and stroke it soothingly. "It's alright soulmate," he murmured, his voice too calm.

I pinched my eyes shut, afraid of what I'd see in his when I faced him.

But I heard him move away from me before I had to look. When he returned, his hand rested on my back. "Try this, instead," he whispered into my ear. I rotated enough to see the blood bag he extended towards me.

Taking it from him, I placed the straw in my mouth. As soon as the blood hit my mouth, I drank voraciously, like a man dying of thirst.

Gently Andre led me away from the evidence of my sickness and back towards the bike while I polished off the blood.

"Feeling better, soulmate?" Andre asked once I finished.

I nodded as he took the now empty bag from me. He reached into the trunk—presumably for another—when he paused.

He cocked his head, his eyes unfocused. Suddenly he snapped into action, closing the trunk. He used his abnormal speed to grab my helmet and press it onto my head.

He patted the seat. "Get on and make sure to hold me tight," he ordered.

"Andre, what's going on?" I asked, hopping onto the seat.

He swung a leg over and dragged me close to him. "The woods have gone quiet. Something's coming our way."

I threw a glance over my surroundings while Andre revved the engine. I got the vague sense that something lurked out there, but whatever it was, it didn't have time to sink its talons into me before Andre yanked on the throttle and got us the hell out of there.

Chapter 7

WE SPENT MOST of the night driving, only taking breaks to stretch our legs and rest for short bits of time. We stuck to back roads and rocky terrain whenever we could, making me think that while we'd been in the saddle for hours, we hadn't moved very far.

At some point the motorcycle slowed. I peered over Andre's shoulder at our destination. I caught sight of a wrought iron fence and tombstones.

What now?

Andre directed the bike onto the cemetery grounds, and we began to weave between grave markers. Eventually those gave way to crypts, each more ostentatious than the last.

I stared at them with no little amount of trepidation. A few turns later, Andre pulled the bike in between two of them and killed the engine.

"What are we doing here?" I asked, removing the helmet.

"We need to set up camp for the night." Andre pushed off the bike and began circling some of the nearby tombs.

Seriously? I glanced around. "But this is a graveyard."

"It is." His hand dragged along the stone, his eyes honing in on details I couldn't see.

I narrowed my gaze on him. "You suck at picking out places for us to stay."

"On the contrary, soulmate," he said, "I've had centuries to memorize those places that are tricky for seers to pinpoint. This is one of them."

I turned my frightened eyes to the structure nearest me. Andre hadn't parked near headstones; he'd stopped right in front of the ones with doors. "I'm going to have to get in there, aren't I?" Despite having an undead boyfriend and being a step away from death myself, ghosts and graveyards gave me the heebie jeebies.

A wind blew through the cemetery, making the frosted grass shiver. It ruffled Andre's hair as he straightened, returning to my side. For a moment, he was almost too much to stare at.

Andre gave me a small smile. "Don't tell me that you're scared of this?"

My attention turned to the crypt. Even from here I caught a whiff of desiccating bodies. I cringed at the thought of being inside the cramped quarters. The absolute darkness, the chill of stone and earth pressing in on me. That smell wrapping itself around us.

Andre brushed my hair away from my face. "I'm sorry, soulmate. I never wanted to expose you to the desperate measures vampires sometimes must take."

I looked at him skeptically. "You mean you've done this before?"

His jaw tightened. "A few times."

I tried to imagine this regal man, an international celebrity in certain circles, slinking into and out of a crypt just as we were about to do, but it was impossible.

I sighed. "I don't get a choice, do I?"

Andre cupped my face. "You always have a choice." His attention drifted up to the horizon. "But if I am to protect you, then *I* have no choice."

Damn his good intentions. The road to hell was paved with them.

"WELL ISN'T THIS cozy?" I said, rubbing my hands together fifteen minutes later. We were inside one of those blasted crypts, and I couldn't see for shit.

I heard the strike of a match, and then a warm orange glow lit up the room as Andre held the small flame in his hand. "The sun will be up soon, soulmate. You will only have to endure this for a few more minutes."

"I wasn't talking to you. I was talking to ... Katarina," I said, reading the placemarker and patting the woman's stone sarcophagus next to me. A small cloud of dust billowed out beneath my hand, and I made a face as I coughed and waved it away. I really hoped I didn't just breathe in the remains of my new friend.

Andre's eyes crinkled with amusement as he lit a candle he'd packed. He set it atop another stone casket and began setting up our bed once more.

Once he finished, he sat down amongst the blankets and furs. The sight of them brought back the memory of last night's intimacy.

"Come here, my little mate," Andre said, his eyes flickering in the firelight. "I want to feel you close to me."

I moved over to where he was, stretching my body out next to his, and he tucked me snugly into the side of his body. One of his arms arced over my head while the other draped itself over my stomach.

His presence consumed my thoughts and temporarily drove away my skittishness. But even as I calmed, I sensed his own tumultuous emotions. There was a restlessness to him, lingering just beneath his skin. Andre didn't panic the way that most people did. Instead he became more protective, more possessive, quicker to draw blood.

"After tomorrow we should hopefully have to hide less," he said, interrupting my thoughts.

"What's happening tomorrow?" I asked, staring up at the darkness above me.

"I can't tell you."

Another one of his precautions. I blew out a breath, already tired of being kept in the dark.

"I will not endanger you again, soulmate. You never should've been placed in harm's way to begin with."

I ran a tentative hand over the one that held me close, my brows furrowing at his words. "Endangering me again? What are you talking about, Andre?" I asked. "You're not playing some weird blame game on yourself, are you?"

"If I hadn't scared you away the night of my birthday, you'd never have run to the Politia. And if you hadn't worked for the Politia, you never would've been at the stone circle on Samhain and you would've never been in Romania." The two places the devil had snatched me.

"Ugh, you *are* playing the blame game. Andre, the fates have been meddling with my life since I was a baby." Since before then, if I considered the myths of Hades and Persephone. "Not to mention I'm cursed. It would've happened one way or another."

Andre didn't respond. Despite my words the man still blamed himself.

"I could simply command you to not feel guilty," I said.

He rolled his body so that he hovered over me. "If you entertain *that* thought any longer, I will make sure you can't talk."

"I'm pretty sure that bag of yours doesn't have duct tape in it."

"I wouldn't have to gag you to quiet your tongue." The sexual undercurrents of his words heated my skin.

I cleared my throat. "I won't glamour you. Pinky promise."

He raised his brows, the first stirrings of amusement lighting his face. "'Pinky promise'? Do I even want to know what that means?"

"This is a pinky promise—" I grabbed his hand and hooked my little finger through his. I got the impression that he was holding back a laugh.

I brought my joined hand to my lips and kissed it. "Now

it's your turn."

"My turn to do what?" The candlelight threw sensual shadows in the hollows beneath Andre's cheekbones. The darkness seemed to caress the edges of his lips and painted his brows with heavy strokes. He was exquisite to look at.

"Kiss your hand."

"I am *not* kissing my hand." He made it sound like it was beneath him.

"You have to," I whispered in the dimly lit room. "That's how it works."

He snatched his hand back. "I'm king of the vampires. I will not make any of these 'pinky promises.' The oaths I make are in blood."

"Fine. Be a boob."

"A *boob?*" He sounded genuinely offended.

I bit the inside of my cheek to keep from laughing.

Andre growled low in his throat. Grabbing my hand, he pressed a kiss to my knuckles. "There, satisfied, soulmate?" Beneath the annoyance, I could hear mirth in his voice, and that's all I really wanted—to make the guilt go away.

Still, Andre sucked at pinky promises.

I pushed him back down to our makeshift bed and lay back against him. "It'll have to do."

He huffed at my words, but I knew he was just posturing. His amusement had become obvious. His hand played with my hair while we laid in companionable silence.

Eventually my mind wandered back to the events that unfolded earlier this evening. "What does my blood taste like?" I asked him.

He fingered a lock of my hair, its ends tickling my cheek. "Ambrosia. Home."

"Oh." His words sank in, warming me from the inside out. Coming from a man who'd lived seven hundred years, that seemed to be saying a lot.

He turned his face so that his mouth was pressed to my ear. "Don't tell me that after everything, you're surprised by this?"

I stared up at the ceiling. "Sometimes it's hard to believe, you know?" I said. "I'd always been that girl that other girls hated. The one who never knew her biological parents. The one who never had money.

"Then I came to Peel and made friends, learned of my family, discovered an inheritance, found my soulmate."

I turned to look at him, our noses brushing. It would be so easy to close those last few inches and kiss him. "Even with everything horrible that's happened to me, sometimes it's hard to believe all the good that's come with it."

He nuzzled my nose. "I understand."

All my attention honed in on Andre. It was hard not to think of other things ... *intimate* things with him this close.

We stared at each other, and just like last night, the mood shifted. My skin began to lightly glow, and heat spread through my belly.

"What about ... ?" My voice trailed off. I couldn't do it. Couldn't bring myself to finish the sentence.

"What about what?" Andre asked, his gaze as intense as ever.

S-E-X. A short, simple word. After last night, it should've been easy to discuss. But my mouth refused to form the words, so instead I coughed. "Um, never mind."

The hand that rested over my waist now tightened. "Ah," he said, his eyebrows lifting. "What did you want to ask?" There was a note to Andre's voice that I couldn't place.

I shook my head.

"Is this about what we did, or what we haven't done?" he asked, running the fingers of his other hand through my hair.

I averted my eyes from his, instead staring at the cobwebbed ceiling. "Forget I asked."

"We're going to have to go over this at some point, soulmate. It might as well be now."

He wasn't going to let this go. Best rip it off like a Band-Aid, nice and quick.

My gaze reluctantly returned to his. "Will it feel like your bite—or like last night?" I cringed even as I spoke.

Andre stopped stroking my hair.

Kill me now.

After considering my question, Andre resumed stroking my hair. "No," he said. "It will feel different. *Better.*"

At his words, my skin brightened, illuminating all the dark corners of the chamber. My heart sped up until it was throwing itself at my ribcage, trying to break free.

Maybe this crypt had a small casket I could crawl into and die. I couldn't remember being this flustered in a long time.

Andre's hand moved up between my breasts and rested over that organ that kept me alive, the one that now belonged to him. "If I had known a little scandalous talk would move this thing into action, I would've spoken on this subject much sooner." What he hadn't mentioned was that he'd already sent it racing yesterday.

I could see him reveling in the sight of my skin and the solid thump of my heartbeat.

"You are beautiful, soulmate, for all those things that no one ever notices."

My throat constricted.

Andre brushed a chaste kiss across my cheekbone. Just as he drew away, his body stiffened.

"Andre?"

He sighed as air escaped his lungs, and then an unnatural stillness took over his body. My eyes searched for a window, seeking out the rising sun, but the only source of light in the tomb was the flickering flame.

My body was tugging me towards sleep, but my mind still raced. So much had happened to us over the last several days. Most bad, but some good.

A cool draft of air gusted through the crypt, blowing out the candle and throwing the room into darkness. I shivered. Andre's cold arms still encircled me, but his presence here was gone.

"Hello, consort."

Chapter 8

THE DEVIL'S BREATH moved the hair near my ear. If I turned, I probably would've brushed his lips.

Choking on my fear, I sat up. The darkness was absolute, and the only sentient thing in the crypt with me was the lord of the Underworld.

"Little bird, I can hear your fragile heart pattering away. It will give out soon, do you know this?" His words skittered over my skin.

"Go away," I whispered, my eyes wildly searching the blackness for him.

"Once you are queen, you will not fear me."

Terror lodged itself in my throat, and I swallowed, trying to tamp it down. "I thought you wanted me to fear you?"

Phantom fingers trailed up my forearms, drawing the

hairs to attention. The touch was oddly sensual. "I lied."

My skin crawled. "You're lying now."

The air shifted and I heard his hollow laugh. It echoed throughout the chamber. "And precisely how would you know that?"

My words hadn't angered him like they once might've. Odd.

"Come away with me," he said.

Next to me I heard Andre stir, like he was trying to rouse himself from the hold of the sun.

"Leave me alone. *Please.*" Was he trying to smoke me out? If so, it was working. I was eyeing the mausoleum's stone door, wondering how long I'd survive out in the sun now that I was more vampire than human. Even if the elements couldn't kill me, someone would find me soon. Then I'd die.

The devil was an evil genius.

"I enjoy tormenting you far too much to ever leave you alone."

"I thought you said you didn't want me to fear—"

"It was a joke."

"Oh." Were we really having a conversation? One based on something other than threats? My heart continued to race at the possibility. It seemed like a fragile sort of peace. One that could only last for a few more minutes—if that.

"You've always known this was supposed to happen?" I asked. I didn't need to clarify what I was asking.

"Always." The word stroked my skin.

"Why would you want a consort?" I asked the darkness. My voice still trembled from his nearness. He might not be threatening me, and he might not be corporeal right now, but he was the devil.

The air shivered. "Come with me and find out."

I stared into the abyss; I could feel his eyes watching me. "I will never willingly join you."

The silence that fell over me was ominous.

"You mortals are so full of promises you can't keep," the devil hissed. "You'll vow one thing today and rescind it tomorrow. Once you join me, that fickleness will fade."

The devil's chill no longer seeped deep into my bones, and that worried me because it should've. His presence should be carving up my soul. But it wasn't.

"What makes you think I'll be joining you at all?"

If darkness could smile, then it just did.

"There are many things that haven't yet come to pass, but there is one vow I can make you: willing or not, you will join me in hell as my consort. Of all things, that is a certainty."

ANDRE'S TOUCH WOKE me.

His fingertips glided down the side of my face and trailed down the curve of my arm. Only in the blackness of the crypt with the devil's presence a vivid memory, I recoiled from it.

I could practically feel Andre's frown through our connection. Even as my body weakened, the link between us had strengthened.

"What's wrong?" he asked.

Only everything.

"Bad dream," I lied.

"Vampires don't dream."

"And I'm not yet—"

Andre cut off my response with a sigh. "I can smell your dishonesty, soulmate."

Well crap, there went that excuse.

A hand fell on my shoulder and squeezed. "I will not mine you for the truth. Tell it to me on your own time."

He stepped away from me then and moved to the doorway. Only once some space separated us was I able to breathe freely again. I didn't want to mention the devil's visits because voicing them worried Andre and made this all the more real.

Andre propped the crypt's door open, and pale moonlight filtered in. My night vision amplified, and suddenly I could see again.

While I began to fold up the sheets of our bed, Andre dug through the bag. He pulled out several clothing items from it and handed two of them to me. It was a leather bustier and a matching jacket.

Very vampire chic.

I scrunched my nose. "Do I have to wear this?"

"No," Andre said, shrugging off his shredded jacket. I watched the bunched muscle beneath it move.

I glanced back down at the clothing in my hands, flustered from something as simple as watching his body. It wasn't as though I hadn't seen him in less. Maybe it was because I felt so achingly close to throwing all care to the wind and finishing here what we'd started a couple nights ago.

"You are embarrassed," Andre said.

I glanced up, realizing with horror that even in the dark he could literally sniff out my emotions.

"Not embarrassed," I said. "Just … overwhelmed by you," I admitted.

"As I am by you," he said, lifting his ruined shirt over his head. Even with the dim lighting I could make out all the areas where the material had been shredded. Areas where he'd been stabbed by the centaurs' spears. "You don't need to fight it. I am your soulmate. I like it that I can affect you this way."

My gaze dropped to his naked torso, my chest rising and falling. Unlike his shirt, his broad expanse of chest was unblemished, save for some smears of dried blood where he'd briefly bled before his skin healed over.

His words sounded like a dare to me, and dammit, I gotten this far in life being a baddie! I wasn't going to stop being one now.

I grabbed the edge of my torn shirt and worked it over my head, uncovering my bra and my pale skin. I stayed like that for only a moment, and then I reached behind me and unsnapped my bra, exposing myself to him.

Andre stilled and his muscles tensed. He hadn't yet put a shirt on, and in that moment it was unclear whether more clothes would be added or subtracted to the equation.

I breathed in the intoxicating smell that rolled off Andre. It was impossible not to in the small confines.

I held up the corset he'd given me. "Will you help me put it on?" I asked.

He prowled over to me by way of answer. Taking the bustier from my hands, he wrapped it around my torso and began hooking it together down the front. His fingers brushed the skin between my breasts, but like the gentleman he was trying to be, he didn't pay them any extra attention. I wish he had.

Once he finished, his hands lingered at my hips. "It might not be the most comfortable outfit, but the leather will offer you the most protection."

Uh huh. Like that was the real reason why a freaking corset was today's casual wear. I probably would've kicked up a fuss, except that it was impossible to focus with him this close.

I placed a hand on his chest, and my thumb moved over the dried blood, rubbing it away. I concentrated on the tan skin in front of me, pulled taut over muscle.

Beneath my touch, he shuddered. I glanced up at him, only to see his eyes closed and a small smile dancing along his lips.

Gently he removed my hand, giving it a squeeze as he opened his eyes. "I'm trying to show some self-restraint," he said, "but with you it's a lot harder than it should be."

"I thought you said that you didn't need to fight it."

A low, pained groan came out of him. "I said that *you* didn't need to fight it. I, however, ..." He ran a hand through his hair. "I'm trying to take things at a pace you're comfortable with, and it's taking every last ounce of control I have."

He turned from me then and crouched next to our bag. Rummaging through it, he pulled out a blood bag and a protein bar. "Eat up," he said, handing them to me. "You'll need your energy today."

I stared down at the two items. It was a sad day when the blood held more appeal for me than the human food. I gave the protein bar back to him.

Andre pushed it back towards me. "Drink the blood first, then see if your appetite returns."

I did so, but it pained me to admit as I finished drinking the liquid that not even the blood held much allure for me today.

Before I could think too much on it, I tore open the protein bar and had a few bites. When my stomach didn't immediately try to upchuck it, I ate more. Eventually I managed to polish the thing off, though I felt a little queasy.

"What about you?" I asked, shoving the wrappers into the bag. Apparently the anti-Christ didn't litter, which made everyone who else did a bunch of royal D-bags. "Aren't you going to ... have breakfast?"

"I'm saving the blood bags for you."

I stared at him, aghast. "But you also need to feed."

"I did last night, if you remember," he said. "I'm in no danger of starving." *But you are.* Those words went unspoken, but I still heard them. Both of us had noticed my diminished appetite.

It had only taken days for me to lose most of my human hungers. I worried that my vampire ones would go just as quickly. The body could only continue so long without food and water. If I stopped drinking blood, I'd have only days to live.

If that.

Chapter 9

"NOW TELL ME again how exactly this place factors into our great escape?" I gazed at club Bleu from the shadows as I covertly picked out the world's worst wedgie. Leather.

"You'll see," Andre said, being cryptic for the five millionth time in the last two days. My hands were itching to shake him until he spilled his secrets—seers be damned.

He took my hand. "C'mon."

I tried not to stare at my surroundings as we crossed the street, but it was impossible not to when human sized windows showcased scantily clad men and women. I'd read about Amsterdam's Red Light District, but reading was different from seeing.

Way different.

Andre strode towards Bleu, his hand tugging mine when I lagged behind. I felt all sorts of exposed walking out in the open like this. Even this late into the evening, the streets were crowded, which meant that someone would inevitably recognize me. Especially if we partied it up inside one of Andre's swanky supernatural clubs, which I was assuming this was.

After slipping out of the crypt, we'd driven for a couple hours until we'd entered Amsterdam. And now we were here, at a nightclub, and I was sure I had the remnants of vomit, blood, and corpse dust clinging to me.

As the line of people waiting outside the club caught sight of Andre, they began to scream excitedly. I'd been through so much with him that it took me a moment to remember that in addition to being old as dirt and the king of vampires, he was also an international celebrity. Maybe it was the swagger or the face that promised danger, but he always, *always* had this effect on crowds that recognized him.

However, as soon as Andre's fan club caught sight of me, the atmosphere shifted. The crowd went from screaming to silent. I could smell their fear, their excitement, their lust.

I was the anti-Christ, and I was walking in their midst.

Andre ignored it all, maneuvering us through the throng of people towards the club's entrance. If he was worried that one of them would attack me, he didn't show it. Just as I'd gone from scared teenager to otherworldly abomination, Andre had gone from affectionate soulmate to a seven-hundred-year-old king.

One of the bouncers glanced from Andre to me. I could smell his growing fear and his righteous anger. Beneath that was a thread of desire that the siren always seemed to coax out.

The bouncer ripped his gaze from me. He hesitated, then, seeming to gather courage, spoke. "I'm sorry, Andre," he said in English, his Dutch accent pronounced, "but we cannot let her inside."

I was sure being told *no* by an employee was a first.

Andre's eyes flashed and he squared his jaw, about ready to bark out an order or, worse, maim the dude like he had Tybalt. Before he got the chance, I placed my hand on the bouncer's forearm.

My skin began to glow. "Evening." I smiled.

The bouncer's eyes widened as my glamour ensnared him. A moment ago he might've yanked his hand away, but now his glassy eyes watched mine, enthralled.

"You'll let us in, and then you'll forget about this." As I spoke, I felt someone behind me reach out and touch me, drawn in by the effects of second-hand glamour.

The bouncer blinked a few times, then jolted, like he'd been caught with his pants down. "Fuck, sorry for the hold up, Andre," the bouncer said. He reached for the rope and unhooked it for us.

Andre raised an eyebrow at me as he pressed a hand to the small of my back, ready to lead me inside.

"Wait." I turned to the waiting crowd. Flashes of light came from camera phones. "You will delete all evidence of our presence, and you will remember only that a celebrity passed through."

Cameras were lowered and murmurs traveled through the line of eager partygoers.

I swiveled back to Andre. He pulled me close so that his nose and mouth were buried in my raven-dark hair. "You definitely came back a little more wicked." It was the same thing he'd said when we were on his jet, right before shit had hit the fan. He'd been referring to my time at Bran Castle.

I absently rubbed my throat, remembering how it had been slit. I'd been dead for a short period of time, and then I had some real one-on-one time with the devil. I suppressed the thought that, if caught, I might soon face more one-on-one time with him.

I forced a smile, determined to not let my fears drag me down. "Don't be jealous that you don't have mad skills like I do," I said.

Andre glanced down at me, raising an eyebrow as he propelled us into the club. "Soulmate, you have not even *begun* to see my mad skills." The pitch of his voice made it clear exactly what skills he was referring to.

My skin flickered a little brighter. Well played, Andre. Well played.

We pushed through the crowd, and people stopped and stared. "Uh, Andre, how are we supposed to get out of here unseen again?" I asked, eyeing them.

His mouth pressed into a tight line. "We're not."

Startled by his words, I stopped walking, only to have him nudge me forward.

"Relax, soulmate, this is my club, my domain. I would not bring you here only to see you hurt." As we passed the bar, he leaned down so that his lips brushed against my ears. "I promise."

I cleared my throat. Even in a crowded room, Andre's nearness had me flustered. "So, why, exactly are we here again?"

"Supply gathering."

He was still being cryptic, but at least he'd given me more information than he had so far.

Andre led us to the club's backrooms and knocked on one of the doors. I could hear a feminine voice murmuring on the other side. When it became clear the woman wasn't going to answer the door, Andre yanked on the handle. Metal snapped and the door swung open.

Inside a woman with glittering skin leaned back in a chair, a cellphone pressed to her ear and her feet propped up on the desk.

"Hey—" The woman's voice cut off when she caught sight of us. She dropped the phone and shot to her feet. "Andre, holy shit, I had no idea you were ..." Her voice died away when she saw me. "Gabrielle Fiori?" Her brows pulled together. "What's going on?" She glanced back at Andre.

"I need a favor, Ophelia."

She whistled, her gaze finding mine again. "You know how we work. Highest bidder ultimately wins."

It was about then that I realized she was a fairy. Like Oliver, only way less cool because ... *Oliver*. 'Nuff said.

She eyed me. "And I seriously doubt you could provide me something big enough to hide her from those that wish to know."

"All my current club holdings in the Netherlands, Belgium, Germany, and Denmark are yours from this day forward," Andre said. "That's my final offer."

Her eyes widened, then a smile lit her face. "I think I can work something out."

"No, Ophelia. I need a hard answer on this. Either you take it, or you don't."

She must've realized that an offer like this didn't come around too often because she nodded. "I'll take it. What do you want from me?"

"I need that seer's shroud of yours."

I gave Andre a strange look. Seer's shroud?

Ophelia was already shaking her head. "I bartered mine away a long time ago."

I saw the hope die from Andre's eyes. I had the horrible suspicion that we were now screwed.

"Wait, Andre—" Ophelia reached out and grabbed his forearm. "I know of a sorceress in Austria who can produce what you seek."

"We do not have the means to travel to Austria."

Now Ophelia smiled. "You may not, but I do."

Chapter 10

MY BOOTS CRUNCHED over the frosted grass of the field that Andre, Ophelia, and I walked along. Amsterdam was no more than a glitzy dream. Supposedly we weren't too far outside the city, but you'd never know it from our surroundings.

"There was a long ago battle here," Ophelia said, breaking the silence, "during the time when the Romans were pushing northwards. The dead were never claimed," she explained. "Their bones still lie beneath us, unburied and restless." Hence why we were here. The restless dead made fitting entrances to the ley lines. Yippee.

We'd been walking single file through the field, but now Ophelia dropped back. Moonlight glinted off of her skin, and I wondered not for the first time why she glittered all the time. Oliver only ever did when he was drunk.

"Never seen a fairy before?" she asked.

I startled from my thoughts. "Actually, one of my best friends is a fairy."

"Oh really?" she raised her eyebrows, her eyes flicking over me. "We do make for powerful friends—or foes."

I couldn't tell if her words were praising my taste in friends or a warning not to put faith in that friendship. She herself had cautioned Andre that her help came with a hefty price.

Mist drifted up from the earth. It was easy to mistake this place for a haunted graveyard. Considering that I still smelled like the last one I visited, I was right at home.

"So," Ophelia said, breaking the silence once more, "what's it like being the anti-Christ?"

I knew this was coming. I'd seen and smelled her burning curiosity.

I shrugged. "It sucks." I shoved my hands in my pockets, wincing as the skintight leather resisted the intrusion.

Her gaze searched me. "You don't seem particularly—"

"Demonic?" I finished for her. I'd seen enough Hollywood movies on the subject to know the role I was supposed to fill.

"I was going to say 'scary'."

Behind me Andre guffawed. *She obviously hasn't seen your bad side.* He spoke low enough that only I could hear him.

I threw an unamused glanced at my soulmate. Andre walked behind us, keeping watch on our surroundings. When he saw me looking, he flashed me a unapologetic smile. His eyes gleamed with that internal fire of his, the one that made me feel both exposed and protected in his presence.

"So are you really his soulmate?" Ophelia asked, dragging my attention back her.

"Who?"

"Andre," she said, dropping her voice.

My lips twitched. Even whispering, Andre could hear our conversation with perfect clarity.

"He is."

"You're lucky, then," Ophelia said. "I wouldn't know a better man to safeguard my life."

I stared down at my feet as I walked. "I know."

But it may not be enough, that cold voice inside me whispered. We were fighting the devil and an ancient prophecy.

"So have you met him?" she asked.

I glanced sharply at her. We were no longer talking about Andre.

"Yes."

Her face was alight with far too much interest. "What's he like?"

"That's enough, Ophelia," Andre said, his voice harsh.

She raised her hands in innocence.

"No, *no*, she wants to know." I grabbed Ophelia's wrist as she dropped her arms and stopped her. "I'll tell you what he's like."

It was my turn to have my expression burn with its own intensity. "He's a cauterized wound—a remedy that hurts worse than the injury itself and leaves behind a nasty scar. He's evil with just enough humanity to make you fall for his tricks over and over." I squeezed her wrist until she yelped.

I released my hold, and turned away from both her and Andre. My final words were for neither of them. "But, worst of all, his very presence carves out bits and pieces of your soul until all of it—every last inch—is his."

WE STOOD IN front of an archaic church, it's roof covered in a sheet of snow.

"This is it," Ophelia said, careful to keep Andre between the two of us. Someone was still spooked from our earlier encounter. I wonder if she'd changed her mind about finding me scary.

"The sorceress lives *here?*" Was I the only one that found it ironic that a powerful practitioner of magic lived in a Christian temple?

"I cannot enter sanctified ground," Andre said, scrutinizing the building ahead of us.

"That won't be an issue," Ophelia said. "It's been repurposed for quite some time now."

I could tell Andre remained unconvinced.

"What happens if you step into a church?" I asked him.

"I burn."

Ouch.

"But not graveyards?" I asked. Weren't those also sanctified? If *Hocus Pocus* lied to me about that, I might just die.

Andre lifted a shoulder. "Loophole."

I rubbed my temples. "That makes no sense." Andre had saint's relics in his house and mosaics of holy men in his bathroom. He walked through cemeteries unscathed. Where was the line drawn?

"No one ever said that magic was supposed to be logical—or fair." Because Andre had tried so hard to save his soul and those of the vampires he'd sired.

"Speaking of magic," I said, "what exactly is a seer's shroud?" It was about time someone told me something.

"She doesn't know?" Ophelia looked between me and Andre.

"No, I don't." *Also, I'm right here.*

"Essentially," she said, "it's a spell or a spelled item that prevents anyone with the Sight from divining your locations. They won't be able to find you."

Now I understood. That would make our movements all but invisible to those with magic.

"So, why are they so difficult to come by?"

"That would be because they are against the law," she said.

Then there was that.

"Not to mention that they're expensive and rare," Ophelia added. "Powerful magic must go into them to be able to block that many seers."

"Ah."

"Now, explanations over, are you two ready?" Ophelia asked. "The sorceress knows we're here, and she is *not* a patient one. We best get moving." With that, she headed towards the church.

Andre and I shared a look. This could end poorly. He gave a pointed glance down at the knives strapped to my legs, and his meaning was clear. If anything were to go wrong, I needed to use them.

"So, what exactly is a sorceress?" I asked Andre, stalling for time.

"A witch of great power." He was apparently stalling for time too.

"A *witch?*" Now her location was particularly ironic.

Andre nodded, distracted. The church grounds lay just a step away, the frosted grass beckoning him across. But centuries of conditioning prevented him from taking that final step across.

I wondered whether there was really a chance that the once hallowed ground would cause Andre to sponta-neously combust. My soul wasn't lily white either; there was a chance I might also go up in flames.

I seriously hoped that these were tales spun by super-stitions, and that time had given them credibility. Other-wise my ass might get creamed the moment I crossed the threshold.

I took a deep breath. *No time like the present.*

Closing my eyes, I crossed onto the church grounds. The instant I did so, the atmosphere changed; the air felt heavier here, as though saturated with ... *something.* Whether it was magic or salvation, I wasn't sure.

When I didn't burn, I turned around. Andre watched me, his eyes a bit wider than usual. I extended my hand to Andre. "Here, we can do this together—if your hand starts to burn, just pull it back."

I expected him to be offended, to puff out his chest and make one of his typical and ridiculous claims about being king of the vampires and yadda yadda yadda. Instead he took my hand, his brow creased.

I pulled it forward until it had passed over the threshold.

Andre stared at his hand in wonder. "It didn't burn."

Braver now, he took a step forward, just enough for the tip of his shoes to cross the boundary. A sweet little laugh escaped him at the sight of his intact foot. He stepped all the way across.

He rubbed his mouth, staring down at his intact body. He swore. "That actually worked." He chuckled again, like he'd just figured out a life cheat.

"Better save your excitement, Andre. We still have the church's threshold to cross."

He swatted my bottom, his expression playful. "Wicked little mate. You're going to pay for that comment later." The way he was looking at me, I didn't think I'd mind my punishment too much.

THE CHURCH SMELLED musty, and its pews needed a new coat of lacquer. Narrow beams of light filtered through the high windows from the streetlamps outside. I looked around, but other than the three of us, I saw no sign of life.

Next to me, Andre seemed rapt, and I realized that he might not have stepped into a church in centuries. It was just another reminder of the sacrifices he was making on my behalf.

A female voice boomed out from the shadows at the back of the room. "*I want to see the girl alone.*"

The three of us paused. The sorceress had finally made herself known.

"Over my dead body," Andre said, recovering the quickest.

The voice chuckled. "Lucky for us, that's already the case."

I took a step forward, pulled by her voice and the magic it wielded. It wasn't like my own ability, which compelled people to do my bidding. More like the sheer power behind her words reeled me in.

Andre caught my wrist. "Soulmate, I don't trust her." He didn't bother lowering his voice.

"You wish to do business with me, vampire, when I know nothing of your motives. Let me see this so-called consort and judge her worthiness."

A muscle in Andre's cheek fluttered and his eyes flashed.

Whether it was my curiosity, her magic, or a restless feeling that we were wasting time, I made the executive decision to face her and whatever came with the contact. I began walking down the aisle.

"Gabrielle," Andre growled.

"It'll be fine," I said, heading towards the voice. I stepped up to the wooden altar and hesitated. I glanced back at Andre, whose hands were fisted at his sides. Next to him, Ophelia's skin shimmered a little more than usual, like apprehension flared it up. That, more than Andre's reaction, had me nervous. If the fairy wasn't in control of her own dealings, I couldn't assume my little tea party with the sorceress would go smoothly.

"Come closer, Gabrielle Fiori," she beckoned from behind the dias.

I stepped around the altar ... only for the floor to dissolve beneath me.

Chapter 11

MY STOMACH BOTTOMED out as I fell. Just when I thought I might continue to fall until I reached hell's gates, my body slammed into a solid surface.

Glass shattered on impact, its jagged edges slicing into my skin in a dozen different locations. Something wet sizzled against my flesh.

"Son of a demon!" This crap required a supernatural curse.

I rolled off the open tomes and the now broken glass jars I'd fallen on only to topple off a table and onto the ground. As I did so, several vials tumbled with me—clinking against the floor.

"And I'd always assumed sirens were graceful."

I moaned and rubbed my backside. "Some warning would've been nice," I managed.

I had fallen into what looked like a mad scientist's room—if that mad scientist happened to also be a practitioner of magic. Beakers connected to elaborate glass tubes bubbled, as did a cauldron that hovered over an open flame.

"You're lucky I don't kill you on the spot. I could use some siren blood and a favor from the devil."

That jolted me to attention. I was on my feet in an instant, my hand hovering near one of my knives, ready to square off with the sorceress.

But as my eyes roved over the vats with their plumes of colored smoke, I saw no one.

"Halt your hand. I will not tolerate drawn weapons in my house."

"Then show yourself," I called, straightening and lifting my hands to indicate that I was unarmed.

"You show yourself."

I scrunched up my face. Huh?

"Siren, *show yourself!*"

Her words seemed to wrap themselves around my siren and drag her to the surface. My back arched as light flared along my skin, bright and immediate.

"Vampire, *show yourself!*"

I'd barely caught my breath when my gums receded and my fangs unsheathed.

"Soulmate, consort, *show yourself!*"

My heart seemed to burn at the command. When the pain became nearly unbearable, the woman grunted her approval.

"Enough," she said.

As quickly as it came, the sharp burn abated, the siren fled, and my fangs receded. I fell to my knees and coughed. "Ow."

"You may step forward."

Oh yeah, because I was *so* eager now. I rose to my feet, but I still saw nothing other than plumes of tinted smoke.

"Come *forward*."

My feet jerked of their own volition, tugging me through the smoke until I caught sight of a woman reclining on an ornate couch. A very, *very* stoned woman.

The sorceress was high as a kite and intimidating as hell.

She sat up, her long white hair shifting about her. She had a third eye tattooed on her forehead, and I had the queerest impression that the thing could actually see me.

"*Stop*," she commanded.

My legs halted as the magic in her voice receded, and I glowered at her. "You could've tried asking nicely."

Her eyes widened at my words, and she tilted her head. "Got a little fire to that tongue, do you now?" Her eyes narrowed as they passed me over. Then her features relaxed. "It's a good thing I can appreciate a hot temper," she said, sucking in a lungful of the pink smoke that billowed around us. "Shame the devil has enough fire as it is." She cackled at that. As she did so, blue smoke curled out from her nose and lips.

I studied it, fascinated.

"Are you planning on gawking at me like the village idiot all evening?"

My lips, which had parted, now snapped shut.

"Much better," she said. "Now come." She patted the seat next to her.

I practically dove to the couch to avoid her compelling magic. That earned me another chuckle. "Maybe you're not the village idiot after all—jury's still out on that one, though."

I kept my smartass mouth shut. The thing had gotten me into trouble before, and I could already tell I'd blow it with this broad if I opened it now.

The sorceress inhaled deeply again. "I am Hestia, Mistress of Potions, Sorceress of Upper Europe."

In the expectant silence that followed, I cleared my throat. "I am—"

"I *know* who you are." She eyed me up and down. "*Consorte del diavolo*. What I want to know is why you think I should help you."

Well that shut me up. ... for about five seconds. "Because I don't want to die and marry the devil."

She leaned back into her seat and appraised me. "Why not?"

Was this a trick question? "Because he's evil?"

"Bah!" She waved her arms. "I don't see what the problem is. You stink of evil."

My fangs dropped down at the comment. "I do *not*." Even as I objected to her words, I covertly sniffed myself. Instead of inhaling my scent, I breathed in a lungful of pink smoke.

I coughed and waved my hand through the air, little puffs of blue smoke trickling out of my mouth. "What is this stuff?" I wheezed.

"*Santus fumus*—holy smoke. Feel honored to breath in the hallowed air of my foremothers, the great Oracles of Delphi."

Yeah, whatever.

She wasn't done. "Some of the world's greatest prophecies were borne in this smoke." She leaned forward. "Even yours." I swear that third eye of hers was squinting at me.

I cocked my head, trying not to wince at the boneless feel of my neck. The smoke was already taking effect. "You're telling me my fate was prophesized by some women who spent their days hanging out and getting high?"

"Precisely!" Hestia's eyes twinkled as she settled back into her seat. "I think I like you," she declared. "You're not so dumb after all." A moue of disappointment pinched her lips. "It's too bad you're marked for death. You've got *verve*."

I only barely stopped myself from snorting. This lady was gone.

"Despite your stink, you are strangely pure of heart." She folded her hands and peered over at me. "Tell me, have you even bedded the vampire yet?"

I sucked in a surprised breath and choked on the pink smoke again. I pounded my chest and coughed, plumes of blue smoke leaving my mouth.

"Well, that's a *no*," she said for me. "Shame. Had life given me that man, I would've already ruined him for all others." She blew out a puff of smoke, her eyes growing distant. "Absolutely *ruined* him," she muttered to herself.

Batty old woman.

When my coughing fit had subsided, I managed to

speak. "Um, I was hoping we could discuss the seer's shroud?" I wheezed. Because that was a waaaaay better option than talking about my nonexistent sex life with this woman, who was a little too trigger happy with her power.

She inhaled deeply. "Ah yes, the seer's shroud." She studied me. "I can make what you seek, but it will not be ready until evening tomorrow."

Crap, could Andre and I rest here for that long? Thinking of him, my gaze moved up, towards the ceiling. I hadn't heard a peep from him or Ophelia since I'd fallen into the sorceress's den, and now that I thought about it, our connection had dimmed. I'd assumed their silence was purposeful, but now I wondered. The last thing Andre would have been was silent.

"Gabrielle Fiori, last of the sirens, queen of vampires, empress of hell, your soulmate is fine. Madder than a hatter, but fine."

"Where is he?"

The sorceress glanced skyward. "Stalking between my pews like a raging bull. If that man breaks anything, he'll be paying for it with his hide—and I do mean that literally."

I bristled at that comment. She'd have to go through me to do so.

"The fairy that led you here," Hestia said, "she is one of a select few who know my location—and her knowledge of this place will be a temporary thing." I swore I heard her grumble under her breath about deals made with fairies. "No seer will locate you before we meet again.

"Stay another day here, and I will get you your seer's

shroud—for a price."

I swayed in my seat, and the room seemed to spin. The smoke was addling my mind.

"Price?" I rubbed my temples. "If it's a soul you want, you're going to need to get in line."

She laughed at that. "Not your soul. Others can fight for that. I want something else."

I dropped my hands. "What is it you want?"

She pursed her lips, the wrinkles around her mouth deepening. "Part of the cost is not knowing what it is I will ask for."

I'd be an idiot to agree to these terms, especially considering the bounty on my head. Intuition told me that she wouldn't hand me over to those that would harm me, but there were other things she could ask for that would come at too steep a cost.

My mind drifted to Andre, who'd sacrificed so much to get us here. He seemed to think we needed this—so badly, in fact, that he'd traded his clubs to Ophelia for the opportunity.

I extended my hand. "Agreed."

She sucked in more of the pink plumes and glanced at my hand. Instead of shaking it, she blew out her breath, and thick, indigo-colored smoke cascaded over it.

"Good," she said. "Then the first part of your payment begins tonight."

The first part? "You never said there would be more than one—"

"*You agreed to my terms.*" She spoke over me, her voice severe. The force of her words pushed me back into my seat. "You *will* fulfill your end of the bargain."

I lifted my hands in supplication. Man, her bossiness could give Andre a run for his money.

"You will not leave here the way you came, and you will not see your mate until tomorrow evening."

Unease pooled in my stomach. What had I agreed to? "How do you plan on keeping us apart?" Even if I didn't seek him out, Andre would surely hunt me down, using our connection to guide him.

"*I* will deal with the vampire. You should be more concerned with your own fate."

She chose those words because, somehow, she knew they'd sober me right up.

"There is a bridge down the street from here," she continued. "On the other side is a dirt trail. Take it and it will lead you to a copse of trees—you can't miss it, they make a perfect ring—and within that copse is a rose bush that only blooms in the dead of winter. Fetch a rose for me and come back here straightaway."

"You want me to retrieve a *rose* for you?" I asked, disbelieving.

Her hooded eyes pierced me. "Yes, insolent girl, I want you to get me a rose."

My voice dropped low. "Why would you have me do this?"

"Like many other things in my collection, this rose is a rarity, and I want it plucked by a special hand."

My eyes moved from her to a wall of jars containing various ingredients—fairy dust, unicorn hair, dragon fire—which continually scorched the inside of its container—

mermaid scales. Rare indeed.

She clapped her hands, and a door manifested itself on the other side of the room. "Now, it's high time you're off."

When she saw my face, she patted my hand. "I am no seer, but I know you will live to see another eve."

Oh, *that* was reassuring.

I stood. "Where am I supposed to go once I deliver the rose to you?" Because, unless this rose bush was a hundred miles away, I'd finish this task quickly.

Her eyes, which had dulled, now sharpened. "One step at a time, consort. But," she leaned forward, placing her wrinkled hand on my thigh, "between you and me, sleeping arrangements are the least of your worries."

I AM THE village idiot, I thought as I trudged down the street. I had no real idea where I was going or what I'd gotten myself into. And all for some seer's shroud, which I might never get my hands on because I'd be dead.

I glanced behind me at the now distant stone chapel, which rested at the edge of the small town, and I willed Andre to walk outside. To see me, to stop me, to prevent me from fulfilling my end of the bargain.

He never exited the church.

I sighed, taking a deep breath. Hestia would keep him away from me until I retrieved the stupid rose. And I had to retrieve it and fulfill my end of the bargain if I wanted to get that seer's shroud.

Lamest quest ever.

The cold air stung my throat and lungs, but I embraced the sensation as it slowly drove away my drug-induced haze. The sorceress sure knew how to hotbox a room.

I swiveled to face the road ahead of me. The town I walked through was impressively small—just a single main road of shops, and then two small neighborhoods on either side. This late at night—or rather, this early in the morning, no one was out.

My ears searched for the sound of heartbeats, and I heard many, but all were slow and steady—the sound of a town fast asleep. Besides them, I didn't hear anything.

Passing through the village, I finally caught a glimpse of the huge stone bridge Hestia had talked about. It had two lanes and ran about the length of a football field. Several lamps lined either side of it, and they were the last bits of illumination before the darkness beyond.

My muscles tensed, and I used my senses to search for any hidden attackers. I didn't trust Hestia's reassurances—not completely. That one was tricky with her words.

I listened closely, but no heartbeats pounded and no breaths were drawn. I scented the air, but smelled nothing out of the ordinary. If someone waited for me, they hid themselves exceptionally well. Still, I grabbed one of the knives strapped to my thigh and held it loosely at my side.

I stopped at the edge of the bridge. I could see straight down the lamp-lined pathway. At this hour it was utterly abandoned—like everything else in this town. The soft lamplight glowed against the stone and cement then gave way to darkness. It was in that darkness where I'd find the dirt path and the ring of trees.

The wind tore through my hair, caressing the nape of my neck. The sooner I did this, the sooner I could get back to Andre and leave this place.

I stepped onto the bridge, turning the knife handle over and over in my hand. The two lamps farthest from me flickered. My breath caught, and I immediately opened my senses up. But just like before, I heard no one, saw no one, smelled no one.

Because no one is here, Einstein. I'd clearly inhaled too much holy smoke.

I strode forward, emboldened by my thoughts. The wind picked up again, pushing past me, and I quickened my pace. I was contemplating using my vampiric speed to get this over with when the two lampposts that bordered the far side of the bridge flickered once more, then died out.

I paused. If my heart beat normally, it would've skipped at the sight. It did, however, speed up slightly.

I resumed walking, my boots clicking against the cement. Another pair of streetlamps, those that were second farthest from me, made a popping noise as their bulbs exploded.

This time when I halted, I took a staggering step back. My breath hiked. Another pair of lights burned out. The darkness was creeping closer, working its way towards me.

The hair on my forearms rose. Something lurked in those shadows, something I couldn't sense but I knew intuitively.

I backed up as another two streetlamps burst. Glass shattered outward, and I jumped at the sight. In the darkness I heard laughter. I knew that laughter, knew the evil being that lurked within it.

Now pairs of lights were extinguishing faster and faster, speeding up like they'd scented me.

My grip on the knife tightened. The time to flee had passed. Maybe it was never there to begin with. I caught the smell of blood and brimstone just as the final two lampposts on either side of me burned out.

And then the darkness swallowed me up.

Chapter 12

I BLINKED MY eyes open as a cold breeze bit into the skin of my cheeks. Above me starlight twinkled. My brows pinched together at the sight.

I sat up, my hands crunching into fallen leaves. As I did so, an object rolled off my torso. I caught it by its long, green stalk and lifted it.

A *rose*, I realized.

I rolled it between my fingers, noticing that its stem was singed where phantom fingertips had touched it. I brought it to my nose, breathing in the smell of brimstone and blood.

The devil.

Last night's events rushed in. He'd taken me. All that is holy, *he'd taken me*.

A small note flapped from the neck of the rose, the

words penned in blood.

Counting the days.

I set the flower aside with a shaky hand and glanced around me. I was lying in what appeared to have been a forest. *Have been* being the key words. The trees that should've surrounded me were flattened, stretching away from me like rays of a child-drawn sun, and I sat at its point of origin. It looked for all the world like a bomb had gone off.

Or like the devil had paid a visit.

I couldn't catch my breath. It wasn't the first time this had happened. The devil—Pluto—had done this months ago when I stayed with Andre at Bishopcourt. I'd assumed it was a one-time thing, something terrifying and unexplainable.

But now it had happened again.

I stood, dusting leaves off of my leather outfit. At least that had remained the same. If I'd woken up dressed in anything else, I'd have to deal with the possibility that the devil had caught a glimpse of nip. And I really didn't want him to catch a glimpse of nip.

I shivered. *I can't believe my thoughts just went there.* I'd been hanging around Oliver for too long.

I gazed up at the night sky again, wondering how much time had passed. A few minutes? An hour?

Sweat beaded my brow, and it wasn't just from the fear that thrummed through me. My body was weak, my muscles tired. I felt ... *sick*. And I couldn't remember the last time I was sick. If ever.

When I reached to dust off my back, my hand came away with ash. I started at the sight of it. Bringing my hand to my face, I scented it. Not simply ash. Ash, brimstone, and a hint of ... rose.

My eyes took in my surroundings anew. The uprooted trees formed a nearly perfect circle around me. I brought my clean hand to my mouth. This was the copse of trees the Hestia spoke of. Beneath me was a pile of ash, all that remained of the bush that once grew here. I bent down and picked up the singed rose that rested next to it.

This rose is a rarity, and I want it plucked by a special hand. Special hand indeed. The devil had harvested it, not me.

The air grew hazy, as though from a heat wave. I caught the scent of light cologne and magic. That was all the warning I got.

"Oh, my effing *gawd*, Buffy called and she wants her outfit back."

I jumped at the voice behind me. Whirling around, I caught sight of ice blond hair and a cocked hip.

"*Oliver?*" The only thing more surprising than my current situation was that he'd pop in to join me.

"In the exquisite flesh." He held up his arms.

I didn't question how he was here, or why he'd dropped in now. I couldn't even answer those questions myself. So I threw myself into his arms and promptly started blubbering.

"Whoa, is my baddie BBF crying?" Oliver's arms dropped around me. He pulled me close and stroked my back. "I promise we can get you new clothes and burn these. No one but us three will have to know."

I sniffled, and drew back a little. "Three?"

"Hey, roomie," Leanne said from over Oliver's shoulder. I hadn't even seen her, so intent was I on tackle-hugging my fairy friend.

I let go of Oliver and dragged Leanne into her own bear hug. She held me close. Something about the way she squeezed me made me think she knew better than anyone else what exactly I was going through.

I stepped away, wiping away bloody tears. "You don't know how good it is to see you two." I took a couple deep breaths, looked between the two of them, then to our surroundings. "Wait," I said as my tears dried up, my gaze traveling back to them, "what *are* you two doing here?"

"Rescuing your skanky ass," Oliver said.

Rescuing me. I could smell the truth to Oliver's words too. They hadn't turned their backs on me, though I didn't know why. I was dangerous to associate with.

"Word on the street is that you're the anti-Christ," he said.

I winced at the name. "That's what they say."

"It's a load of ogre crap," Leanne said.

I couldn't meet her eyes. "I'm not sure that it is," I said, rolling the stem of the rose between my fingers.

I drew in a deep breath. "How did you find me?" I asked her. Hestia had said that no seer would be able to locate me.

"She didn't find you, Buffy," Oliver said, pursing his lips. "I did."

My eyebrows lifted.

"Apparently the ley lines have been blowing up with demonic activity," Leanne supplied, "all circling this location."

"Pssh." Oliver buffed his nails on his button-down. "She makes it sound like it was a simple matter of plotting lines down on a chart. Do you know how many favors I cashed in on your behalf, Sabertooth? So. Many. Not to mention all of the demons lurking on the ley lines that I had to crotch kick." He glanced down at his shoes and pouted. "Their dongs melted my new Jimmy Choos. Boo."

Movement flickered on my peripherals, but when I turned to look, nothing was there. Still, it was enough to spook me.

"Neither of you should be here," I said, my panic rising. If Oliver had to fight off demons just to traverse a ley line, what would happen to him and Leanne once Underworld beings realized they were my friends?

"Don't be ridiculous. You need us," Leanne said. "Oliver has the connections—and the means of travel—and I have the foresight."

God, they weren't going to back down, and I didn't know whether the dominating emotion was terror or soul-deep gratitude. "But you could both get hurt."

"Do I look frightened?" Oliver asked. "I'm James-fuck-ing-Bond with wings. Oh—" Oliver snapped his fingers, his eyes lighting up, "before I forget, I had something made for you."

Even in dire circumstances, some things never changed, like Oliver's impressively short attention span.

He dug through the bag he carried until he pulled out

a folded fitted shirt. Shaking it out, he held it up and presented it to me. "Do you like it?"

The shirt read, *I Kissed Satan and All I Got Was This Shitty Shirt.*

I choked a little. "Oh my God."

"I figured we needed evidence that you got somewhere with some guy. Lord knows your sex life is slower than the journey to Mordor."

He folded the shirt back up. "Don't worry, Sabertooth, I'll hold this for you," he eyed my leather outfit, "seeing as how you have no place to store it."

"How ... thoughtful of you."

"I thought so."

My breath caught, and a sharp pain wedged itself in the center of my chest. Happiness that my friends were here with me. Fear for them and worry that they'd located me so easily.

Speaking of locating people ...

"I need to find Andre." He'd been at the back of my mind since I'd woken, and now I couldn't ignore my thoughts concerning him. As soon as he realized I was gone, he'd begin moving heaven and earth to find me, and that usually meant human casualties. I didn't want anymore blood on my hands.

Oliver cocked his head. "You don't know where he is ... ?" As if seeing it all for the first time, Oliver surveyed me, then my surroundings. His head drew back, affronted. "Wait, fuck that question: what are *you* doing here?"

I rolled the stem of the flower in my hand, causing his eyes to dart to it and his head to tilt in the other direction.

"No clue," I said.

Olive grabbed the note tied to the rose and turned it over. "'Counting the days'?" He pursed his lips. "Is it … written in blood? *Ew*." He dropped the note.

His eyes met mine as did Leanne's, and my mouth began to move, words tumbling out before I could think twice about them. "The devil kidnapped me—just like he did at the beginning of the school year."

"Kidnapped you?" Leanne repeated, her eyes going wide.

I nodded, a frown tugging down the corners of my lips.

Oliver made a sound at the back of his throat. "Ooooh, ten euro says your big, scary hunk of burning love has ripped out at least one throat trying to find you."

"Oliver, that's inappropriate and savage." Leanne turned to me. "Do you know where Andre might be? Oliver can take us to him."

"Pfft, there you go, just offering out my services."

She rolled her eyes. "As if you had anything different in mind."

I cut in. "A sorceress lives a little less than a mile away." I nodded in the direction. "That's where I last left him."

"Awesome," Leanne said. "Let's get going." She made a grab for Oliver's hand, but he pulled it out of reach.

"Whoa," he said, "eff-no to the nature hike—my shoes are ruined enough as is." He wiped something dark off of his shoe and onto the leaves. I really hoped it was just melted rubber. Turning to me he asked, "This is *the* sorceress we're talking about, right?"

I shrugged. "She seemed pretty self-important."

136

"Then she'll have her one ley line portal, which we'll use."

"Still going to get demon all over you," Leanne said.

"Then I'll just have to use you as a shield. Now," he said, turning to me, "where did you say this crone's lair was?"

While I gave Oliver directions, he tugged Leanne and me over to the pile of ash.

"Got it," he said, after I finished. "M'kay hoes, On the count of three: one, twooooooooo—" His voice dragged out as we were torn from where we stood and shoved through the ley line.

As soon as my feet touched the ground, a wave of queasiness washed over me. I stumbled, forcing the nausea down.

"Dammit, that demon singed my shirt," Oliver said, shaking it out. "I'm going smell like crispy-fried critters for the rest of the evening." While Leanne and I couldn't experience anything traveling along a ley line, Oliver clearly could.

"Told you," Leanne said.

We stood in a small dank hallway, the air hazy with smoke. Some faded photos hung on the wall, along with fossilized jars of I-don't-want-to-know. I could hear the mucous-y pop of boiling liquids coming from the room at the end of the hall.

Oliver had landed us right inside the sorceress's den.

"What time is it?" I asked.

Leanne pulled out her phone. "A little after seven."

I waved away some of the familiar-smoke. I'd like to

leave this place sober for once. "Seven a.m.?" I said, moving down the hall. Strange that I wasn't sleepy this close to dawn. I'd have to be quick about this—give the sorceress her rose then find Andre before the sun rose.

"Not seven a.m., Gabrielle," Leanne said from behind me. "Seven at night."

I rotated to face her. She stared at me with a mixture of horror and pity, and if I had to guess, I'd say my expression began to mirror her own.

"Seven p.m.?" I'd lost an entire day.

I squeezed my eyes shut. I wouldn't think about what happened to me.

"*Once you three mongrels are done socializing, I suggest you come join me,*" Hestia's voice drifted down from the room at the far end. "*Preferably before the king of vampires tears my home to shreds.*"

I could hear dull thumps from somewhere above us. They sounded as though they were muffled by a body of water, making me wonder just how far below the chapel we were and just how much enchantment had gone into this place if Andre was still up there, tearing into furniture, instead of down here, tearing into jugulars.

I strode into Hestia's opium den. Just like yesterday, rose-colored smoke hung throughout the room, thickest in the corner where the sorceress lounged.

The smoke cleared enough for me to catch a glimpse of her. I could see she was no less high today than she was yesterday. Her eyes traveled over me. That unnerving third eye of hers also seemed to hone in on me. She tsked. "Well, that answers that."

I took a step forward, noticing the glint in her eyes. She knew what happened to me. It made me clench the rose in my hand tighter. One of the thorns dug into my flesh, and I smelled the bead of blood it drew from me.

Hestia's eyes flicked to Oliver and Leanne, the former who was staring at a jar of crushed fairy wings with obvious horror.

"You two may leave us. And please, when you find him, tell the vampire that his soulmate is safe—and that I expect him to reimburse me for any damage he's caused."

Oliver didn't need anyone to tell him twice. Faster than you could say *pixie dust*, he was out of there.

Leanne hesitated, her mouth opening. She closed it and reluctantly left us.

Once we were alone, the sorceress turned her attention back to me. "You've surrounded yourself with very formidable people. Both the seer and the fairy are exceptionally powerful." She sucked in a lungful of the holy smoke billowing around her head. "Come, consort," she said, patting the seat next to her, we have much to discuss.

"Don't call me that."

She raised an eyebrow, her face shrewd. "If you seek to hide from the truth, then the truth will be your undoing."

I stalked forward and slammed the rose down on a side table next to her, ignoring how the plant's thorns pierced my skin. "Happy? I got you your fucking rose."

Her eyes narrowed. "*Sit.*" Immediately my muscles drew me forward and down to the seat next to Hestia. "I have not risen to power to be at the whim of some dying teenager, no matter how important she might one day be." Her words snapped like a whiplash.

"You sent me to meet the devil. *The devil.* And you knew it." It was never about the rose.

I should've known. The ring of trees, the winter-blooming rose. Fairytales were made of more mundane descriptions than that.

"I sent you to claim your destiny, and destiny spoke." Hestia's words held power, and they reminded me of why the events last night had come to pass.

"So that's it? I can't retrieve a flower without getting accosted by the devil, and now what? I'm doomed?"

"No, you were always doomed, I just wanted to prove it to you. And I wanted my tainted rose." She leaned forward and drew the flower to her.

I threw my hands up. "I already knew I was."

Hestia rubbed the fingerprints singed onto the flower's stem. "You lie to yourself. You've been running your entire life—from people, lovers, and now your fate. Perhaps if you owned it for once, you'd make a little more headway."

I didn't ask how she could know these intimate things about me.

Hestia stood. "The seer's shroud is ready." The pink smoke engulfed her as she moved to the other side of the room.

My head swayed as I stared at the smoke. Dang it, I wasn't leaving this place sober.

Hestia came back to me with four stopped vials. When I made no move to get up and take them from her, she nodded to her hand. "They're yours."

"*That's* the seer shroud?"

"What, you thought I'd give you some enchanted cape, so you could look like a superhero twat?"

I kept my mouth shut because, yeah, I kind of thought a seer's shroud was, well, a shroud.

I extended my hand towards the vials, but she withdrew her hand from reach. "Before I hand these over, I expect the rest of my payment.

I dropped my arm. "What else do you want?"

"A lock of your hair and a draught of your blood."

"What use are they to you?" I asked, even as I stood and bared a wrist to Hestia.

"What is that phrase you Americans have?" She set the vials down on the counter next to her. "Ah, yes: 'A magician never reveals her secrets.' I will not share mine. Suffice it to say that they have their purpose."

She lowered my arm before retrieving a knife from a nearby shelf. When she came back, she grabbed a clump of my hair. Muttering an incantation, she sawed off the lock and shoved it into an empty glass jar sitting amongst the clutter on the table next to us.

Murmuring something in a language that definitely wasn't English, her papery hand skimmed over the odds and ends stacked on the table until they landed on a goblet. "Hold your arm out," she commanded, "and keep this under your wrist." She thrust the goblet at me.

I took it, nestling the cup beneath the pale skin of my forearm and ignoring the way my hand shook. It was fatigue, not fright that caused the jitter, though I'd be lying if I said that I wasn't also scared out of my mind at what might've happened to me yesterday. And at what was happening to my body all on its own.

Hestia still clasped the knife she'd used earlier, and now, grabbing my wrist, she sliced down hard through the skin. My arm jerked against the pain.

"Steady," she said, like I was a skiddish mare. "The more you cooperate, the swifter this will go." Easy for her to say; she wasn't the one getting cut into.

"Do you know what happened to me last night?" I asked, my blood trickling down my wrist and into the chalice.

For a long time Hestia didn't speak, simply watched as my blood dripped out. She seesawed the knife to prevent the wound from closing.

"The devil tasted you," she finally said.

That took several seconds to sink in, mostly because my mind refused to wrap itself around the idea. Once it did, the nausea I'd felt earlier came roaring back.

"What do you mean by 'tasted me'?" *Please let that not be sex. Please not sex.*

Hestia seemed to know where my thoughts had taken me because she shook her head and cackled. "Who would've ever thought a siren was afraid of knocking boots? No, he will not consummate your union on this realm."

Ew. Gag. Even the mention of consummation had my innards folding up on themselves. At least that meant that we hadn't done the nasty yet. But it didn't matter, did it? All evidence suggested that if we hadn't already, at some point we would. I drew in a shaky breath. I wouldn't think about that.

"Then what exactly did he taste?" I asked.

Once the cup had been filled nearly to the rim with my blood, Hestia removed the knife from my skin. "Your soul," she said, taking the goblet from me and placing it on the counter. "He tasted your soul."

I rubbed my wrist as the skin slowly sealed over and thought back to my first weeks on the Isle of Man. "He's done it before."

Hestia retrieved the rose I'd brought her and plucked three petals from it. "He thinks you are his, and he's keen to collect your soul. A little overeager in my opinion," she said.

"Is my soul ... okay?" I couldn't help but think that getting tasted by the devil would somehow sully it.

"You are a vampire. Your soul is damned. It's no more corrupted today than it was yesterday."

Gee, that was reassuring.

She dropped the three rose petals she held into the chalice. As soon as they came into contact with my blood, they bubbled and sizzled until nothing of them remained.

"Hmm, interesting," Hestia murmured.

My eyes flicked between her and the goblet. "What's interesting?"

She grabbed the four vials of seer's shroud and took my hand. "You asked if your soul was okay. His smell lingers on you. That is all."

She made light of it when she shouldn't have. To the supernatural world, carrying someone's scent on you was as good as being claimed by them.

Hestia pressed the four tiny bottles into my hand. "One

for you, your lover, and one for each of your companions."

I furrowed my brow, her words raising several questions.

"Yes," she said before I had a chance to speak, "I threw in some additional vials, and yes, those two friends of yours are going to need them.

"Now, each of you are to drink a vial. It will shield you from seers for an entire lunar cycle."

"That's it?" So little time?

She leveled her gaze on me. "If things go the way they appear to, that's more time than you'll need."

Chills ran down my arms. "What do you mean?"

Her intimidating stare ratcheted up a notch. "You know exactly what I mean. My parting advice to you is this: Best you get in a victory lap or two with that man up there before time's up."

Chapter 13

I WANDERED DOWN the long hallway I appeared in fifteen minutes ago and out a door that led to the back of the church. As soon as I left the building, the cord that connected me to Andre flared up. Distantly I realized that until now, magic must've suppressed it, perhaps since as long ago as last night.

A small cemetery sat next to the church, and my feet took me here. It had begun to snow outside, and small tendrils caught in my hair as I passed by the somber stone angels and weathered crosses.

I knelt before one of the tombstones and bowed my head. A tear slipped out, then another. Once they started, I couldn't stop them. Rivulets snaked down my face and crimson drops dripped off my cheeks. It seemed fitting that when I wept, I bled.

I wasn't long for this world. I already knew that. So why did I feel like I was choking on this despair?

Because there is truly no hope.

The vials tinkled in my hand as it shook. I was finally breaking down, and it felt good. I'd been strong for so long. There was something peaceful in giving up and letting go.

The cord that connected me to Andre throbbed; I could feel his tension from the very nature of our connection. Without using any of my other senses, I could tell he left the church.

But then I did hear the powerful, insistent footsteps of my soulmate crunch first along the dead leaves scattered between the chapel and the cemetery, and then against the dead, icy grass that grew between tombstones.

"Gabrielle?" The calm note to his voice alerted me that he was anything but. As he neared me, he slowed, like if he moved too quickly I'd startle and flee.

"I can't do this forever, Andre," I said. "I'm going to slip up, and when I do, someone will kill me."

His footsteps neared until he was right behind me. "What happened?" He might as well have asked who he needed to kill, with the menace that laced his tone.

I rubbed my eyes, and my fingers came away with streaks of blood. "It doesn't matter." My chin shook. "He's going to get me." It was only a matter of time before I was well and truly damned.

Andre knelt beside me and turned my face. "He's not going to get you. I'm not going to let him."

"Stop making empty promises, Andre," I whispered.

His grip tightened on my chin and his mouth thinned. "The promise wasn't an empty one." I could see the fierce determination in his eyes. He'd kill for me. He'd even die for me, though it would mean the death of every other vampire still living. He wouldn't hesitate to do either.

But it wasn't his sacrifice to make. It was mine.

He took the vials from my hand, not commenting on the fact that there were four of them. He unstopped one and handed it back to me. "Drink," he said.

I took the bottle from him and dumped its contents down my throat. My body seemed to close up at the intrusion, but I managed to choke it down.

Like the elixir given to me at my Awakening, Hestia's concoction was both sweet and bitter. I wondered if that was the taste of the ingredients or the taste of powerful magic.

God, what does it matter?

A frown pressed into Andre's features, as did a vertical wrinkle between his brows. Anger and anguish looked the same on his face. "Stop it," he whispered.

"What?"

"Acting like you don't care. Where is your faith?"

Gone. My faith was gone.

"Do you remember what I told you in Romania?" he asked.

I shook my head. He'd told me a lot of things.

"Belief—not fate—rules the world. And I believe in us."

I waited until I knew my voice was under control before I spoke. "I do too, Andre," I said. "I do. But between heaven, hell, and earth, I don't think my belief holds much sway."

"Damnit, Gabrielle," he gathered me into his arms, "I haven't waited centuries for you just to watch you *die*." His voice broke at the end of that last word.

A seven hundred year old vampire, a damned creature who had supposedly lost his humanity long before we'd ever met, was coming apart around me.

"We are going to see this thing through," he said, "and while there's life in you, you are going to live."

I nodded, not because I agreed with him, but because I couldn't stand the thought of Andre fighting for the both of us alone.

"Can you promise me something?" I asked as I stood up.

"Depends," Andre said. He sure wasn't in the most agreeable of moods.

"If I die—"

"No, soulmate," he stopped me.

"*Yes*," I said. "If I die, you need to promise me that you'll live on."

His eyes flashed. "You *cannot* ask that of me."

"But I am. Promise me, Andre."

"No." The muscle in his jaw ticked and he stared back at me defiantly.

"I'm not saying I'm going to die, I just need to hear you say it. I've escaped the devil twice now. Who's to say I can't do it again?" The words felt like a lie as I spoke them. True, I had escaped the devil twice, and technically there might be a way to extricate myself from his clutches yet again. But I didn't believe it. Not really.

Andre stared at me, his eyes stormy. "Fine," he said, "I'll agree to it, but you have to promise me something."

"Go ahead."

"Promise me that you'll never stop fighting. Not now, not ever. Not here, and—God save us all—if you find yourself in hell."

The wind was picking up, lifting my hair so that it brushed against my face. I'd spent mere months fighting the devil in earnest, and I was already beaten down. I couldn't fathom fighting more. But gazing at Andre's face and seeing his despair and his resolve gave me courage. Seven hundred years ago his father made a deal with the devil, a deal that damned Andre's soul, and for seven hundred years Andre had kept the devil at bay. I could try holding Pluto off a little longer myself.

"I promise."

He nodded, his face grim. "Good." He stood and pulled me to my feet.

His nostrils flared, and his gaze sharpened. "Why do you smell of unholy things?"

Aw, crap, I'd forgotten.

"Demons on the ley lines," I squeaked out.

Andre looked alarmed at this. "Ley lines?"

"Oliver and Leanne brought me back." Only after the words had left my mouth did I realize they raised more questions than they answered.

The lines along Andre's face deepened. "Where have you been for the last day?"

My throat closed at the memory of the bridge and waking up in that ring of fallen trees.

He must've seen the terror in my eyes, because he swore. "I'm going to kill that woman." He started back for the church.

"No," I grabbed his arm, "it was part of the deal I made with her."

"Deal?" Andre's brows slammed down. "Soulmate," he said carefully, "we talked about this: you are not to make deals."

Oh, he was being *real* reasonable.

"You wanted the seer's shroud and I got it for us."

He twisted out of my hold so he could grip my upper arms. "I *never* intended for you to pay for it."

"I know that, Andre, but I didn't have much choice."

"What did you promise?" he demanded.

I opened my mouth to respond when I heard Oliver shout, "Skanks, are you done making little Andres? My ass is about to get as fried as those demons if I stay on church grounds much longer."

A moment later he came sauntering out around the church, Leanne on his heels.

"Where's Ophelia?" I asked Andre, noticing her absence.

"Don't change the subject."

"Oh, is he getting bossy?" Oliver yelled, picking his way through the tombstones to get to us. "I *love* it when he gets bossy."

I could tell Andre was now torn between extracting my secrets and throttling the fairy. His mood was darkening by the second.

"Let me guess," Oliver said, "you finally told him about

last night's preview of thunder from down under, eh?" Oliver waggled his eyebrows.

Andre went still as stone, and I winced. Oliver just *had* to drop a bomb like that.

Andre's fangs slid out. "What is he talking about, soulmate?"

Eep.

Before I could answer, Leanne said, "Cough it up, Oliver."

"What?" He tried to look innocent.

"Oh, you damn well know what. You lost the bet."

"What bet?" I asked.

"The bet where Oliver insisted he could hold out on all sexual references to the devil—T-shirt aside—for a full day." Leanne gave me a pitying glance. "Sorry, babe."

Oliver huffed, folding his arms. "I was under the influence of pixie dust when the bet was made. It doesn't count."

"Does too. Now hand over the dinero buddy, or I'm not going to tell you how to run into that merman you'll have a fling with on your—"

Oliver whipped his wallet out so fast you'd have thought someone put a gun to his head.

"That's what I thought. Never bet a mother-effing seer," she said as he dolled out several bills. "We'll come and collect on your ass."

Oliver grumbled. "Taking advantage of poor, unsuspecting fairies ..."

Andre growled. "Enough of this. What happened last night, soulmate?" he demanded, recapturing my attention.

I shook my head, my throat closing up at his intensity. "Nothing."

He stepped into me. "You're lying," he stated.

"Lover's quarrel," Oliver said as he dragged Leanne away. "You don't want to be here when shit hits the fan ..."

Andre lifted a lock of my hair and fingered it before bringing it to his nose. He drew in a deep breath, closing his eyes. They snapped open. "*The devil.*"

His eyes widened with horror. "What did that hag have you do last night?"

Should I tell Andre when he was like this? I'd inevitably have to talk him down from running the sorceress through with that sword of his. "I had to fetch Hestia a rose as part of my payment for the seer's shroud," I said. "I ran into some complications."

"Complications?" He ran a shaky hand over his mouth. "What do you mean *complications*? You come back to me with four vials of seer's shroud and bleakness in your eyes." His eyes unfocused. "You smell of brimstone ..."

His gaze sharpened and the connection between us flared as some terrifying thought hit him. He grabbed for my wrist and brought it to his face. For a moment I thought he'd bite me, but instead he inhaled.

I tried to step away from him, but his grip held firm.

"His scent is woven through yours." Andre's eyes snapped to mine. "What have you—?"

A bloodcurdling scream interrupted us. Another joined it a moment later. My breath caught in my throat at the sound.

My gaze met Andre's. "Oliver and Leanne," I whispered.

Our pursuers had found my friends.

I yanked my wrist from Andre's grip and sprinted towards the source of the screams just as my two friends rounded the church, moving like hell was nipping at their toes. I smelled the metallic tang of blood the same instant I saw it seeping from Oliver's temple.

"They shot me!" Oliver screamed as he ran. "Oh my God, I'm going to die!"

Next to him Leanne was white as a sheet.

Andre's form blurred as he ran to Oliver and threw the fairy fireman-style over his shoulders. I followed suit, grabbing Leanne and wrapping her body around my neck like a shawl.

"We need to move. *Now.*"

"Hestia might help." As I spoke, I heard footfalls on the other side of the church moving quickly in our direction. Our attackers weren't as fast as us, but they'd still spot us in another several seconds if we didn't get going.

"She will not interfere further, soulmate." Andre readjusted Oliver's weight, and then he took off, running faster than human eyes could track.

I followed Andre blindly, not sure where he was going, but trusting him to know what to do.

"I never saw it coming," Leanne said as I ran. "I've been so worried about your future that I didn't foresee his."

"Shh," I said, vaulting over a rock. "It's okay."

"It's not."

Something whizzed by me, so close it stirred my hair. It thwacked into a tree, and when I caught sight of it, I had to give it a double take.

Iridescent feathers tipped the shaft of the arrow lodged into the tree.

Did none of these people use modern weapons?

"Keep moving," Andre ordered, not turning, "and use your hearing to avoid getting hit."

Behind me I could hear whoops and strange calls.

"Who are they?" I said, ducking as an arrow whizzed by. Did anyone use guns these days.

"Amazons," Andre ground out.

I balked even as I ran. "You mean the chicks that fought in the Trojan War? The ones that cut off their right breasts to better shoot? Those ones?"

"Unfortunately, yes," he gritted out.

Shit, shit, shit. And they were after my ass?

I stopped, swiveled around, and caught sight of several women who looked just as badass as I had pictured.

"*Gabrielle!*" Panic laced Andre's voice.

"Ceasefire!" I yelled at our assailants, willing the siren to enter my voice.

One of them laughed in my face as she loaded and released another arrow. I jumped out of the way just as the arrow zipped by. Andre jerked my hand, and we began to run once more.

"That should've worked."

"Earplugs, soulmate."

Well, there went that advantage. As we ran, Andre's hair lifted, and from the snappy static that was coming off of him, I didn't think the wind that was causing it.

Andre was going into berserker mode.

Crap.

He still seemed to have some of his faculties with him, however, because I could hear Oliver murmuring directions to him and see him nod in response.

A minute later, we entered the clearing I'd woken up in, and Andre slowed to a stop. He set a bloody Oliver down, and I slid Leanne off my shoulders. She stumbled over to Oliver, and I could hear her quiet sobs.

Andre took in the felled trees. His nostrils flared, and I breathed in as well, not sure what I was scenting for. Beneath the smell of my friends, there was the stench of the damned ... and me.

He straightened, his expression turning malevolent.

Going ... going ... *gone.*

Andre's inner demons consumed him, just like that night at Bishopcourt. His hair lifted and his coat flapped in an invisible breeze. He dragged his attention from me to our pursuers just as they came into our line of sight. I could hear their footfalls and their easy breathing. They hadn't seen us yet—not surprising considering that most supernaturals didn't have night vision—but already they had their arrows notched into their bows, ready to aim and fire the moment they caught sight of us.

Now that I got a good look at them, I could see their wide shoulders and impressive height. The metallic armor they wore glinted in the moonlight. They moved lithely, their footfalls light against the ground.

They were beautiful, deadly, and even scarier than I had

imagined.

The moment they noticed us their weapons went up.

Andre lifted his arms, and flames blossomed at his feet. A wall of fire roared to life in front of the four of us, arcing across the ground until it formed a protective circle.

Under normal circumstances, turning one's back on approaching Amazons was probably a death sentence. But having a vampire king channel his unholy power to protect you afforded me certain luxuries ... like temporarily leaving him to his own devices.

I made my way to my friends, who were huddled near the remains of the rose bush. Oliver's usually coiffed ice blond hair was now matted with blood.

I crouched next to him so that I could brush his hair out of his face. As soon as my fingers touched his face, I felt his feverish skin. "You're burning up." My voice quivered.

He shivered. "Doesn't help ... that your boyfriend ... lit the place ... on fire."

I smiled at the fairy's attempt at humor.

"I can ... get us out ... of here," Oliver rasped. "Get ... Andre."

I pressed my lips together and stood up. My eyes met Leanne's. She'd been zoning out—which likely meant she was foreseeing something—but as soon as our gazes met, her attention refocused.

She nodded. "He's going to be okay."

I blew out a breath and made my way to my possessed boyfriend.

He stood at the edge of the circle, staring down the

approaching Amazons.

As soon as they caught sight of me, one let loose an arrow.

Wrong move on her part.

Andre blurred, stepping in front of me and catching the arrow before it ever had the chance to land. He studied the arrow, and he seemed calm enough, but the fire pulsed, expanding with his growing anger.

He flipped the arrow in his hand, then threw it like a missile back at the shooter. The Amazon barely leapt out of the way in time.

The remaining women had their weapons raised, but they held them in check now that they knew their opponent far outgunned them.

Andre began walking towards the fire, his hair whipping about him.

I grabbed his arm. "Andre, no."

He turned to me, his eyes unseeing. His fangs were down, and his lips twitched, like he was holding back a hiss.

"We need to go."

His gaze moved back to the Amazons. "They need to die," he said, his voice resonating. The fire pulsed outward.

Well damn.

"Maybe later, Andre." I grabbed his hand.

"Not later," he said, staring them down. "Now."

At least I could reason with him.

Not.

Andre jerked his chin up and the bows the Amazons

carried were yanked from their grip, as if by an invisible hand. And then that invisible hand crushed them. Wood splintered and metal crunched as the weapons splintered and broke.

These Amazons may be scary-ass women, but they were also smart ones. As soon as their bows were destroyed, they hauled butt out of there. I didn't doubt they had other weapons—I could see one's holstered knife as she tore away from us—but I'm sure they already figured that those too would get destroyed the moment they pulled them out.

And if metal could be pulverized that easily, human flesh—no matter how strong—would be putty at the hands of a deranged vampire king.

Andre strode towards the fire that ringed us in, looking like he had every intention of following them. He stepped into the fire, and without thinking, I lunged after him.

The flames licked up my body, and I screamed as they flayed open my exposed flesh.

A moment later, I heard a roar, and then I was scooped out of the fire and laid down on the ground, the flames creeping along my clothes smothered by the press of gentle hands.

Andre stared down at me with frightened eyes, and I could tell that whatever had possessed him now fled in the wake of my injury.

"Gabrielle," he choked out, "are you alright?"

My skin still felt like it was burning, but I nodded. "Take me to Oliver." He frowned but picked me up and brought me to my friends.

Heat radiated from Oliver's body and a tainted smell rose from his blood.

He cracked his eyes open. "'Bout damn time." He mouthed the words more than spoke them. "Touch me."

At any other time I would've said this was Oliver being lewd. Any other time but now. The three of us each laid a hand on Oliver's chest. A moment later the ring of fire and the felled trees disappeared.

Warm wind tore through my clothes from where I crouched amongst wild grass. Wherever we were, the night had the touch of summer to it.

In front of me, Oliver moaned, drawing my attention back to him. That stench rose again from his blood. "What is that?" I asked.

"Poison," Andre stated. "Their arrows were tipped with it. You can tell by the smell."

Andre leaned over the fairy. "It's a flesh wound. There's a lot more bleeding than actual tissue damage, but the poison can still spread. I'm going to need to suck it out."

"I always ... wanted ... you to say ... that ... to me."

"Stop hitting on my soulmate," I teased, earning myself a smile from the fairy. I wouldn't mention how relieved I was to hear a joke coming out of him. It meant that he'd be okay.

Andre bent to the wound. "This might hurt a bit," he said, and then he placed his mouth against the fairy's temple. Air hissed between Oliver's teeth as Andre drew the poisoned blood out of him.

Staring at the two of them, I couldn't decide whether the situation looked more awkward or oddly erotic. Either way, it had me shifting my weight uncomfortably.

Next to Oliver, Leanne held his hand tightly, whispering soothing platitudes in his ear. Gradually the smell of tainted blood left him.

Andre pulled away from Oliver and leaned back on his haunches. "The poison is mostly gone from your system," he said, discreetly wiping his mouth. "How do you feel?"

Oliver groaned. "Like I got nailed with a tire iron—and I do mean *iron*." From some dim recess of my mind I remembered that the metal was lethal to fairies.

Andre nodded. "You'll live—though you'll have to ride off the last of the fever and you'll need to eat soon to replenish your blood."

Andre stood and leveled a look at me. "Soulmate, we need to talk."

WE STOOD ON top of a rock formation that jutted far above the surrounding jungle, giving me a panoramic view. Wherever we were, it was lovely.

Behind us, Leanne murmured to Oliver as the fairy came down from his fever.

Andre and I stared out at the jungle for several seconds before either one of us spoke.

"I'm sorry," he said.

I glanced over at him, vaguely alarmed. I was expecting him to say a lot of things, but not that. "For what?"

He took my hand, the one that sported his mother's—and now my—ruby ring.

"For worsening your burden. I'm sure I haven't been

the easiest person to deal with for the last several days." He smiled ruefully." The truth of the matter is—" he stared at my hand as he spoke, "I'm petrified of losing you."

He glanced up at me, his thumb rubbing over my knuckles. "I've lived for a long time. Long enough to grow apathetic to people, to the world. I've wished to die more times than I can remember, and the thing that has always stayed my hand is fear for my people and what lay on the other side of death. Now, for the first time in a long time, I'm eager to live. Yet now I fear something far more greatly than even my people. I can't lose you."

There wasn't anything to say to that, so I didn't bother. Instead I pressed our joined hands to my heart.

Andre's fangs slid out, and eyes bright, he kissed me. I hadn't realized how much I'd craved the touch until he was there, pressing himself into me and enveloping me in his taste.

My mouth parted, and his tongue stroked mine. Against the fire-burned tatters of my outfit, I could feel his taught muscles.

My fangs slid out, nicking Andre's tongue in the process. He groaned into my mouth as I tasted him. My skin began to glow at the sound. I'd forgotten that my undead boyfriend had a blood fetish. And while that still disturbed me on some levels, a much larger part of me was turned on at the thought.

I was officially a freak—which was why I ran my tongue along one of his fangs until I drew blood. I was rewarded with another one of those delectable groans.

Andre broke off the kiss suddenly, his grip tightening

on me. I blinked up at him, dazed and a bit confused as to why we stopped.

"Your scent is mixed with the devil's," he stated. The muscle in his jaw jumped.

Well, that just took the fun out of everything. My skin dimmed and my fangs retracted.

"What happened last night?" he asked, his voice gentling.

I extricated myself from Andre's touch. The devil kept coming between us.

I toed a nearby pebble. "Last night the devil took me." I kicked the pebble off the side of the outcropping. "I woke up this evening in that circle of fallen trees—that's where Leanne and Oliver found me—with no memory of what happened after he took me."

My eyes finally met his. "Hestia called it *tasting*. He's essentially getting a preview of my soul. That's what happened when he took me, though I don't remember it."

Andre's brow wrinkled, his dark eyes shining in the moonlight. His expression was inscrutable, but I imagined horror dawned behind those lovely eyes of his.

"*Tasting*." Andre tried the word out. "I've never heard of it."

"I doubt the devil does it very often," I said.

That muscle in Andre's jaw ticked. "He took you and he tasted you, and you lost a full day somewhere in there?"

I sucked in my cheeks, then nodded.

Andre brought his hand up to his mouth again and shook his head. I saw the moment Andre truly realized that he couldn't do a damn thing about the situation. His expression didn't change, but a drop of blood snaked out from the corner of his eye.

I reached up and wiped the tear away. Andre caught my wrist and pulled me into his embrace. His arms enfolded me, and his chin rested on my head. He whispered to me in Romanian things he knew I couldn't understand and held onto me like I might blow away.

"Thank you for telling me," he said, letting me go.

I searched his face. "Of course." My words were silly, careless; I hadn't planned on telling him.

Andre gave me a sharp nod and that was the end of that conversation.

I couldn't decide whether I was relieved or frightened that he hadn't made any false promises.

Andre fished out the remaining bottles of seer's shroud from his pocket. Unstopping one, he downed it like it was a shot of something strong.

He held up the remaining two. "I'm presuming these are for your friends?"

I nodded.

"Then let's get these to them. We'll all be safer once they drink this." He turned away from the edge of the outcropping.

"Hey Andre?" I said, stopping him.

"Hmm?"

"What did you do while I was gone?"

Andre's face darkened. "Hestia placed an enchantment on the church. I couldn't leave it. I destroyed what I could before she bound me up with magic. Then I seethed."

"Ah."

His evening sounded almost as fun as mine. Almost.

"WHAT IS IT?" Leanne asked, when we returned back to where she and Oliver rested.

She held the bottle of seer's shroud up to the moonlit sky. I almost laughed; there was no way her human vision would make out details of the liquid in this lighting.

I swayed a little on my feet as a wave of dizziness passed over me.

"It's called seer's shroud," Andre said, casting me a concerned glance. "It hides your movement from seers. Highly illegal."

"Breaking the law? Oh, I'm game," Oliver said, his voice still weak. Limply, he accepted the vial Andre handed him.

In one smooth motion, he uncorked the bottle, and downed the fluid. I noted the way he forced his throat to push the liquid down. I was perversely happy that I wasn't the only one who had a hard time drinking the liquid. He grimaced. "Ugh, that tastes fucking horrible. Like unwashed asshole."

It wasn't *that* bad. Even the girl without an appetite could attest to that.

"Ugh, Oliver," Leanne made a face. "I still have to drink it." She hesitated. "Highly illegal?"

"Highly," Andre confirmed. "You do not have to drink it, but for Gabrielle's safety, you cannot travel with us if you're not under its protection."

Leanne chewed her lower lip. "I understand. Give me a

minute." She closed her eyes, her breath deepening.

As I watched her, I grew lightheaded.

"She does nothing by the seat of her knickers anymore," Oliver stage-whispered. "I'm telling you, that doppelganger fucked her up."

"Shhhh," she said, overlooking the barb. Beneath her closed lids, her eyes darted back and forth, watching our phantom futures play out.

Darkness crept up from the corners of my vision.

When she finally opened her eyes, she nodded. "Oliver and I should be fine."

She unstopped the bottle and chugged its contents.

Blackness swallowed my eyesight as another wave of dizziness slammed into me. I stumbled forward.

"Soulmate?"

I reached out for Andre, but I never felt his touch before sweet oblivion consumed me.

Chapter 14

Wʜᴇɴ I ᴄᴀᴍᴇ to, the first thing I noticed was the tang of blood at the back of my mouth and the arm that cradled my head.

My eyes fluttered open, and I stared into the dark, concerned gaze of my soulmate, who held me in his lap.

He handed me a blood bag with a single command. "Drink, love."

Using the tube at the top of the bag, I began pulling the thick liquid into my mouth, not stopping until I'd finished the bag off.

I set the empty bag aside and stared up at him. "What happened to me?"

"You fainted."

I raised my eyebrows. "I *fainted?*"

"Looked like a beached whale too, all pasty and belly

up," Oliver added helpfully.

"You seem to have made a complete recovery," I noted, eyeing him.

He guffawed. "As if there was any doubt. There's a reason no one messes with fairies. Can't kill us that easily. Best not to try, really, because if you can't off us on the first go, we'll up and go Attila the Hun on you."

"Culturally insensitive," Leanne said.

Oliver sighed and, with a roll of his eyes, turned to Leanne. "Just because you sacrificed your pettiness doesn't mean you have to go and slaughter everyone else's. Geez." He swiveled back to me and shook his head. "It's culturally insensitive of *some people*," his eyes slid to Leanne pointedly, "to expect a fairy to act like a saint.

"Anyway," he continued, "those Amazons will rue the day they shot me. I'm going to be that cold sore that won't go away. That chlamydia that you accidently picked up from that one time you went to a rave over the summer and decided to participate in an orgy with a bunch of male sprites."

I wrinkled my nose.

"*Oliver*," Leanne said.

"Bad idea," he muttered, shaking his head. "Bad idea—but at least it wasn't the herps, which is what I'll totally be to those Amazons—persistent and uncomfortable."

Andre cleared his throat and gazed down at me. I could tell from his pained expression that he'd only just managed to sit through the last two minutes. For a guy that had lived for seven centuries, one would think he'd have a little more patience.

"Feel any better?" he asked.

"I'm okay," I said, sitting up.

He readjusted his grip to accommodate me, but I noticed that he wouldn't let me stray far from his lap. It wasn't like I was dying to leave him. I cringed at the thought; that literally *was* what was happening.

Andre's thumb rubbed the skin beneath my eye. "You need rest, soulmate. All of this running around isn't good for you."

I smiled at that. He was still clucking over me like the most troublesome thing about my life right now was my exhaustion. Considering the horde of supernaturals after my scrawny butt, rest was the last thing I needed to worry about.

"I fear your body isn't replenishing your blood the way it should," he said.

I worried he was right.

His hand drifted down my face, his touch soft. It was odd to think that we were equally matched in wicked-ness—the girl that was promised to the devil, and a living extension of him. And here we were, redeeming one an-other. If there was ever a case for salvation, we were it.

I leaned into his touch, my eyes closing. "I want to go back to that tent in the woods."

"What tent in the woods?" Oliver shattered our privacy.

When I opened my eyes, Andre was giving me a heated look ... and Oliver's eager face peered over his shoulder.

Moment ruiner.

"So do I," Andre said.

Oliver glanced between me and Andre. "*What* tent?"

I cleared my throat. "How do you think the Amazons found us?" I asked Andre, getting back to business.

"No, no, no, Sabertooth, you do *not* get to change the subject after you drop a bomb like that."

"Let it go, Oliver," Leanne said. "You'll have plenty of time to badger her later."

Oliver huffed, but quieted.

"The Amazons must've used circumstantial evidence to figure out where you were and who you were with. They're mercenaries—they're used to finding people who wish to stay hidden."

"Crazy bitches," Oliver muttered.

"Fairy," Andre said, "are you well enough to take us to the Isle of Man?"

"You want to go *there*? I hate being the voice of reason, but that is not wise—"

"Are. You. Well. Enough?" Andre repeated.

"Yes—"

"Then we need to go—preferably now."

Andre's attention turned to me. "Soulmate," he said, his tone softening, "we have to leave. Can you walk, or would you prefer me carrying you?"

"I'm fine," I said. Heaven forbid I let Andre haul me around in his arms. He'd never put me down.

"Oh, he gives her the royal treatment," Oliver muttered. "Real fair, Andre."

"I am not *fair*," Andre said, his gaze lingering on me. "I am lawless, and I have little empathy for anything other than the woman in my arms." Aw, Andre was proclaiming his love. Too bad he was going about it as abrasively as possible. "You should never forget that, fairy."

"Hmph. Well, not the best response ever," Oliver said, rising to his feet and dusting himself off, "but I have more important things to worry about, like the horrid state of my clothes." He reached up to pat his hair, only to pause. "My hair's a mess too, isn't it? Dammit, I'm no longer the hottest one of the group."

"*Are* you okay to travel?" Andre asked me, his voice low.

"I'm fine, Andre," I said.

"'I'm fine,'" Andre repeated. "I learned long ago I should never trust a woman who utters those words."

"You really shouldn't," Leanne threw in.

I huffed out a laugh, rising to my feet. "The sooner we get back to the Isle of Man, the sooner I can take a hot shower."

And the sooner I'd have to face down a murderous coven of vampires, among other things.

Awesome.

Chapter 15

WILDERNESS GREW OVER the ruins of the small stone house we stood in front of. Bright green grasses and wooded trees surrounded the four of us.

"Home sweet home," Oliver said. "We're finally back to bloody civilization," his upper lip curled at the sight of the ruins, "though you'd never know it."

For a fairy, he was oddly anti-nature.

Andre stepped up next to me, taking my hand in his. His eyes scanned the forest, searching for any hints of ambush. While he did so, he brought the back of my hand to his lips and absently kissed it, like affection for me came unconsciously to him. My heart picked up its pace at the action.

He glanced down at me, arching an eyebrow, a small smile tugging at his lips. That only made my heart thump faster.

His other arm snaked around my waist, and his eyes told me that he was thinking illicit thoughts.

"You guys done eye-banging, or should I give you another minute?"

I turned to face Oliver. "You are worse than that little voice inside my head."

He raised a shoulder. "I'd like to say I try, but I was just born this fabulous."

I turned to our surroundings. "So we're back to the Isle of Man?" I asked.

"Mmhmm."

"Why not exit at the Braaid?" I asked. The stone circle located near the center of the island seemed like the most obvious portal here.

"Because that's where the Politia will be expecting you to exit."

Oh.

"This exit is one us fairies *exclusively* know about." Oliver seemed mighty proud about that fact.

Andre stiffened next to me, his nostrils flaring. A moment later he pushed me behind him. "Who's there?" his voice thundered.

The wild grass rustled and shifted as though someone moved through it. I breathed in the forest air, but I smelled nothing over Andre and my friends.

The grass stilled, and Cecilia stepped out from the ruins of the house.

"You're late."

"DID YOU SELL the bed and breakfast?" I asked, staring at our surroundings. A warm fire burned in the hearth, heating up the small cottage. A cottage that, from the outside, was nothing more than crumbling stones. Just like Peel Academy, Cecilia's home here had been enchanted.

The five of us sat in Cecilia's living room, drinking tea like we weren't a bunch of savages. We were a ragtag bunch. Andre, with his sheathed swords, Oliver with his blood-caked hair. Leanne with her dirtied face and stained clothes, and me smelling of graveyards and ash. We looked like something the cat dragged in. The sight of us drinking Earl Grey from porcelain cups and eating dainty cookies was almost comical.

Andre lounged back on a side chair, one leg slung over the other. His foot tapped impatiently on the ground. I guess niceties weren't really his thing.

"No," she chuckled, "I still own it. Like your soulmate, I've acquired several homes over the years. The bed and breakfast is one of them, as is this house."

Calling this a house was being generous. From what I could tell, the place in its entirety was probably no bigger than two of the girl's dormitory rooms butted together.

"Enough of this," Andre said, leaning forward. "How can we save Gabrielle?"

"That is a discussion I'm afraid I need to have with Gabrielle alone," Cecilia said.

Andre stood, looking menacing. "The last time a powerful woman demanded that, the devil took my soulmate. I will not let that happen twice."

"Andre de Leon, shame on you," Cecilia said, setting

down her teacup and standing as well. "I helped raise this child during the first years of her life, and if my memory serves me correctly I saved her from *your* right-hand man when he sought to kill her. Do not confuse my intentions for those of some scheming sorceress."

Andre frowned. He stared at her for a long moment, then bowed his head in acquiescence. When he lifted his chin, his gaze landed meaningfully on me, and it lingered there for a long moment. Then he turned on his heal and strode out of the cottage.

"Really?" Oliver said around a partially masticated cookie he'd shoved in his mouth. "After all that huffing and puffing he just ... leaves?"

"Yeah, which means we need to skedaddle too." Leanne stood, brushing crumbs off her hands.

Oliver grumbled. He swallowed his tea down and grabbed a fistful of cookies. "This so does not count as dinner."

"Really?" I said, eyebrows lifting. "Had me fooled, eating like there's no tomorrow."

"Just because your skanky ass is on a liquid diet doesn't mean you got to go and be rude to the rest of us."

Leanne headed over to Cecilia and clasped the fate's hand. "It was good to see you again," Leanne said.

"Oh, you too my dear," Cecilia said, patting the side of her face.

My friends left shortly after that, and then it was just Cecilia and me.

"*Mi tesoro*," she said, opening her arms, "you have had a trying few days."

I walked into her embrace, breathing in her lavender perfume as I fiercely clung to her. It would've been proper to let her go after a couple of seconds, but I didn't. She had insight that no one else had.

"I'm frightened," I admitted, my voice barely a whisper.

"Good. I'd be worried if you weren't." She smiled as she pulled away from me and clasped my cheeks.

"Is it going to get worse?" I asked.

"Yes," she said bluntly, "but you already knew this."

I bit the inside of my cheek and nodded.

She moved to the scattered teacups and began stacking them on a serving tray. Mine and Andre's cups were still filled to the brim with cooling tea. "Won't be needing these anymore, will we now?" she said as she lifted them onto the tray. She didn't bother asking whether I wanted the rest of tea, and I was grateful that we were dealing solely with the truth, no matter how unpleasant it might be.

"Will I get my appetite back?" I asked.

She made a humming noise at the back of her throat. "Eventually." She hoisted the tray in her arms and porcelain clattered.

I hustled over to help her. "Let me take that from you."

"Nonsense, *mi tesoro*. Just give me a second to put these away. And please," she nodded to the living space, "get comfortable. *Mia casa è tua casa*." With that, she took the dishes into the kitchen.

As she began banging around in there, I perused her living room. Even after all these years, it was still strange to see her living a life completely separate from mine. But to a fate, I must be one small blip in the great expanse of her lifetime.

I ran a hand along the fireplace's mantle, noticing the bundles of dried heather. On a side table, a series of framed photos had been placed on display. I moved over to them. What pictures did a fate hold dear?

It was a strange collection that spanned at least a century. A grainy sepia photo of a stiff couple rested next to a photo from the sixties of a family standing in front of a tinseled tree.

I did a double take when I glimpsed a picture of my mother. I grabbed the frame, drawn just as much by my desperate desire to see her as I was by the pull of her face. Even trapped in a photo she had that effect.

Her complexion looked nothing like mine, save for the pale skin. Her hair was strawberry blonde, and the warm eyes that looked heavenward were hazel. The photographer caught her mid-laugh, and even frozen in place, I wanted to laugh along with her.

Next to her was another girl, her cheek smudged with flour. Their hands were buried in a bowl of dough. The picture was so full of life that it was hard to believe the woman who'd given birth to me no longer lived.

"She loved you so much," Cecilia said, stepping up next to me.

"I know nothing about her," I said, my thumb rubbing over her face.

"She was fiery—she could cut a man down with her words alone. Your father was no exception. But God did he love her." She sighed. "I thought I would have more time to tell you about them."

My throat tightened. "You're a fate. Shouldn't you have known?"

"Perhaps. I'm not omniscient—not in this form—regardless of what the myths say about me."

I turned back to the photo. "Where is she buried?"

"Lemnos—it's an island on the Aegean. It's where your family is from."

Up until this point, I hadn't known that. I wanted to shake Cecilia, to yell and ask her why she had failed so epically to tell me about my parents, but then that would make me a hypocrite.

I'd never asked about them. Sure, I'd done searches for them, read up on their histories, memorized their faces and printed out pictures of them, which I'd shoved between pages of my textbooks. But I'd never forced Andre to tell me all he knew of Santiago—a man he'd been close friends with for half a millennia. And I'd never sought out Cecilia before this to learn more about them.

I think as much as I wanted to know, I didn't want the what-ifs to well within me. They were gone, I'd survived, and I was forced to live out my life without the shine of their personalities.

"She did it all for you," Cecilia said staring down at the photo.

"What do you mean?"

"The child that never should've existed. She was the only one who knew for certain that you were Santiago's. Not even he could be sure—not until you grew old enough to take on his features." She shrugged helplessly. "I'm afraid a siren's reputation long precedes her.

I turned to more fully face Cecilia. "Vampires don't have children—they can't."

"You're right, they can't. But you *are* Santiago's daughter."

I searched her face. "How is that possible?"

"Just as the devil tricks humans, sometimes God tricks the devil."

I breathed in and out, letting that settle on my shoulders. "You're saying *God* made me this way?"

Cecilia shrugged. "I, as you might imagine, am not well acquainted with Christian religion. That's ultimately for you to decide.

"Most of the time the world's religions coexist in—relative—harmony. But not always. You are one such case. The prophecy is true—you are Pluto's Proserpine, and he will do everything in his power to take you back to the Underworld with him. But it is also true that some great being out there tweaked the rules of our world so that you could exist at all."

She glanced at the photo I still held. "Your mother knew about the prophecy before you were ever born, and she spent the last years of her life doing everything she could to protect you from your fate." Cecilia touched the skin just beneath my eye. "And like you, she knew when her time was coming to a close."

My heartbeat increased. "She knew she was going to die?"

Cecilia gave a slight nod. She moved away from the framed photo and to the window. I followed her over there.

Outside Leanne and Oliver played some game that involved slapping each other's hands. Beyond them, Andre leaned against a tree, his body tense. His entire focus seemed to be trained on this house. That man was a force of nature.

Cecilia nodded to him. "He's impossible to be around right now, isn't he?"

I shook my head. "You have no idea."

"He's only going to get more difficult, I'm afraid. Fear does that to men like him. Nothing for it."

He hadn't moved since we came to the window.

"He's a good man." She smiled. "You brought him back from the edge; he was getting tired of life." She paused. "I don't know everything, but I can tell you this: he loves you more than he's ever loved anything. Losing you is going to gut him."

So we were still talking in truths.

I placed a trembling hand on the cold windowpane and stared out at him. "I know." It was barely a whisper.

I longed to take away his pain. Instead I'd be adding to it. "Will he survive it?"

Cecilia turned my face to her. "I shouldn't be surprised that you ask about him rather than yourself."

I lifted my shoulders and glanced down at my shoes. "I'm trying not to think about what's going to happen to me."

"Ah. That I can understand."

She wasn't denying that my fate would be everything my nightmares suggested it would be.

She sighed. "I can't answer your question about the

vampire. It would alter the way events must unfold."

She twisted away from the window. "There is a very specific reason why I called you here," Cecilia said. "As much as you do not want to dwell on your future, we must discuss it.

"There has always been a balance to things," she said, "but the balance has been thrown off for some time. The Celestial Plane—heaven—doesn't involve itself in earthly skirmishes, but the devil has gotten too powerful. He thinks to overreach."

I narrowed my eyes. "And I have something to do with that?"

Cecilia drew in a deep breath. "He wants access to earth. And in order to get that, he needs a woman with the flesh of the earth and born with the blood of the tainted—he needs *you*. You offer him power. Lots of it."

Her words reminded me of a long ago conversation with Andre. He had said the same thing.

I put a hand to my head. "Wait." Her words echoed in my head. "Are you saying that because my father was a vampire, I was born ... *tainted*?" I used the word she provided.

Cecilia nodded.

"And you're saying that some bigger being allowed me to be born?"

"Not allowed, *mi tesoro*. Facilitated. Your birth was facilitated."

Now there was some news to knock you on your ass.

"*Wow*." I had to shelve that one; I had no idea what to make of it.

"Is there a way to stop the devil?" I asked.

"To stop him means stopping you."

I rubbed my eyes, suddenly feeling a million years old—so, about the same age as Andre. "If I thought dying would help, I wouldn't be running from certain death, Cecilia. Is there another way?"

She looked at me from the corner of her eye, a sly smile curving her mouth. I'd asked the question out of desperation, but it seemed that there was actually validity to it.

"There is, isn't there?" I didn't mean to sound so shocked. It was just that after visiting Hestia, I'd resigned myself to my fate.

"There is always salvation for those who want it." Cecilia's eyes flicked back to the window before returning to me. "You must talk to the third and final fate, Decima. She's currently undecided on the matter of your life and the balance between good and evil."

No pressure or anything.

"And you want me to convince her of what? My goodness?"

"*Mi tesoro*, we fates are far-seeing, but we also dwell in human bodies with all of their limitations. We are subjective, and we make mistakes. A person's future is a pattern of possibilities. They collapse together into one reality only when they happen. And right now, the number of possibilities that end well for you, for vampires, for the balance of good and evil … well, the odds are against you."

I swallowed, remembering the chill of the devil's presence, the desolation of a place without God. The thought of going back to that had my heart hammering. "I've beaten the odds more than once," I said.

"That you have, which is why you need to talk with Decima. The third fate watches you even now. She is the swing vote. Find her."

"How will I find her?"

"She waits for you inside Peel Academy. A certain hell-hound will lead you to her. Word is that dog is very taken with you"

"Scooby?" I said quietly. Yeah, I'd named the *Moddey Dhoo*, Peel Castle's demonic dog. He'd become my buddy.

I cleared my throat. "When should I meet Decima?"

"She is a fate. You'll meet her exactly when the time is right."

Typical cryptic response.

A grandfather clock chimed in the corner.

Cecilia took the photo from me, returning it to its place. "Enemies approach, *mi tesoro*. It is time to be on your way."

She led me to the door. "Do you still have that card I gave you?"

"Mhm." It was buried somewhere in that enchanted bag Andre had hauled around, shoved inside one of my pants' pockets.

"Good," she said absentmindedly, a faraway look in her eyes. "Keep it safe. You'll need it in the future."

Trusting me with a flimsy piece of paper was probably not Cecilia's wisest decision, but I nodded anyway.

I hesitated, then leaned in to hug her tightly. I had so many more things that I wanted to ask, to say, and I feared I'd never get the chance.

When I pulled away, she patted my cheek. "Have faith. We are the weavers of time. Everything will go as it should."

I wanted to believe her, but the truth was, I was earthborn, hellbound, and absolutely screwed.

I LEFT HER small cottage, dazed by what I'd learned. As soon as Andre caught sight of me, that singular focus of his was honed in on me.

He loves you more than he's ever loved anything.

I took in a ragged breath. Hope might not be lost. Not completely.

"Done with your little tête-à-tête?" Oliver asked when he saw me. "Sure you don't want a little longer? I don't think all ten of my fingers have gotten frostbite yet."

"Shut up, Oliver," Leanne said, elbowing him.

"Ow!" he rubbed his side. "Keep your elbows to yourself. The only boney things I want poking me are—"

Leanne covered his mouth with her hand before he had time to finish the sentence. "Sometimes I seriously wonder why we're friends."

Oliver's protest was muffled.

When Andre reached me, he laid his hands on my upper arms and gently kneaded them. "All went well, soulmate?"

I nodded, trying to keep eye contact in spite of the knowledge I'd learned between Hestia and Cecilia.

"I need to meet with the third fate and convince her that I'm worth saving."

Andre's face broke into a brilliant smile. "That's excellent, soulmate. Where and when are you to meet her?"

"Peel Academy, and on fate time—so whenever."

His smile dropped. "No."

"No?" *Is he serious?*

"Peel Academy is way too dangerous."

Oh Lordy, he is.

I raised my eyebrows. "I don't remember asking for your permission."

"There will be Politia everywhere, soulmate. Let's find a different location."

"Sure, why don't I just call up Decima with a number *I don't have*. I'm sure a fate that might not even like me is eager to accommodate my needs."

I don't even know why I was arguing with Andre. It's not like he was going to change my mind. Not if this fate could save me from the devil. I'd risk death for that.

Andre glowered at me.

"Is someone having another lover's quarrel?" Oliver asked, wandering over.

"Soulmate, this is a bad idea."

"What's a bad idea?" Oliver asked, gripping my arm. "I love bad ideas. Especially yours."

"I need to get inside Peel Academy unnoticed."

Oliver snorted. "Bitch please, that's *too* easy."

All of us turned to the fairy, including Leanne, who'd so far stayed out of the fray.

"Really?" Oliver let us all know with a single look that he thought we were imbeciles. "They're called persecution tunnels."

Andre stepped forward. "These tunnels can get my soulmate in and out of the school *completely* undetected?"

"That is the idea."

"Perfect," I said, clapping my hands together. "That solves that." I'd be going back on campus. I could already feel my excitement bubbling. I missed my old school.

"I don't like this," Andre grumbled, but he didn't fight it.

Once we made plans to meet up again tomorrow to find Decima, Andre and I parted ways with Oliver and Leanne. Those two headed back to Peel Academy, while we headed for Bishopcourt.

It wasn't until we'd reached Andre's place that I thought back on my conversation with Cecilia. I realized I never asked her who the other woman in the photo was. Or, more importantly, what a random photo of my mother was doing there in the first place.

Chapter 16

I PASSED A saint's relic Andre had on display along the hall at Bishopcourt. It wasn't the original one he had here; that one had been lost in the fire several months ago.

I reached out and touched the relic, whispering a desperate prayer under my breath. Even knowing it hadn't saved Andre or any other vampire didn't matter at the moment. Time and reverence had made the thing holy.

Andre paused to wait for me, but he didn't comment on my behavior. If anything, something like understanding flickered in his eyes. He'd done this before, perhaps many times. He knew what it was like to ask for salvation even if deliverance would never come.

He called over a servant. "Please get Gabrielle a clean set of clothes and leave them in my room.

Once the servant left, he placed a hand on my back and

steered me farther down the hall. "Soon they will know you're here."

Andre didn't have to clarify who "they" were. Considering the entire supernatural community wanted my head, I might as well assume he meant all of them.

"And," Andre continued, "later tonight I will have to contact the coven and schedule a meeting."

I cringed. "They're going to eat me alive—right after they draw and quarter me."

We came to the door of his room, and he held it open for me. "Soulmate, our coven will not harm you."

Andre didn't close it after I entered, and I swiveled to look at him. He nodded to the bathroom. "Get clean. I need to set my coven's business in order, among other things. I'll be back here shortly."

He didn't need to tell me twice. I slipped into the bathroom and turned on the shower. I sighed as I peeled off the leather pants and the matching bustier. I could die a happy woman if I never had to wear leather again.

When I stepped into the shower, days' worth of grime slid off my body. I practically moaned at the hot water beating down my back. Up until now I hadn't noticed just how cold I'd gotten, not until the steam and the warm spray thawed my body.

The air outside the glass shower stall rippled, the steam seeming to displace itself. I stared, first transfixed then horrified, as a figure coalesced from the mist.

Not *just* a figure. A black suit, custom tailored, hugged wide shoulders. It tapered inward at a narrow waist. The slacks beneath it were crisp, a starched line running down the middle of each pant leg. Gleaming leather shoes crossed at the ankle. Almond eyes stared at me through the mist.

The devil lounged against the nearby wall, scrutinizing me. His mouth didn't move, but his words tickled my ear.

"Miss me?"

I covered myself as fear coursed through me.

"Nothing I haven't seen many times before." Again, the devil's mouth didn't move, but his voice spoke in my ear. I didn't know if he was referring to the female form in general, or mine in particular. I seriously hoped it was the former.

"What is with you and bathrooms?" I said over my fear.

He ignored my question and pushed off the wall, heading towards me. All that separated us was the clear glass stall that encased me. Filmsy protection against a man that could appear at will.

I backed up. "Stay away from me," I warned him.

"Or else what?" he challenged.

I drew in a shaky breath. I had nothing. No threat of mine could scare off Pluto, the devil—whatever and whoever he was.

The steam inside the shower stirred, and then he stood in front of me. I stumbled back. While he appeared corporeal, water passed right through him.

His eyes flicked over me, and my skin crawled. "The vampire's time with you is coming to a close. Shame that he's wasting it, too."

"He's not wasting it."

"Oh?" The devil's brows rose in mock surprise. He

stepped forward, crowding me. This was the closest he'd ever come to me here on earth. His voice dropped low. "And yet I'm the one in the shower with you."

Goosebumps broke out along my flesh at the wanting in his eyes. "I didn't invite you."

"I didn't ask for your consent."

We stared each other down, and I flared my nostrils, anger rising. But even it couldn't compete with the sheer panic that flooded my veins.

The devil leaned in, removing the last space between us. "Coming back here will be the death of you."

Despite the hot water, a shiver tore through me at his words.

He lies for a living. This is no different, I told myself.

But I couldn't pretend away the subtle palsy my limbs had taken on in the last day, or the way my heart sometimes slowed to a crawl. My appetite was going too. I wouldn't need someone to gun me down; my body was doing a great job of dying all on its own.

The devil didn't step back, not immediately. Instead he lingered, not touching, but only just. Having him this close reminded me that he'd taken me—twice—to do with as he pleased. While he hadn't physically violated me, he'd tasted my soul. That was another type of desecration.

"Did you expect anything differently of me?" he asked, reading my thoughts.

His sharp words held a hidden meaning in them. If I was to believe what I'd learned of him, then he wasn't just the devil—and he wasn't just Pluto, either. He was all those primordial gods of the Underworld, and there were many of them with their own myths, and not all were terrible.

Osiris, the Egyptian version of him, for all intents and purposes, seemed like a half decent guy. He'd loved his wife, Isis, and judging from the fact that after he'd been chopped to little pieces by his brother—ew—she'd painstakingly collected them all and put him back together, I'd say she might've had the hots for him as well.

In no universe would I put the devil back together like Humpty Dumpty if someone slaughtered him. I was far more likely to do the jig on top of his grave—or help kill him myself. Believing he was capable of good felt too much like I was excusing the infinite evil he'd orchestrated throughout lifetimes.

"Give me a reason to," I finally said.

I assumed my words would anger him. Instead he tipped his head forward. "I just might, consort. I just might."

On shaky legs, I stepped into Andre's room. He was rubbing his hair with a towel, his skin damp. I guess he'd slipped into another shower while I used his.

I was certain he forgot to wash something. That, or he used his super speed to get clean. There was no other explanation for how he'd managed to get all his business finished *and* take a shower in the same time it took me to get clean.

That, or my visit with the devil took even longer than it felt. And it felt *long*. I pushed down the panic that rose whenever I thought of him. He was always there, waiting in the wings of my mind. If I let myself get consumed by thoughts of him, I'd be his long before I ever set foot in hell.

Seeing me, Andre paused. Other than a pair of low-slung jeans, he was blissfully naked.

They just don't make men the same way they used to.

I braced an arm against the wall. Praise Jesus for hormones and short attention spans. I needed a distraction right about now and Andre was just about as good as it got.

His gaze flicked over my towel-clad body, and I shuddered at his appraisal. It reminded me too much of the devil's.

Andre's brow puckered. "Soulmate, are you okay?"

So much for a distraction. I considered lying, but, oh hell with it. I shook my head. "No, I'm really not."

He crossed the room. "What's wrong?" He pushed some damp strands of hair behind my ear.

"The devil visited me while I was in the shower."

"While you were ... in the shower?" Andre repeated.

I gave him something between a headshake and a nod. It conveyed perfectly my own uncertainty.

Andre's face blackened with rage. "That bastard."

He came to me, his hands lightly touching my shoulders. "What did he do to you?"

"Nothing physical." Even as I spoke, my mind drifted back to the encounter. The devil hadn't seemed nearly so hostile lately. Disconcerting, as usual, but not violent.

Andre's eyes roved over me, as if he couldn't believe it. Or maybe he was realizing that the devil had gotten an eyeful of naked Gabrielle.

"What did he say to you?"

I shook my head. No way was I repeating some of the things he said. "It doesn't matter. It's over. He's gone."

Andre's troubled eyes lifted from mine to the air beyond. I could tell he was thinking the same thing I was: the devil might be gone, but he was never far.

My gaze moved to Andre's bed. I'd now slept several days in his arms. But as my gaze took in the soft sheets, Hestia's words echoed in my mind. Hell, *fate* echoed in my mind. Unless I could convince Decima otherwise, I had less than a lunar cycle—twenty-eight days—to live.

"Soulmate?" Andre stepped up next to me.

When I turned to face him, he must've seen the direction of my thoughts because he stilled, his nostrils flaring.

My skin lightly glowed, but I was in control. I placed my hands on his bare chest. Warmth that shouldn't be there emanated from him. That was the thing about magic. It made no logical sense, and yet it simply was.

I swallowed, staring at the expanse of chiseled muscle in front of me. I didn't know what to do next.

The back of Andre's hand slid along my jaw. He cupped the back of my neck and tilted my head up to face him. His eyes searched mine.

I scented the air, breathing in Andre's spicy smell.

"Gabrielle ..." Andre's hands skimmed down my sides. They caressed the swell of my hips.

"Do you want this as much as I do?" I asked.

His jaw clenched, but for once it was out of self-restraint, not anger. "More."

I ran my hands down his torso, pausing at the edge of

his jeans. He didn't stop me when I undid his pants' top button. He used to.

Andre functioned so differently from me. I'd simply wanted him since the beginning. It was an ache in my bones, the need to be close to him. But for Andre, who had practiced so much self-restraint over his long life, he didn't just give into his every whim and desire. At least, not when it came to me.

I think that now, after all we'd been through, he finally figured we'd earned the right to do this. You can only cross paths with death and damnation so many times.

I tugged his zipper down then moved my hands back up his torso, running them over his shoulders and down his arms, feeling every sculpted edge of muscle there. His body shuddered at the sensation.

A half-smile curved Andre's mouth, but his eyes were serious. He took my chin and angled my head up, brushing a kiss along my lips. "Are you sure?" he whispered.

"*Andre.*" I gave him a look, and he laughed, the sound made husky by his rising passion.

I backed up from him. Unhooking the edges of my towel, I let it slide off my body.

I heard him growl ominously as he prowled after me. He scooped me up in his arms, and I yelped as he carried me to the bed. His scent wafted around us, mingling with mine.

He set me down on his soft mattress. His gaze trailed over my body, drinking in every inch of exposed skin. I moved to cover myself, suddenly shy.

He took my hands and kissed the knuckles of each.

"You have nothing to hide, soulmate. And trust me when I say there is no reason to be embarrassed. *None.*" His voice had roughened as he spoke, and his gaze slid back to my body. He placed my hands at my sides and ran one of his palms over a piece of exposed flesh, feeling the gentle dip and rise of my curves.

His gaze seared my skin, making it shine brighter. "You've never been lovelier than you are right now," he breathed.

I looked pointedly at his pants, which, despite being unzipped, had remained on his hips. I didn't blame those pants; I'd suction myself to him if I got the chance. Correction: I would suction myself to him once they were gone. "You have two pieces of clothing on. I have none. This needs to change."

Andre's eyes smoldered. Never tearing his gaze from me, he shoved his jeans off of him. When he straightened, he still wore a pair of boxer briefs. This was as much as I'd ever seen of him, and all that is holy, it was a beautiful sight.

His hands dropped to his waistband, and he arched an eyebrow, a sly—and oddly vulnerable—grin gracing his lips. It was his last silent request for me to back out.

But I wouldn't.

He slid the material down his legs and stepped out of them.

The next time he straightened, I caught my first glimpse of Andre completely naked. I shifted impatiently, my desire for him only increasing. Too bad for me I was a living mood ring when it came to this. My skin brightened at the sight.

His gaze caressed my body as he joined me on the bed.

Skin met skin, and my mouth parted as I felt all of him brushing against all of me for the first time. Ever so carefully he settled himself over me, keeping most of his weight off. We stared at each other.

"Love of my life," Andre whispered, "I have waited centuries for this. For you." He captured my mouth with his and pressed a hard, feverish kiss to my lips, his body moving against mine.

My back arched at the feel of him so close, and it ached to remove the last of the distance that lingered between us.

One of his hands slid up my bare thigh, the touch leaving me breathless. I'd seen Hollywood's version of romance, I'd even made the unfortunate mistake to read about some overblown rendition of it once or twice, but never had I lived it.

It seemed forbidden, and tonight it was my reality. The thought had my head spinning.

I grabbed Andre's wrist. "If ... if the devil tries to stop us again, I want you to keep going."

Andre's passion-drunk gaze sharpened. His brow pressed together. "Soulmate, I can't agree to that. Not if you get scared." He smoothed back a strand of my hair.

"But if I hear him and I tell you to keep going, will you?"

Andre frowned but nodded—albeit, reluctantly. "Only if it is truly what you wish."

I knew what he really meant: if he scented something

that contradicted my words, he'd stop anyway.

He leaned in slowly, kissing me softly, and I moved against him, my body thrumming with excitement. Impatience. Nerves.

"You're shaking," Andre noted. His naked chest glided over mine, the warm light of the room casting his skin in golds. He pressed a kiss at the juncture of my jaw and my neck, "but not scared," he breathed, scenting me.

"Can I tell you a secret?" he said, his lips trailing little kisses across my jaw before moving down.

"Mmhmm." I bit back the Bedlam that was moving through my body, lest it bleed into my voice.

"I'm nervous too."

That made me pause.

"Seven hundred years of yearning for something to fill the hollow inside me. And now she's beneath me," his eyes landed tenderly on me, "waiting for me to rock her world." Andre smiled down at me.

I laughed, the sound echoing melodically as the siren joined in. She wasn't nervous, but oh was she eager.

Our bond rang between my ears the closer we got. It lit my skin from the inside out until it felt as though I bathed in a pool of warmth. The sensation cast out the shadows that lingered in my soul.

"Protection?" I whispered.

"Soulmate, I can't create children."

I nodded, swallowing down something thick. Technically, neither could I. Why, on top of everything else, was that so sad? I pushed away the thought, refocusing my attention on the man in front of me.

Andre's hips flexed, and he aligned himself with me. My heart beat like mad.

I could tell Andre watched for signs that the devil had joined our little party; he kept a close eye on my expression. I wanted to tell him that if anything, the devil's absence unnerved me. He hadn't made a sound.

The siren lingered just below the surface, not in control, but unwilling to miss out on what was about to happen. For once we'd drawn some sort of truce; she didn't take over and I didn't suppress her.

And here I thought I didn't play well with others.

Andre kept his eyes on me as he gently slid inside. The bond between us—the one I could always feel—now ... *melded*. The two of us were finally, *finally* together.

He stared down at me, his eyes wide with wonder. Something haunted left his features, and he smiled. "Centuries of wearisome existence. Eternal damnation. And because of you, soulmate, I regret none of it."

We moved against each other until we'd banished every shadowy corner of our souls and every dark deed we'd ever done. Until there was just us—two people madly, hopelessly in love.

Chapter 17

ANDRE PULLED ME close, nuzzling my neck, and I just about died from happiness. His hair was mussed from my fingers, and a persistent little grin kept tugging the corners of his mouth.

"Soulmate, I've been thinking about it, and I've come to the decision that you're not to leave my arms again."

I ran a hand through his hair, reveling in this new intimacy. "Oh, that's real reasonable."

His head dipped between my breasts, and his lips paid homage to the skin there. I could feel him beginning to get aroused anew.

My lips twitched. "Isn't there supposed to be a recovery period for you dudes?" I asked.

He nipped at the flesh beneath his mouth, making my siren rise.

"You'll find that vampires have extremely quick recovery periods."

I moved one of my legs against him, and he trapped it between his.

"Lucky me."

That sinful grin of his widened. "No, soulmate. Lucky me."

I CURLED UP next to him much later, and for a moment, just a moment, I felt pure and utter bliss. This was as close as I'd ever get to heaven.

He held me close, and things felt different. Deeper. More intimate.

Andre's naked chest stilled beneath me. Whatever animated him during the evening fled as dawn broke along the horizon.

I pulled away from him and stared at his face. Princely. That was the kind of beauty he had. Strong jaw, high cheekbones, straight brows, sensual lips. In sleep his expression gentled.

I risked losing this.

I glanced away, the sight of him suddenly making the pain of that future more acute.

As I laid there, letting my happiness slip through my fingers like grains of sand, the notes of some haunting song drifted in from beyond the walls of Andre's room.

I pushed out of Andre's bed and slipped on the clothes left for me earlier.

That painting of Andre clad in his crusader gear

watched me as I moved throughout the room and pulled on my boots. I swear those troubled eyes beseeched me, but to do what, I had no clue.

Why does the spider weave its web?
Why do the fates spin their thread?
For you. For you. For you.

The song's lyrics drifted out from behind Andre's bookshelf, and I stiffened at them.

I knew that voice. I'd know it from anywhere.

My mother.

She wasn't using her glamour, but her voice was still lovely enough to convince me of anything.

Without thinking, I moved to the shelf and drew the trap door back. The bookshelf swung out, revealing the passage that led to Andre's secret library, his equivalent of a panic room.

Light spilled up the stairs from the room below. I couldn't for the life of me remember if those lights came on when the passage was opened. If they didn't, then Andre's hidden library wasn't so hidden after all.

I closed my eyes, letting my other senses take over. As far as I could tell, nothing living was down there.

I crept down the staircase, drawn by the music.

Why does the morning lark find me dead?
Why does the devil want you wed?
It's true. It's true. It's true.

The hairs on my forearms rose as I entered the room. To

anyone else, these lyrics were eloquent gibberish. But to me, they actually meant something. I could swear she was singing to me.

Why do we lay in prophecy's bed?
Why does the world want your head?
If only they knew. They knew. They knew.

I crossed the room, heading for the source of the music. An iPod sat on one of the shelves at the back of the room. Attached to it were two speakers.

You can't run from destiny
You can't run from history
Fate will find you.
They will find you.
He will find you.

My forsaken one.

The song ended there, the notes echoing into silence. The effect was haunting.

"It is lucky for you that I am benevolent."

I yelped and whirled around. The devil stood on the opposite end of the room, blocking the passage out. The shadows gathered around him, darkening the already dimly lit room. And, uh, the dude looked pissed.

His eyes narrowed and he folded his arms. "You fucked the vampire."

I flinched at the devil's words. I didn't shy away from cursing, but something about the word used in its true context and spoken with such casual venom shocked me.

A chill entered the room as we stared at each other.

"Not that I should be surprised," the devil continued. "The fates didn't fashion me some lilywhite saint for a consort—though that would've been fun to corrupt."

He stepped forward, and I backed up, banging into the shelf I stood next to and jostling the iPod. There was nowhere for me to go.

Best get used to this, a small voice inside me said. The thought sickened me.

"I warned you not to get intimate, and I don't make idle threats."

"Then why didn't you stop me?" He could have, just like last time. I wasn't sure it would've made a difference.

His unflinching gaze unnerved me. "You keep crossing me, as though I have not built my very reputation on punishment and pain. I figured it was time to remind you. You needed to be taught a lesson.

The devil's quiet menace had unease unfurling inside me, and my siren responded. My skin began to glow. "What are you going to do?"

He took another step forward, beginning to close the distance that separated us. "Oh, I have a few things in mind."

My breathing quickened and his stare dropped to my chest. I closed my eyes against the expression he wore.

"I could kill your friends—the ones that so dutifully protect you. That seer and I do have unfinished business. I'd torture them slowly, make it clear with every painful injury why they were receiving my wrath. That they put their loyalty in the wrong woman. All she had to do was remain chaste. But she didn't, and her betrayal caused their suffering."

Trapped as I was between the bookcase and the devil, I couldn't move. Couldn't escape.

He stopped just short of me. This close to him, I could see his dark beauty. It scared me that his presence no longer caused the same sick reaction it normally did. I could still feel a dull ache around him, like something vital was being sucked from me, but the sensation should've been sharper, more powerful.

Hestia had called me tainted. Somehow, somewhere along the way, I'd become immune to the devil's wickedness. Or, more likely, he'd poisoned my soul.

"Or I could kill your adopted mother," he said. "That's the one I'm leaning towards."

My mother. Oh God, he would too. This needed to end.

"What do you want?" My voice came out harsh.

He cocked his head. Amusement twinkled in his eyes. "I thought I made that very clear from the start. I've lived for an eternity and waited for you for nearly as long." He came up close to me, his eyes traveling over my body. "It's almost too much. The waiting."

A cold sweat had broken out across my body.

His form seemed to flicker. Whatever force allowed him to visit here, it was running out. "I was there the moment you took your first step. The moment you spoke your first word—'da,' in case you were wondering. I heard your wails when your mother never returned home, drank in your fear the night your father entered my kingdom.

"I've seen the way girls scorn you, the nights you cried yourself to sleep, the lonely walks you sometimes take by yourself. I've watched over you since the day you were born. I've been there for everything, and I will continue to be by your side even after you leave this realm."

He almost touched me then. At the last second he dropped his hand. Something about him here and now reminded me that he wasn't just the devil; he was also Hades, a being that wasn't quite as evil. Still, I was pretty sure there was a reason our myth was often referred to as "the rape of Persephone." Not exactly the kind of title that gave you warm fuzzies.

"Why are you telling me this?" I asked, gripping the shelves behind me to keep my shaking legs from buckling.

"You keep fighting this, little bird. Us."

I closed my eyes and swallowed. *Us.* The word reverberated in my mind. I'd gotten used to it referring to Andre and me. I wasn't ready to give that up, not now after I'd fully experienced what eternity might be like with him.

"Open your eyes," the devil commanded.

Afraid to defy him, they snapped open.

His almond-shaped eyes drank me in. They'd always unsettled me, those eyes. In the past I'd assumed it was because they were windows to the soul and his—if he had one—was pure evil. But now I wondered if it might be simply the fact that they weren't human.

"I want to make a deal," I said.

"I'm listening."

"Their lives for mine." I couldn't have him or his minions murder my friends and family.

He watched me, his gaze unreadable, so I pressed forward. "Give me—" I swallowed, "twenty-eight days to say goodbye."

The devil laughed. "You won't live twenty-eight days, regardless, and you expect me to agree to that?"

Shit.

He gave me an appraising look. "You have no bargaining power." The corner of the devil's mouth tipped up. "But I'm feeling generous, so I'll give you three days."

Three days? I controlled my features to prevent my horror from showing. "Two weeks."

"Three days is my final offer. If no one's managed to kill you off by then—you'll come to me freely."

I could hear Andre inside my head, screaming at me to not consider this. The devil's deals were laced with poison. The thing was, I was hurling towards that date with death, devils and killers aside.

"And if I don't come to you at the end of three days?" Was I actually considering this?

He smiled and those disturbing eyes of his lit with excitement. "Consort, it would please me beyond reason and terrify you beyond belief if you went back on your end of the deal."

I'd been cornered; I needed to protect my loved ones, and the devil knew it.

I swallowed and nodded. "Fine," I rasped out. "You have a deal." I reached out to shake his hand.

He eyed it, and then a slow, sensual smile spread across his face. Reaching out, his hand grasped my wrist rather than my hand. His skin—it might've been a stretch to call what touched me that—was ice cold, and the chill burned my flesh down to the bone.

I screamed at the sensation, my legs buckling at the pain. He brought the back of my hand up to his mouth and kissed it. Then he released me.

I cradled my arm, which still bore a ghostly handprint for several more seconds before fading away.

"Sleep tight, consort." He tipped his head to me, and the darkness that surrounded him grew. He'd disappear in another moment.

On shaky legs, I stood. "I know that you've tasted me. Twice."

The devil smiled at me as the shadows around him began to move and expand. "An eternity is a long time to wait for you, and I am not a patient man."

"You're not a man at all." Though I'd seen few monsters lovelier than the one in front of me.

"No, consort, I am much, much more." The shadows twisted around the devil. All at once they collapsed in on themselves and sucked the devil up. And then he was gone.

I STAYED IN Andre's library long after the devil left, listening to my mother's music on the mystery iPod, shivering and absently rubbing my forearm.

A horrifying thought hit me: Could he know I was going to visit Decima?

Oh God, he must've. *That* was why he made a deal with

me. A shit deal that gave me three days to live.

What have I done?

I shivered again and fought off the sleep that all but demanded I give in. Instead my thumb flipped over the playlist of my mother's songs. There was an entire library of them. The tracks were some strange combination of Brit pop and radio hits mixed with darker, more personal songs. All of them were utterly haunting.

Like me, my biological mother had known when she was about to die. Had she cloistered herself away from my father like I did from Andre? Had she been scared? I craved knowing her now more than ever.

I listened to the final song on the playlist, this one a ballad.

There was a girl,
A lovely, laughing girl,
Fairer than thou ere did see,
There was a girl,
A sweet, strange girl,
And that girl loved me.

There was a man,
A dark, dangerous man,
Who fancied she,
There was a man,
A wild, wicked man,
And that man stole her from me.

There was a girl,

A sad, solemn girl,
Her hair as black as night,
There was a girl,
A desperate, doomed girl,
Whose soul too soon took flight.

There was a man,
A mad, monstrous man,
Whose soul couldn't be,
There was a man,
A bleak, broken man,
And that broken man was me.

I sighed. My biological mother—like my father—was an ache in my heart that would never heal. And if—no, when—the devil made good on his end of our deal, I'd meet at least one parent in the fiery gates of hell. I could only hope I wouldn't meet both.

That would be one bitch of a reunion.

Chapter 18

THE NEXT EVENING Oliver and Leanne slipped out of Peel Academy to visit me at Bishopcourt before we snuck back onto school grounds.

As soon as Oliver saw me, his jaw went a little slack. "Oh. My. Gawd!" he squealed. "My baby's no longer a virgin! Get it gurl!"

Just about every servant in the entryway paused what they were doing to glance over at us.

Well this wasn't mortifying or anything.

"Will you please keep your voice down?" I hissed at him. Did I have a giant sign on me that said "deflowered" or something?

Leanne shook her head. "He is *such* a liability."

"*You have to tell me everything.*"

I could feel the pull of Andre as he moved towards the

commotion. I bit back a groan. He'd only just alerted the coven that we were at Bishopcourt—we were scheduled to meet with them tomorrow—*yippee!* Now he probably assumed some vampire had decided to visit early, which meant he thought a fight was about to break out. Awesome. All I needed was an extra-aggressive Andre.

A moment later he strode to my side, his hand resting proprietarily around my waist. I shivered at his touch, remembering last night.

Oliver waggled his eyebrows as Andre leaned in and gave my temple a kiss before nodding to my friends. "Oliver, Leanne, I trust you weren't followed?"

"Hello to you too," Oliver said, sassy as ever.

"We weren't," Leanne said.

"Well come in," Andre beckoned. "Can I get you two anything to eat or drink?"

"I thought you'd never ask," Oliver replied.

Andre glanced down at me. "Soulmate, have you eaten yet?"

My stomach clenched at the thought of food—or blood.

"You haven't," he stated, reading my expression. "Come," he said to my friends, placing a hand on my lower back and steering me towards Bishopcourt's informal dining room.

After he arranged dinner for my friends, Andre set a blood bag in front of me. I grimaced.

"You need to feed." Worry drew sharp lines along his face.

I pushed the blood away from me. "I'm not that hungry yet."

Andre pushed it back. "You need your energy for to-night."

"It doesn't look appetizing at the moment." That was the truth. The lie was pretending that it might look more appetizing in a few hours.

Andre grabbed the bag. "I'll heat it up."

Reheated blood. The thought had my stomach churning.

I grabbed Andre's wrist. "If I have to drink it, I'd prefer it cold." Said no vampire ever. Until now.

He studied my hand, then my face. "If you don't want the blood bag, then I can get one of my servants."

Oh, that would be so much worse.

"This is fine." My hands shook as they clasped the bag.

A handful of days. That was all I got. And I was going to have to pretend that I didn't flitter away my life so soon after I'd learned the third fate might be able to save it. Because there was no way in hell I was admitting my stupid, stupid decision to bargain with the devil. I'd have to go through the motions, which meant visiting the fate, regardless of how damned I was.

"Ew, are you going to drink that in front of me?" Oliver asked, snapping me out of my thoughts. He unwrapped the first of a pile of truffles set in front of him—his version of dinner. "I love you and all, Sabertooth, but that's like, *really* gross."

Andre's jaw hardened, his arms folding. Clearly someone was feeling extra protective.

By way of response, I stuck the blood bag's straw in my mouth.

Oliver curled his upper lip. "Ugh, that's disgusting."

I smiled around the straw, flashing fang, and flipped him the bird.

He tilted his head. "I'll give you this: you're really showing off your amazing sucking skills. I bet you'd be great at BJ's."

Oh. My. God. *Ew*. I spit out the straw. "All that is *holy*, Oliver, could you for once ..."

I didn't finish. Andre already had him by the neck and was dragging him out of the kitchen. Oliver scrambled to keep his footing as he was hauled off.

I pushed myself to my feet, following them out. "Whoa. Andre, let him go."

Andre ignored me. "You have no business talking to a lady like that."

Aw damn, Andre was up and getting all chivalrous on my behalf.

"A lady?" Oliver said raising his eyebrows. He glanced at me like the thought was precious.

I shook my head at him to keep his mouth shut, but the fairy just smirked, like he couldn't help himself.

"Me thinks her reputation's been sullied a bit after last night. Bow-chicka-wow-w—*ack*." He began making choking noises as Andre squeezed his neck.

Oliver was an idiot.

I jumped in between the two of them and tried to pry Andre's finger's off of him. "Oliver, just—shut up for five seconds."

I swiveled to face my soulmate. "Please let my friend go."

"If he was one of my subjects he'd be whipped for this."

Whipped? Nope, not going to ask.

"He's my friend, and he promises he'll be respectful from now on, don't you Oliver?" I glared at him.

He gave me a look that said, *Are you crazy?* But when his gaze moved to Andre, he nodded eagerly. "Best behavior," he wheezed.

Andre snarled and roughly let his neck go. "Your word means little when your actions don't match."

Oliver rubbed his neck and mouthed, *Holy fuck.*

Andre was breathing heavily, and I put a bracing hand on his arm. "It's okay. He meant nothing by it." As far as Oliver's remarks went, that one hardly made a blip on the Richter scale.

"Friend or not, I will not tolerate slander."

It was a bit late for that, considering all the stories circulating about me.

I rubbed my forehead. For the love of—"Can we please choose our battles? I have enough enemies as it is."

The muscle in Andre's cheek jumped as his jaw clenched and unclenched. His eyes moved to Oliver, who was retreating back to the kitchen. Andre's lips pressed tightly together, like he tasted something bitter, then he nodded once.

I let out a breath. My soulmate was wound way too tightly from recent events. He was lashing out from things outside of his control, and Oliver had been one his targets.

The anger slowly drained from his eyes as he turned his attention back to me. He reached out to tuck a lock of hair behind my ear. "I don't want you to ever think that what we do together is something lewd. Last night—"

Andre's cell phone buzzed, interrupting him. He hesitated to reach for it.

"Take the call. We can finish discussing this later." I gave him a soft smile.

He pulled me in close, resting his forehead against mine before letting me go to grab his cell.

"That was cray-cray," Oliver said when I re-entered the kitchen. "He went bat-shit crazy on me."

"He's the king of vampires, Oliver," Leanne said with a roll of her eyes. "He's used to running his own agenda."

"He was ready to off me!"

While Oliver talked, I grabbed the blood bag and squeezed the rest of its contents down the kitchen drain. I silently apologized to all the hospitals that could've used the blood.

"You mistreated his mate," Leanne said.

I ran the tap water, just to wipe away any signs of my little treachery. I couldn't stomach the liquid without it coming back up, and I wasn't going to waste the evening praying to the porcelain god when I didn't have to.

Oliver guffawed. "Now that is just ridiculous. Did I mistreat you, Gabrielle?"

"Hm, what?" I glanced up, still holding the blood bag.

"Ooooh, is someone doing naughty things over there?"

"Do you want me to sic my bloodthirsty boyfriend on you? Here—" I said, walking to the door, "I can go get him."

"Geez, your secret is safe with me—hey, do you think

214

I can get more of these?" Oliver asked, pointing to his wrapper-strewn plate.

"No clue. You'll have to ask the kitchen dude." I nodded my head to the door that led to an attached industrial kitchen.

"Chef," Leanne corrected.

Oliver gave me a pointed look. "Does it not drive you insane when she does that?"

I suppressed a smile. "You both have your own, unique charm."

Leanne snorted. "As do you."

I stuck my tongue out at her. I was real mature like that.

Oliver hopped off the barstool he sat on and wandered back to the kitchen, muttering about chocolate.

As soon as we were alone, I swiveled to face my roommate. My *former* roommate, I thought with a twinge of regret. I wouldn't ever attend Peel Academy again.

"Are you okay, roomie?" she asked.

I shook my head. "Have you seen anything?" I asked, fearing Leanne's response but also perversely eager to hear it. One could get addicted to hearing their fortunes told.

She shrugged. "Not since you drank that seer's shroud."

Duh. I'd almost forgotten. Oliver wasn't the only idiot.

I ran my fingers over the table, following the veins in the polished wood. "Back when we were visiting the sorceress, Hestia told me that I had less than a month to live." I wasn't ready to admit the deal I'd made, but I'd admit this.

Leanne's pulse picked up, and I could smell her nervousness, but when I looked up, her face looked almost

... *guilty*.

It dawned on me. "You already knew."

I pushed a hand through my hair. It was really hitting me. I was going to hell in less than a week. And then I'd have to play house with the devil.

"So, before I drank the seer's shroud, you saw my future?"

She heaved a great sigh. "Vaguely. I was far away from you, and I didn't have any objects of yours close at hand. I foresaw only the most likely of your futures."

"And what was that?"

She hesitated, then spoke. "I saw you murdered—shot straight through the heart. Within a minute you were gone." Her voice cut off after that, and she glanced down at her hands. Her heart beat madly, and I could smell her fear.

Fear for me. I'd be touched if I wasn't also scared shitless.

"So that's it." Seventeen short years of life snuffed out in under a minute.

Leanne tore her gaze from her lap to meet my stare.

"No," she said simply, "that's not it. I saw you surrounded by darkness so deep and complete it made my chest ache."

My eyes rounded. Sounded like hell to me.

"You wore a black crown, and behind you stood the devil. He—he wrapped an arm around you. The darkness enveloped you then, but before you both disappeared completely, he looked at me ... and he smiled."

I rubbed the goose bumps that had broken out along

my skin. That didn't sound horrifying or anything.

Both of us were quiet for a few minutes, neither really knowing what to say.

"It's really going to happen." I finally spoke, tracing the veins of the table once more.

"Not if you can convince that final fate."

My eyes slowly traveled up to Leanne's. My throat tightened as I nodded. The truth wanted to claw its way out, and it might've if not for the sound of something banging in the kitchen and the sound of Oliver's squawk.

I rolled my eyes and stood up, trying to shake off my fear.

She chose her words carefully. "The future is nothing like the past," she said. "What has been is immovable and unchanging; what will be is full of infinite possibilities—some more likely than others. Nothing is certain until it happens."

I didn't have the heart to tell her that her optimism was misplaced. Since last night, my doom was, in fact, certain.

Chapter 19

LATER THAT EVENING, I found myself back inside one of Peel Academy's godforsaken persecution tunnels. I'd never taken this particular one, though Oliver clearly had.

Said fairy grumbled in front of me as we sloshed through puddles. "Break into the school, she said. It'll be fun, she said."

I ducked under a clump of roots that hung from the ceiling. "If I remember correctly, you were the one that suggested this."

Oliver harrumphed. "That was before it started raining buckets." The storm had rolled in while we'd been at Bishopcourt.

I fingered the hilt of one of the daggers strapped to my side. I'd told Andre I would only visit Decima alone. Initially he kicked up a fuss, but as pushy as he was, the man couldn't deny me much, and what I wanted was a frank conversation with the fate. The weapons were his compromise: *Go in without me soulmate, then you'll go in armed to the teeth.*

Now Andre waited for us at the tunnel's exit. My last glimpse of him had been his controlled pacing. He reminded me of a leopard I'd seen once at the zoo. It had prowled the wall of its cage with the same agitation.

"Shhhh," Leanne said from behind Oliver, angling the flashlight on her phone around him to see far into the tunnel.

"Why are you shushing me?" Oliver looked over his shoulder to catch my eye. "Why is she shushing me? Who could possibly overhear us?"

Not three seconds after he spoke we heard a distant hiss.

"That's why," Leanne said.

Oliver huffed, but fell silent … for about a minute.

"So … our baby girl is no longer a virgin."

I bit back a groan.

"Be thankful it took him this long to bring the subject up," Leanne said.

"It's not like he hasn't tried," I said, remembering how Andre manhandled him back at Bishopcourt. God, my life was a clusterfuck of unreasonable people. I wasn't even going to exclude myself from that group either.

"True."

"So," Oliver said, "tell me: how hung is that man?"

"*Oliver!*" both Leanne and I said.

Off in the distance we heard another hiss.

"For the record," Oliver said, "if that thing comes at us, I'm blaming you two."

I listened a little longer, but wherever the creature was, it sounded as though it was moving away from us.

"Bet he's huge," Oliver said. "Lucky fuck."

I pinched the bridge of my nose. "Can we not talk about this?"

"Ugh, Leanne, she's still a prude."

"There is a distinction between a prude and refusing to kiss and tell," Leanne said.

"Fine, gang up on me you two."

A thoughtful silence descended on us.

"So, did he bite you while you were going at it?" the fairy asked.

"Oli-*ver*," I said.

"Okay, geez. Forget I asked. Someone clearly needs to get laid again," he grumbled.

The puddles became more frequent and bigger.

"We're slogging through a mote here," Oliver complained. "Another beautiful pair of shoes ruined."

Leanne and I ignored him. Ahead Leanne's light shone eerily on a patch of wall still cast in darkness. Another passage.

"That's where we leave you," Leanne said nodding to it. "Right Oliver?"

"Yea—*wait*, we're not going with you, Sabertooth?" Oliver asked.

"You and I are going back to our rooms," Leanne said. "We have appearances to keep up."

Oliver looked at her like she was mad. "Appearances?

You want me to show up in my dorm looking—and smelling—like a hobo?"

"No one will notice you."

"Like hell they won't. I got suspicious written all over me."

"If anyone asks, you'll just tell them you met up with the chief constable of the Politia for some late night lovin'.'"

"Wait, Chief Constable Morgan? As in, my former boss?" I put up a hand as soon as I spoke. "You know what? I don't want to know."

"That's right you don't," Oliver said. "You can't *handle* my love life!"

Truer words had never been spoken.

"Gabrielle," Leanne said, turning to me, "This tunnel will take you to the library." She nodded to the darkness that branched to our right."

I pulled out the phone Andre had gifted me earlier this evening and shined its built-in flashlight down the dark passage. I could hear a skittering sound somewhere beyond my sight.

Just what I wanted to be doing at the beginning of my night. "Wish me luck."

"You got this, Sabertooth. And if you don't, just glamour the shit out of that woman."

I didn't bother telling Oliver that fates couldn't be glamoured.

"Good luck, roomie," Leanne said. "Call me later and tell me how it went." It was strange to hear her ask for news that a seer would normally foresee.

"Will do." I left them there, watching me descend into darkness.

My boots splashed through the water. I heard a rustling sound. I aimed the beam of light towards the noise, only to see a rat scampering away. I grimaced but didn't slow. Vermin were the least of my concerns at the moment.

The farther I went, the deeper the puddle became, until it went up to mid-calf. Even the boots I wore couldn't prevent the grimy water from seeping in.

I could hear rhythmic dripping from the earthen roof above me. I wiped away cobwebs and scrunched my nostrils against the musty smell of the passage.

A chilled breath brushed against my ear. I flinched and turned, dragging the beam of light with me. Nothing was there.

I gripped my phone tighter, afraid to drop it. I was getting spooked at nothing.

A creature howled in the distance. A normal person would've turned tail and ran. I, however, exhaled, my body relaxing.

A minute later, Scooby materialized ahead of me, his ruby eyes gleaming in the dim light. I reached a hand out and scratched him behind his ears.

"Who's a good demon doggie?"

He whined happily.

"Yes, you are," I cooed. I was beyond caring that I sounded like an idiot. Scooby saved me from myself.

When I began walking again, he trotted ahead of me, his tail wagging. His paws didn't stir the water, reminding me that while I might be able to touch him, he couldn't interact with the physical world for the most part.

A short distance later I came upon a severely rusted ladder. Above it someone had already opened a trap door set into passage's ceiling.

I placed my heel on the first rung and placed part of my weight on it. It crumbled almost immediately.

Crap. This was going to prove interesting.

Next to me Scooby vanished, only to reappear above me. His head peaked over the trap door.

"Make it look easy, why don't you?"

Five minutes and two broken rungs later, I pushed myself onto the cobblestone floor of what looked to be Peel's basement. I stood and brushed dirt and dust off my body. There was nothing to do about my soaked lower legs. I caught a whiff of myself and winced. Not the best start to my conversation.

Scooby began to trot away from me, so I hurried after him, clicking off my flashlight as I did so. Around me firelight glowed from scones set into the castle walls. Unconsciously I pressed my hand to my heart.

Boy, had I missed this place.

The *Moddey Dhoo* led me to Peel Academy's back library. This had been the same place where I first encountered Scooby all those months ago. Then we hadn't been such buddies. He'd been a death omen, and he'd wanted nothing more than to tear me to shreds. Since surviving that encounter, he'd warmed up to me.

At this late hour, no students lingered. This was a good thing ... and yet my heart ached to be surrounded by my peers once more.

My hand slid along the wall as I passed into the library, and I breathed in the musty smell of books. Tarp rustled beneath my feet.

"So you don't get the carpet dirty," a female voice explained.

My head snapped up, and I met the eyes of Lydia Thyme, Peel Academy's head librarian.

And, apparently, the third fate.

Chapter 20

"You're right on time." Lydia stood behind the check out desk, but now she came around and directed me to a nearby table, the floor beneath it also covered with tarp.

"You?" I squinted my eyes at her. She'd been there at my Awakening, and I'd chatted with her numerous times since then. She'd helped me more than once.

"Yes, me."

Like Cecilia, Lydia was older. Her skin was a dark, burnished brown, and her black hair was shot through with streaks of white.

"Please sit," she gestured to a chair covered with a towel. "We have much to talk about and not much time to spare." She gave me a meaningful look, and I hesitated.

"Do you know—?"

"About your deal with Pluto?" Lydia—Decima—finished

for me. "I do."

I twisted my hands together. "I'm such a fool." Being here was pointless. It was me going through the motions for the benefit of those few people who still cared about me.

She sighed, sliding into the seat across from me. "You're human, and this is a game Pluto has played with desperate people just like you for thousands of years. He uses persuasive, believable lies and half-truths to get you to agree to his desires. And, as you already know, it's you he desires."

Lydia placed a folder she'd been carrying on the table. "He scouted you, you know."

"W-what? What does that mean?"

Lydia Thyme opened the manila folder and pulled out a sheet of paper. She slid it across the table, and I took it from her.

It was a printed excel sheet titled "Displaced Supernatural Children." All but one row had been blacked out. On that row two names had been highlighted. One was my own, and the other ...

"'Rex Inferni'?"

The candlelight flickered at my words.

Lydia nodded. "That's Latin for 'King of Hell'."

I released the paper like it burned me.

"He alerted Peel Academy of your existence. He's the one that set these events into motion."

If not for him, I would still be in Los Angeles. I would've never been hunted, I would've never been Awoken.

I would've never met Andre.

"How could no one have caught this?" Seemed to me

that if the king of hell wrote in to say that a really special girl he knew should come to Peel Academy, not only would I not be invited, the Politia would probably burn and raze my house while I was inside ... then salt the land for good measure.

"The same way no one foresaw that you'd Awake a vampire. Mistakes happen."

That was the second time I'd heard a fate utter that line. Seemed like a lot of people were dropping the ball when they shouldn't be.

In the distance, I could hear the sound of sirens. I had no doubt that they were meant for me. Only Oliver, Leanne, and Lydia had seen me, and I suspected none of them were responsible for the sirens. Perhaps the school had been enchanted to notify authorities of my presence as soon as I stepped foot on campus.

My legs tensed, but I didn't get up. Not yet. "Is there any way at all for me to survive this?" I had to ask, even though I was fucked three ways to Wednesday. I didn't try hiding the terror in my voice.

"You mean, can I save you?" Lydia clarified.

I lifted my shoulders and my hands, trying to convey that at this point, I was beyond nuances. Any hope would be good enough.

She shook her head. "I was never in a position to save you," she said. "I'm sorry if someone gave you that impression. Only you can save yourself. It's always been that way."

I breathed in the smell of books. A hollowness had established itself at the base of my stomach, and now with her words, it grew, numbing me. I was past saving myself. I'd given that power away to the devil when I traded my life for that of my friends and family.

From somewhere far outside the library, I heard someone hammering on the front door.

"You need to leave now," Lydia Thyme whispered.

I stood, blinking back the blood that had gathered in my eyes. "Why did Nona send me? If it was all for nothing, then why?" If she said it was another mistake, I might just maim this fate.

Lydia lifted my chin. "It wasn't all for nothing." Her thumb moved across my cheek, and for a second I caught a shadow of a smile. "Remember this: the only way out is through."

She pushed me away. "Goodbye, Gabrielle Fiori, the last of the sirens, the first born vampire, the future queen of the Underworld."

I SLID ON the slick stone as I fled, going down on one knee as I turned a corner. Scooby ran alongside me. We fled through the castle back to the trap door. My surroundings were tinted in shades of pink, and it took me a moment to realize that was because I still had tears in my eyes.

I skidded to a halt in front of the door cut into the floor. The smell of mold and decay emanated from it.

I really didn't want to go back down. I didn't want to wind my way through the darkness only to find Andre on the other side, waiting to hear how I convinced this fate to tip the scales in my favor. I didn't want to tell him that she wouldn't help—that she couldn't.

I shut my eyes. The sound of footfalls was moving closer. I could hear the shouts of officers. I winced when Maggie, the woman I'd once worked under during my time with the Politia, yelled something.

My coworkers were here, hunting me like I'd hunted killers. I could still hear that last monster's words echoing in my head. They came from the cambion I'd killed.

The good guys? she'd said. *The ones you think you represent? They will hunt you down and steal your life from you. The saddest part of all is that they will think the world is a better place because you are no longer in it. That will be your legacy.*

"Gabrielle." The hairs on my forearms rose at the familiar, masculine voice at my back.

I swiveled around in time to see Caleb.

Chapter 21

I JOLTED AT the sight of him. He still had the same gorgeous features that were responsible for half the school crushing on him and the ruffled, golden hair that made me think of long days out in the sun.

I might never stand under the sun again.

He looked tired, and I could smell the sadness wafting off of him even from the other side of the hall.

Next to me, Scooby growled low in his throat. For once, my demonic companion didn't dissolve into mist. I hope that had more to do with my presence and less to do with the dog being a death omen.

"Caleb?" My voice broke. He wore the Politia's official uniform.

Because he's here on official business.

Caleb's wide eyes traveled to the dog, then back to me.

This was what I'd tried to explain to him all those times he minimized my nature. He'd been convinced that we were not so different; that there wasn't some insurmountable chasm between creatures deemed good and creatures deemed evil. But he'd never understand what it felt like to be hated—and to be hunted—for simply existing. To consort with the things of nightmares and superstition—things spoken of in whispers and told only late at night.

He just had to kill them.

We stared each other down—former partners turned enemies. This felt like a bad rendition of *The Fox and the Hound*, one with an even shittier ending.

Beyond him, I could her the Politia officers getting closer. One spoke in low tones to Lydia, and the others moved through the library, down the hall. A couple more turns and they would be on us.

The trap door was behind me. I edged back—

"Wait!" Caleb lunged forward.

As soon as he shouted, I heard a flurry of movement far behind him. Officers now knew where we were.

Time to go.

I stepped back into the hole, letting my supernatural reflexes take over as I dropped. I landed in a crouch, water splashing out on impact. Above me I heard Scooby snarl and Caleb shout.

I really hoped the dog didn't kill him.

Forgoing my phone's flashlight, I reached out a hand and touched the slimy wall. I bit back a cringe—now was not the time to be squeamish—and began sprinting down the tunnel, using the curve of the wall to direct me.

The encounter had my heart picking up speed. I gasped out a breath, feeling healthier than I had in a while.

The only way out is through.

The footfalls and shouts sounded more distant now, and I paused to grab my phone from my pocket and switch on its flashlight.

As soon as it clicked on, I moved the beam of light over the walls and began running again. Strange shapes danced in the shadows. It didn't take long for my mind to return to the demons that had peeled off the walls, their shadowy limbs filling with flesh as they reached for me.

"*Miiiiine,*" the air seemed to hiss.

Oh hell to the no. I lengthened my stride and *moved it.* As soon as I hit the intersection, I hung a left and splashed through the puddles.

I burst through the persecution tunnel and body-slammed Andre, which was like tackling a wall. A.k.a., I lost.

His arms wrapped around me as I drew in ragged breaths, and he shoved me behind him, his eyes locked on the exit. Vines and plants hung over the entrance, obscuring the passage, but even so, it didn't take long for Andre to realize that no other heartbeat followed me out.

He turned to face me. "The devil?" he asked.

I caught my breath and shook my head. "Just scared of my own shadow—oh and the Politia paid a visit."

He captured my jaw in his hand and pressed a kiss to my lips. "I heard them but could do nothing. Luckily, they are incompetent fools. You were the best thing that ever happened to them."

Even as he spoke, Andre directed me back to the car. Flattering as his words were, we both knew that it wouldn't take long for the Politia to retrace my steps—incompetent or not.

The persecution tunnel let out to a rocky outcropping that overlooked the ocean. Peel Academy was off to our left, sitting on a tiny piece of land that jutted out into the water. A narrow, grassy trail cut through the sloping bluffs we stood on, and we clambered up it like billy goats to get back to Andre's car.

Okay, *I* clambered up it like a billy goat. Andre just looked like the badass mutha-effer he always was.

"How did it go?" he asked when he swung into the driver's side of the vehicle, sliding the key into the ignition. The engine roared to life.

I concentrated on buckling my seatbelt. The metal buckle tapped against the clip. I missed the slot once, twice, three times.

Andre placed a hand over mine.

I drew in a shaky breath and glanced up at him. His gaze was concerned. He squeezed my hands.

"It's okay," he whispered, understanding what I didn't say. "It's going to be fine."

I nodded quickly—too quickly.

"My soulmate took care of herself. That's all I care about."

I still hadn't gathered together the courage to let him know what I had done.

I was a coward.

Andre gunned the car, pulling us onto the road.

I pressed a hand to the window and watched the ruins of Peel Castle disappear behind me. I'd only attended for mere months, but I'd come to love the place. The warm glow of the wall sconces, the smell of musty books, the casual magic that wrapped itself around the buildings themselves. I finally understood what made this place, this island, so very appealing. There was some part of it that called to the primordial magic that ran through my veins.

We careened through the town of Peel, the dark storefronts staring back at me. How many weekends had Oliver, Leanne, and I come here to drink coffee and eat pastries? Never would that happen again. I caught sight of the zany fondue restaurant Caleb had taken me to all those months ago, when I was just the dark, strange girl that captured his attention.

Caleb. A lump rose in my throat. He'd been so sad. What I would give to know his thoughts. Did he hate me as much as the rest of them? I didn't think so, but who knew? People were complex. They could be reasonable when you expected them not to be, but they could also be unreasonable when you thought they'd understand.

My breath fogged the glass, and I drew a frowning smiley face. Gah, I was depressing.

Next to me, I could feel Andre's tension seeping into my bones. I wasn't sure I was the only mess in this car. He just did it while looking regal and broody as all get out.

Outside, the city fell away, hills and glens replacing the small town. Even this scenery tugged at my heartstrings. On that first trip from the airport to Peel, Leanne had explained that the small mounds that dotted the landscape were from ancient burials.

Just as I reached up to add a tear to the frown-y face I drew, a shadow streaked across my vision.

I rubbed my eyes. Just one more thing falling apart these days.

Andre's hand fell to my thigh and gave it a squeeze. I glanced down at its comforting presence. This was how lovers touched each other. I still hadn't gotten used to it—that we could touch each other like this, not just in the bedroom, but outside of it as well. The reminder sent a thrill through me.

I glanced up at him, my skin beginning to shimmer. The glow of it reflected in his eyes, which watched me.

Another shadow caught my eye. My head whipped to the window. Only this time, the shadow didn't disappear.

Ghostly sentinels stood at the edge of the field that bordered the road. I recognized them at once for what they were—the devil's minions.

"Uh, Andre?"

He slammed on the brakes. "I see them."

He turned the car off and the door opened in the next second. "Stay here, soulmate," Andre ordered, never taking his eyes off the demons.

I guffawed. "Oh, *right*. Sit here on my ass while you're busy slaying incorporeal beings. I don't think so," I said, unbuckling my seatbelt.

"*Soulmate*."

"We already have enough enemies to fight. It's going to be hard if you're trying to get me to cooperate on top of that."

Andre ran a hand through his hair. "Why must you always be so stubborn?" he grumbled as I slid out the daggers I carried on me.

"It's one of my charms." I smiled at him.

Oatthhhh breakerrrr, the wind hissed.

I turned my attention to the demons that watched us. These weren't the good guys. The underbelly of the supernatural world had come out to play. "Why aren't they attacking?"

In fact, several of them folded in on themselves. I realized belatedly they were bowing.

To me.

My stomach contracted. I might not have the Sight like Leanne did, but my instincts were going off, and they were telling me that we'd fallen into the middle of something we shouldn't have.

The shadows stirred, their smoky bodies rippling as something passed through them. Then the darkness condensed, and there, from the shadows, emerged a man.

No, not a man. The devil, clad in one of his usual suits. He only had eyes for me.

"Evening, consort." His gaze had me pinned to the spot.

"Why are you here?" I asked, clutching my weapons even tighter.

"Soulmate, we need to go."

"It's too late for that, dear Andre," the devil said.

Just like the centaurs had done, the demons circled us. I still didn't understand their motives. They couldn't attack me here, nor could the devil. They were incorporeal.

The devil's eyes fell to my weapons. "How precious. You mean to stave us off with your crude tools."

Andre stepped in front of me, and the devil's attention turned to him. "And the king of vampires, here to defend the siren against his creator." The devil's upper lip curled back. "I would smite you where you stand for touching *my* consort if I did not know that her parting would ruin you worse than my lashes ever could.

"Does it frighten you to think that one day soon she'll leave you? And once that day comes, she will warm *my* bed, and she will stand faithfully by *my* side for all eternity?"

My gooseflesh rose at his words. He said it to get under Andre's skin, and it worked. Our connection pulsed as a wave of Andre's power washed over me. The crowd of demons stirred at the sensation.

"He pushes you behind him, consort, as though you cannot protect yourself."

The devil was doing this on purpose. Baiting me. He knew Andre's overprotectiveness annoyed me.

"As though," the devil continued, folding his arms, "you aren't far more powerful than he is."

My breath caught. In front of me Andre stiffened, either from insult or from the shocking possibility.

The devil let out a surprised laugh. "You both genuinely never knew?" The devil clasped his hands together. "Well, cat's out of the bag. She's far stronger than you, vampire, old as you may be. She *is* my mate, after all."

I glanced down, seeing myself for the first time. Could he be right? I'd never tested the extent of my powers because of how frightening they were. But as I took in my heavy limbs, the slight palsy I'd developed, and my slow heartbeat, the last thing I felt was powerful.

"She's nothing of yours," Andre spat.

"That's where you're wrong." The devil turned to me. "Isn't he, consort?" He took a step forward, something behind his eyes shifting and curling like a flame might. It mesmerized me. "I am something to you, aren't I? You've known this from your first memories of me."

The man in the suit standing in the flames of my house as it burned. Yes, even then I'd known that I belonged to that fire as much as he did. And then there had been the time shortly after I'd been adopted when he visited. The first time I'd seen him since the fire. By then, I'd lost everything I'd ever known.

Everything, save for him.

He scared me even then, sitting on the neighbor's roof, just watching me through my bedroom window. But another part of me found relief in his presence. He'd been the only person who'd ever consistently stuck around.

I touched a hand to my forehead, the knife I still gripped now coming dangerously close to my face. "Stop it." He did this on purpose, digging up memories better left buried and seeding emotions where there had been none.

"All you need to do is die, and then you will come into your powers."

"That will not be happening tonight, Lucifer," Andre said.

The devil shoved his hands in his pockets and strolled around us. "Another empty promise, Andre? Really, you can only disappoint people so many times before they stop trusting you."

The devil swiveled to me. "You know he cannot prevent your death anymore than you can." He was that dark voice inside my head, the one that probed for my weaknesses, then exploited them, and right now he was trying to drive a wedge between Andre and me.

The devil's attention returned to my soulmate. "But not to worry, brute, I'm not here to take my consort home this evening."

Andre's hair ruffled, and I couldn't tell whether the breeze that moved it came from the island's wind or Andre himself.

I stepped forward. "What *are* you doing here?" I demanded. I pretended not to hear tremor in my voice.

The devil's eyes narrowed on me. "Enjoying bloodsport."

I looked around, taking in the ephemeral beings. "What bloodsport?"

He smiled and my stomach plummeted.

"Soulmate, let's go."

Andre placed a hand on my back, angling me towards his car. We were almost to the ring of shadows when the devil spoke.

"You haven't told him, have you?"

I stopped, closing my eyes. I could feel Andre's probing gaze on me, even without looking.

In the distance I heard the rumble of an engine approaching, coming up fast. A small part of me hoped they would see us as they passed and stop to help. A much larger part of me already knew that no one who stopped would be as well equipped to face the devil as Andre and I. They'd just be casualties.

"Tut, tut, keeping secrets from the vampire. Though I don't blame you, consort. This one is a doozy."

I opened my eyes. Next to me, Andre's jaw had tightened, his gaze trained over his shoulder at the devil. His hair flicked like the tail of an agitated cat.

The car slowed down, drawn to the sight of us undoubtedly.

"Ah," the devil held his hands out, "look, we have company."

Would they be supernaturals, like us, or regular humans? The Politia was still after me. Maybe it was an officer. But if it was, then they drove a civilian vehicle.

The engine cut off, and the driver-side door swung open. A man stepped out of the car, and my senses kicked into gear. His gaunt face and bloodshot eyes were a far cry from the dark perfection of the devil's own features. He smelled of black magic, alcohol, and sickness. This man, like me, was dying.

Liver failure. My nose could detect that. It could also detect what he was. It washed over me, the smell unlocking a memory of a stainless steel table, a still heartbeat, and the touch of death. I'd come across one like him before, though the last man's life force had been long gone by the time I'd ever laid eyes on him.

Necromancer.

They practiced dark magic, so definitely not the Politia.

When I swiveled back around, I caught the devil smirking. Never a good sign.

Another heartbeat came from the car.

"There's someone in there with him," I said to Andre.
"I know."

Around us, the demons and even the devil had fallen silent.

"Necromancer," Andre called, "get back in the car and drive home to your loved ones. This place holds only death for you."

Rather than taking Andre's advice, the necromancer pulled out a knife.

Something told me this dude wasn't on team Andriel— yeah, I'd made Andre and me a celebrity name.

The man brought the knife down, the weapon biting into his skin. Andre swore, his form blurring as he ran to the man.

Was I the only one who had no idea what was going on?

The sharp tang of blood filled the air, making my fangs slide out.

"See, little bird?" the devil whispered in my ear. I jumped at his voice, but when I rotated to face him, he still stood a great distance away. "Bloodsport."

The two grappled, which is really to say that Andre quickly put the necromancer in a chokehold and was threatening to kill the man if he didn't cooperate.

That heartbeat in the car still thumped away, calling me towards it. I moved forward, trying to pick up the person's scent.

Smoke congealed in front of me, and out of it stepped the devil. "Ah, ah, ah, consort. All in good time."

His words were only proof that I'd taken the right course of action.

I continued forward, undaunted at the prospect of passing the devil. I'd go through him if I had to.

The ground rolled, knocking me onto my ass.

The necromancer laughed, drawing my attention to him. "It's too late, vampire! My blood stains the—"

Andre took the man's head between his hands. A deft yank was all it took. Bone cracked and his neck snapped.

I felt Andre's power wash over the field as his anger took over. "*What is the meaning of this?*" he roared, swiveling to face the devil.

What had I missed?

Suddenly the shadowy demons shifted, their forms filling out as they solidified.

Uh oh. They weren't supposed to do that.

I crab crawled backwards.

"Get back in the car, soulmate. *Now.*"

For once I listened to Andre. I scrambled to my feet and ran towards the car. Fifteen feet, ten feet—

A shadow plummeted down from the sky. It crashed onto the roof of Andre's sports car, crushing the frame beneath its body. A very solid, very sinister demon chuckled low in its throat, the sound more monster than man.

"Uh, Andre? I think it's too late for a quick getaway," I said, watching the being step down, its entire focus trained on me.

When I glanced over my shoulder, Andre was already in the heat of battle. Black blood littered the ground and stained his clothing. He withdrew his dagger from a demon's chest just as another jumped on his back, its razor sharp teeth lunging for Andre's throat.

I opened my mouth to scream, only to feel a hand grab a chunk of hair. The demon who'd smashed Andre's car yanked my head back. His lips receded, revealing a set of pointy teeth. And his breath—ugh, dude had never been introduced to a toothbrush.

I brought the blades I still held up and slashed them across his neck. Inky blood splattered across my face, and I cringed at the putrid liquid. The demon fell to his knees. His form shimmered, then disappeared altogether.

"Well done, consort." The devil had strolled over and watched me with folded arms. He seemed to drag the night with him as he did so.

I had no time to flip the devil off before another demon came at me, this one with slitted pupils and claws. I sidestepped him, shoving one of my daggers into his back. Not a mortal wound; just enough to piss him off something good.

"I thought necromancers only animated the dead," I said to the devil as the demon recovered.

"Most do," he said, "but some can do the opposite—give bodies to those without."

The clawed being rushed me again, and feeling like a matador, I once again sidestepped him, only attacking him the moment he passed me. As my blade carved into my opponent, I noticed that several of the demons had focused their attention on the necromancer's car.

That second heartbeat. I took a step towards it, only to be distracted by my opponent's snarl.

I turned my attention back to the fight a second too late. The demon plowed into me. Air whistled out of my lungs as he tackled me to the ground. His claws lunged for my heart, ready to dig it out.

I brought my forearm up to block the attack. I let out a choked cry as his talons dug into the skin of my arm and sliced up the side of my face.

Grunting, I brought a leg up and kneed him in the crotch. The creature on top of me let out an inhuman howl and reflexively curled in on itself. Demons may not be human, but apparently they do in fact come with the same plumbing.

I didn't waste the time I'd bought myself. I rolled on top of the demon and plunged one of my knives into the creature's heart.

A car door slammed, and my head jerked up. From the necromancer's vehicle, several demons dragged an inert woman. Her shoulders slumped, her dark hair dangling loosely in front of her.

I sucked in a breath.

No.

I was up in an instant, running towards her. "Let her go!" I screamed. My skin had already begun to glow, and in my panic it brightened. Only here, among creatures not from this world, my glamour carried no power.

Demons closed in on me from all sides, and I brought my daggers up, slashing with abandon. Between their numbers and my injuries, I couldn't cut my way through them. They yanked away my weapons and dragged my hands behind me, pinning me in place.

"*Cease!*" the devil boomed. Immediately his legion of followers fell back, giving me a view of our battlefield.

My gaze landed on Andre. Like me, he was held in place by demons. His clothing had jagged tears in several places, where claws or teeth had ripped the material. His shirt was drenched, and it had suctioned itself to his torso. Vampires didn't sweat; blood had plastered his shirt to his chest.

Crimson and black liquid peeked above its collar and congealed along his arms. God, he looked fierce, like some strange death deity come to carry away souls. Ironic that the unsullied man in the crisp suit was just that deity.

Andre's eyes found mine. He took in my bloody face and torn clothing and yanked at his wrists, but the demons held him fast. We might have exceptional strength amongst supernaturals, but not amongst Underworld creatures. "Soulmate!" he shouted.

"I'm fine," I said, though I felt anything but. My wounds burned, and my emotions roiled.

My eyes searched for the demon's third captive. I finally caught sight of her, her body slumped between two demons that held her fast.

I'd recognize that face anywhere. It was the woman who'd helped me escape the devil several times before. The woman who raised me as an infant.

"Cecilia!" I cried out.

She shook her head and glanced about her, noticing her surroundings for perhaps the first time. She appeared as though she'd been drugged, but how could that be? She was a fate. Couldn't she have prevented this situation in the first place?

I turned my attention to the devil, who wore a pleased smirk as he watched me.

"Let her go." My voice broke.

"I don't think so," he said, stepping in front of me. "You defied me." His voice boomed for all our audience to hear. "Now you're to be punished."

"But you *promised*."

His lips quirked, his expression amused.

Hestia was right—I was in fact the village idiot. How could I for a moment have assumed the devil was to be trusted? Or that I could ever have the upper hand with him? He'd gotten me to place the last nail in my own coffin.

"Not a promise, consort. A *deal*." The devil's eyes slid to Andre. Only too late did I realize that my soulmate had heard, and he stared at the devil with murder in his eyes.

"An ill-stated one on your part," the devil continued. "You named the people that were not to be hurt. I chose someone you had not mentioned."

The intent of my request had been clear—he wasn't to harm my friends or family. Cecilia counted as both. But he was right, I hadn't mentioned her. A sociopath would take advantage of something like that, and the devil was far, far worse than a sociopath.

"Really, Gabrielle," he continued, "I expect better if you are to stand by my side one day."

My stomach dropped. "Don't punish her. Punish me."

"Soulmate, no," Andre said, jerking once more against his captors. He growled at them, his hair rippling with his rising anger. I could feel the power surge tug at our connection.

The devil stepped in close, his eyes alight. They were too bright. "It doesn't work like that, consort," he said. "I will never break you. Others will pay the price for your offenses."

"You're breaking your promise."

"*You* are the oathbreaker," he said, his rage seeping into his voice, "not me."

He swiveled away, agitation written in his features. "Bring Nona forward."

The demons dragged her towards the devil. I fought against my captors, bloody tears obscuring my vision. He'd done this once before, to Leanne. Luckily he'd only killed off her doppelganger.

My breath caught.

Her doppelganger. Cecilia had helped Leanne then, which meant Cecilia knew how to create a doppelganger. Perhaps the woman in front of me was only her doppelganger. Hope bloomed within me.

"Cecilia?"

She looked up and stared at me with tired, heavy eyes.

"Are you ... ? Are you ... ?" I didn't dare utter what I was thinking, but maybe she'd understand.

"*Mi tesoro,*" she said gently, "tonight will not be like Samhain. But it will be okay. Everything is going to be okay."

It wasn't a direct answer, but it ripped my heart all the same. There was no doppelganger. Just this kind woman who had helped me over and over again. And for knowing me, she would now die.

I shook my head, feeling several tears roll down my cheeks. "I am so sorry. Please forgive me, Cecilia."

"There is nothing to forgive, *mi tesoro.*"

"Moving, but time's up, I'm afraid," the devil said, moving between Cecilia and me. He sauntered over to Cecilia and stared down at her. "You have been a pain in my side for quite some time now."

She laughed at the devil. "Killing me off will not stop me from helping, Gabrielle. It is too late for that. You are not the only one to set events in motion long before they've come to pass."

Rage colored the devil's face. His lips curled inward and his nostrils flared. I could tell he wanted to hit her by the way his fists clenched and unclenched.

He swooped in close. "You will die slowly, and I will make her watch. And she will know what comes to those who cross me."

"Pain doesn't scare me, nor do you, Pluto."

The devil leaned back on his heels, studying her for a second "Perhaps it doesn't scare you, Nona, but I fear it will frighten my future queen."

His gaze returned to me. "Let this be a warning: next time you will think twice before defying me."

He snapped his fingers and all those demons holding my arms now released me. I glanced around at the sudden melee, only to see them descend on Cecilia. They'd clustered around the fate, obscuring her form with their dark bodies. Her shrieks ripped through the night air.

I screamed along with her and tore my way towards the

demons. I was now weaponless, but that was only a minor detail at this point. I'd pull them off of her with my bare hands if I had to.

Arms encircled my waist and dragged me away from the swarm. I kicked against my captor.

"Soulmate, it's me. We have to go."

"*No*," I sobbed, my eyes blind with tears. "They have Cecilia."

"It's too late for her," he said quietly.

I knew he was right. Already her screams were becoming moans.

"*Consort!*" the devil yelled. "You are *not* to leave."

Several demons paused what they were doing, glancing up, their eyes reflecting in the moonlight.

Andre's grip on me tightened. "Hold on." Our surroundings blurred as he sprinted away from the devil and the carnage we left.

Above us I heard the flap of wings as a demon pursued us. Already it fell behind. Demons might be stronger than us, but apparently they couldn't keep pace.

That, or the demon just wanted to get back to its kill.

My throat closed up at the thought.

"Andre," I croaked, "you can put me down."

He ignored me, but I began to wiggle in his arms. "Seriously, put me down."

He kept running, cutting across dark fields. If anything, he clenched me tighter to his chest.

"*Put me down.*"

At the tone in my voice, Andre said, "We need to keep running."

"I know."

He set me to my feet but didn't let go of my hand. I began to jog, my pace increasing until I sprinted. Eventually the sound of the demons vanished completely. We were only running from our shadows at this point. Still, I didn't slow.

Andre didn't say anything but kept pace at my side. I could feel his eyes on me, waiting for me to break. But with the wind in my hair and my lungs drawing in deep gulps of air, for a moment I could pretend away all the grisly events that had come to pass.

And then that unfeeling outer shell began to crack. My mind began to play out all sorts of horrible scenarios of what might've happened to Cecilia—what might still be happening to her.

"Don't think of her pain," Andre whispered. "She wouldn't want that. Think of better memories of her." Only after he spoke did I realize that I must've let out a sob.

I wish I could do as Andre suggested, but her screams still echoed in my ears. I pressed the back of my hand to my mouth. The monster that orchestrated it all would take me two days from now.

I stumbled, then fell to my knees. Once I landed, I decided I didn't want to get up. My entire body shook. Cecilia was dead.

Andre picked me up, and cradled me in his lap. "Shhhh, soulmate," he soothed. "She's immortal. She'll be back."

But not before I died.

250

I pressed my face into his chest, allowing the material to muffle my cries. He'd have questions for me. Questions I'd never meant to answer.

Andre shifted me to pull out his phone. He made a quick call to his servants for a car and a cleanup crew before turning his attention back to me. His fingers brushed aside my own, and he lifted my wrist.

Deep gouges had shredded the skin there where the demon's claws had swiped at me. They'd scabbed over, but the injury should've been a distant memory by now. Gently he probed the wounds, his expression unreadable.

When he caught me looking, his gaze flicked to my face. He hissed in a breath and reached a hand out. It came away with blood.

I touched my cheek, feeling the wetness there. "They're just tears Andre."

His thumb rubbed away some of the blood. "No, soulmate," he said solemnly, tilting my head, "they're not." His brows pressed together as he studied the marks on my face. "The scratches are somewhat shallow. I'm ... surprised they haven't healed yet."

Not surprised. *Frightened.* I could read it all over his face. He paused, then his nostrils flared.

Andre leaned into my neck. I thought he might bite or kiss me, but instead he drew in a deep breath. Beneath me, his body went rigid.

I wiped my bloody cheeks with the back of my hand, though it did nothing but smear the blood. "What is it?" I asked.

Ignoring my question, he pressed an ear to my chest.

"Take a deep breath for me, soulmate," he said.

I drew in air, stopping when I felt I might cough.

"Deeper," he encouraged.

I did, and a wet, rattling cough wracked my lungs. It shook my body, and it didn't resolve itself.

When Andre pulled away, that muscle in his jaw fluttered and his throat worked. "We need to get some blood in you," he said, revealing none of his thoughts.

My stomach clenched uncomfortably at the thought. I'd have to force it down. Again.

I stared at him for several seconds, the truth lingering in the space between us.

Our time together was almost up.

Chapter 22

BY THE TIME we'd returned to Bishopcourt, my horror no longer cut like a blade. Maybe it was simply my exhaustion, or the sobering realization that I'd soon join Cecilia, but I'd become blissfully numb to it all.

Power cackled off Andre as he led me into his estate. I swear he was secretly hungering for another fight. His mood had plummeted since he'd seen my cuts and heard my wheezy breath.

"Would you prefer bagged blood or fresh?" Andre asked, leading me towards the kitchen.

I dragged ass, letting Andre drift ahead of me a step or two. "I already drank once this evening."

"I can smell your lie," Andre said, not bothering to turn around as he tugged me after him.

Dammit. "I'm not thirsty."

"You're not hungry either, which leaves me few options," he said as we entered the kitchen. "You must imbibe something, soulmate. Otherwise you'll waste away." His eyes flicked back to me. "You've already lost too much weight—"

"Sir," one of the servants said, following us into the kitchen. Human, by the smell of him, "the Politia called while you were out." He might be human, but he was obviously in-the-know.

Andre dropped my hand and headed to the industrial refrigerator. Inside, rows and rows of blood bags hung.

"About time," he said as he reached for one.

"They wanted to alert you that they're aware of your presence on the island."

Andre raised his eyebrows in acknowledgement while he emptied the bag's contents into a cup.

"That better not be for me," I said, nodding to the blood bag.

"Soulmate," Andre said, like I was being unreasonable. He put the cup into the microwave and nuked it. Microwaved blood—*yum*.

Not.

Andre pulled off his torn, damp shirt, and *holy baby Jesus and all the wise men*, that torso looked airbrushed. He tossed the shirt into an industrial sink, and it hit the bottom with a wet slap.

A shirtless Andre leaned back against the kitchen countertop and, folding his arms, finally turned his full attention to the messenger. "And?" he said.

The servant fidgeted, glancing my way, a detail Andre

noticed. "They said that they know you harbor an international fugitive. They said the truce is in danger of dissolving. That you can prevent it by handing the girl over to the authorities."

Andre nodded, looking deep in thought.

Just then the microwave dinged.

Andre sauntered over to it, and I took the time to admire his backside.

Damn, son.

He grabbed the mug of blood and came back over to me. "Please drink the blood, soulmate." His eyes pleaded with me. They slid to the side of my head, where the scratches likely still lingered.

I took the cup from him and stared down into it. The smell had my gag reflex working. "I … don't have an appetite anymore," I admitted.

I glanced up. Andre's stoic façade had slipped and I stared at raw agony—there was no other term for it. He placed a hand on the side of my neck and squeezed it lightly. "Please try," he rasped.

My lips rolled inward and I nodded. "I think I need to be alone for a little bit."

Judging from Andre's expression, the idea of alone time seemed to disturb him greatly, like I might use it to juggle knives or scrawl poetry onto my arm with razors.

The servant shifted, reminding me that we had an audience. Before Andre could protest further, I left the room. He didn't need me here while he had to make tough decisions concerning me and his coven.

His voice drifted back to me as he returned to business

with his servant. *"Get ahold of the Politia and tell them they have more important things to take care of at the moment, such as the two dozen full-bodied demons that have been set loose on the island."*

I caught a whiff of the blood I clutched to my chest. Despite being repulsed at the smell, my fangs descended. Idiot fangs.

I took a tentative sip, then made a face as the spicy liquid hit the back of my throat. I'd gone from being disgusted by blood to craving it back to being disgusted by it. But I'd completely lost my appetite for food, and I couldn't live off of water, so I would choke this down.

The next swallow I took was larger, and I gagged a little at the taste.

Screw it. I plugged my nose and began gulping the blood down. At last I finished it all, swallowing thickly. The metallic taste lingered, so similar to the smell of Cecilia's blood when ...

I shut the thought down before it made me physically ill. But at the reminder of Cecilia, I headed for Andre's room, where I'd unofficially taken up residence.

Once inside, I moved over to my pile of belongings. They were exactly where I'd dropped them when we first arrived.

I dug through my dirty, travel-worn clothes looking for the one memento I still had from the woman who'd saved me numerous times. The woman I'd indirectly killed, for sleeping with Andre no less.

My stomach churned, and I pushed down the nausea, but—

Nope, nope, nope. Not staying down.

I ran to the bathroom, barely making it before my stomach purged itself of the blood I'd so recently drunk. I flushed the toilet, and straightened, my legs shaky.

I went over to the sink and ran the water. Cupping my hands under the stream, I collected a small pool of it and used it to rinse out my mouth. I spit out the water when I tasted something putrid.

I drew my hands away from me. Black blood still covered them from where the demons bled on me.

Ew, ew, *ew*. Was that what I'd just tasted? Demon blood? *Not chill.*

I scrubbed my hands furiously, until they were raw. And then I glanced up.

Crimson blood covered an entire side of my face where I'd been scratched, mixing with the black blood splattered across my cheeks and over my nose. I sucked in a breath and touched the side of my face.

I ducked my head close to the sink and splashed water onto my face, scrubbing it all down. Everything felt dirty—my hands, my face, and all those places water couldn't touch. Gripping the edge of the sink, I let the cool liquid drip down my cheeks.

I should take a shower.

No amount of stream and scrubbing, however, would change the fact that Cecilia died today—her body, at least.

I swiveled away from the counter, my attention returning to my belongings. I left the bathroom and resumed tearing through them. Right now, I didn't need to feel clean; I just needed to feel close to the woman who'd given up her life for me.

"Where the hell did I put that thing?" It had switched pockets at some point, but I couldn't remember when that was or what I'd been wearing.

For one horrible second I feared I'd lost it. Then I slipped a hand into one of my tattered pants pockets and my hand closed over the sheet of paper.

The birthday card Cecilia had given me.

I yanked it out. It was bent and smudged, but not lost. A drop of blood that had rolled down my cheek now dripped onto the note. Even after all this time I still had the enchanted card.

I ran my fingers over the soft linen finish, tracing her writing. It took me a second to realize the words were not the same ones I'd read with Andre shortly after we'd landed in Germany.

A new set of instructions was scrawled onto the cream-colored paper.

Jericho Aquinas
Find him.
He knows how to save you.

I choked back a sob at the words. She must've written it before I'd made a deal with the devil.

We fates are far-seeing, but we also dwell in human bodies with all of their limitations. We are subjective, and we make mistakes.

She'd made a mistake.

I fell back on my haunches and rubbed my eyes. Defeat

had a bitter, metallic taste.

My connection with Andre thrummed, building on itself as I felt him move towards his room.

I hurriedly wiped my eyes and stashed away Cecilia's note just as the door opened. Andre entered, closing the door behind him. "We have much to discuss, don't we, soulmate?"

I swallowed from where I knelt on the floor.

Andre moved over to the bed and sat on the edge of it. "I've bought us some time with the Politia. They will not attack for a while longer."

I nodded, knowing that wasn't really what he wanted to talk about.

Andre leaned a forearm on his thighs and ran his other hand through his hair. When he looked up at me, resolve colored his face. "What deal did you make with the devil?"

I hadn't thought about what to tell him. My mouth opened, ready to tell him the truth. I bit back my response before I voiced it. How would he react if I told him what I'd promised?

"A kiss," I said in a rush.

I almost groaned as soon as the lie spilled out. A *kiss*? That was the best I could come up with?

"He asked for a kiss in return for not harming the people I loved," I continued. "He ... was angry that we'd ..."

"Made love?" Andre finished for me. His face went soft, like it had been doing every time the subject crossed his mind.

I nodded and bit the inside of my cheek, my body and my conscience feeling sick at the falsehood.

"He asked for a kiss?"

I nodded, averting my eyes.

Andre stood suddenly, his presence filling the room. "You're lying. I can see it, I can smell it." A muscle ticked in Andre's jaw. "There should be no lies between us, no secrets, soulmate. I'd die for you. I deserve the truth."

Now I stood, my fear morphing into anger. "No lies? No secrets? You are seven centuries old! You have more of them than the desert has sand. I don't demand you tell me yours—not the names of all the women before me, not the number of people you've killed, nor your plans for the coven. Give me mine."

Andre crossed the distance between us and clutched my jaw. "I can't, my little mate. I *can't*." Anguish slipped into his voice. "Not when your body wastes away and the devil cleaves to you like a second shadow. If I am to save you, all must be known." He searched my eyes, as if they would give up my secrets.

Before I had a chance to respond, someone rapped on the door, saving me.

"Come in—" "Give us a moment—" we said in unison.

Whoever stood outside our door lingered, uncertain which voice to listen to.

I pushed past Andre and opened the door, eager for the excuse to leave my soulmate and his questions.

"A seer arrived looking for Miss Fiori," the servant said to Andre, ignoring me completely.

Andre growled, running a hand over his jaw. He pointed at me. "Soulmate, this conversation is *not* over." I shivered at the determined note in his voice. He would wheedle the truth out of me; it was only a matter of time.

"Where is this seer?" Andre asked.

"We detained her in the tearoom." Only a vampire would have a room as frivolous and outdated as a tearoom. They didn't even drink the stuff.

I followed the servant to the room, ignoring the brooding vampire king that strode behind me. He was full of pent up frustration. I could feel it like a hot breath on my back.

The man stopped in front of one of many closed doors that lined the halls of Bishopcourt, and with a final glance at Andre and me, he opened the door.

I'd been so distracted by my confrontation with Andre that I hadn't thought about this visitor—that she'd been detained. But when the door swung open and revealed a red-eyed Leanne, I quickly forgot my own issues.

Leanne stumbled towards me. "Nona," she said. She fell into my arms and I held her close as she wept, her own tears coaxing mine back to the surface.

I didn't ask her how she knew.

Behind me I heard Andre whisper to the servant. "*She is a friend of my soulmate. Leave them here, and tell the servants that no one is to bother them.*" Then the door closed behind us.

Even amidst our fight, my heart swelled for that man. He only ever had my best interest at heart. Even if his delivery could suck balls.

I ran my hand over Leanne's hair. She had worked closely with Cecilia only months ago, and for all I knew, they still kept in touch.

I held her for a long time, until her cries became quiet whimpers, and then sniffles.

"It's my fault. He killed her because of me," I whispered into her ear as we held each other.

I bit my lip after I spoke. I hadn't meant to confess this. It felt selfish to draw attention to myself in the wake of someone else's death, but guilt was riding me hard.

She shook her head, pulling back and wiping her tears away. "No, Gabrielle, it's not. *He* killed her—not you."

Leanne placed a hand on my shoulder, then it was her turn to hug me. We'd both witnessed the devil's horrors. She knew better than most how perverse and frightening he was.

I pulled away. "Can I ask you a strange question?"

"Shoot."

"Have you ever heard of Jericho Aquinas?"

She started at the name.

"You have." I so needed to read up on important people of the supernatural world. I was clearly lagging behind.

"What do you want to know about him?" Leanne asked.

"Cecilia had asked me to find him."

She cocked her head. "Why?"

"She thought he might be able to save me." Before I bartered away my life, that was.

Leanne's eyes brightened, bringing me back to the present.

"He owns a shop in Douglas—Jericho's Emporium," she said. "It's less than an hour's drive from here. But ..." She bit the cuticle near her thumb, "before you visit him, there's something you should know."

I hadn't planned on seeking him out, but I didn't bother correcting Leanne. "And what's that?"

"Jericho Aquinas is not of this world."

Chapter 23

WE HUNG OUT in that tearoom for another hour before Leanne had to go. I led her out to the car someone had called for her.

"You sure you're going to be okay?" I asked, eyeing the vehicle and the driver. She and Oliver had given up so much on my behalf. Each one of these excursions put her more at risk for being discovered. If authorities knew my friends were helping me, the anti-Christ—cringe—there was no telling what kind of punishment they'd receive.

But it would be bad.

Leanne gave me a watery smile. "I think I cried out the worst of my emotions."

"That's not what I'm talking about." Though the reminder of Cecilia had my eyes stinging all over again.

She blew out a breath, the smile drooping. "I know.

And I wasn't going to tell you this, but the Politia already talked to me and Oliver."

That drew me up short. "What?" I stiffened. "Why didn't you tell me?"

Leanne leaned against the car. "Because you already have enough to worry about, and it wasn't a big deal."

"How is that not a big deal?" And how had Oliver not brought up the subject? His lips were looser than his morals—well, most of the time, anyway.

"They talked to me and Oliver shortly after we returned. Oliver fed them some story about how we've been trying to convince you to turn yourself in. So that's our official story."

I shoved my hands into my pockets, grimacing when my hand brushed against a crusted patch of dried blood on my pants. "And they bought that?"

"They think you're the embodiment of evil. They assumed we were good supernatural folk that got hoodwinked by you. It wasn't that difficult to convince them."

I pulled a hand from my pocket to rub my eyes. "So even the seer's shroud—?"

"We explained it all away," Leanne said. "I could stand here all night telling you everything we said, but the point is, they believed us, Gabrielle. They *believed* us."

Leanne opened the door to the back of the car and tossed her purse inside. "Oliver and I have been encouraged to continue persuading you, so these visits won't get us into trouble. You really don't need to be worrying about us."

I nodded, pressing my lips together. I couldn't help it.

I'd bartered my soul for their lives.

"I'll see you soon," she said, and then she stepped into the car.

I stood outside a long time after Leanne's vehicle drove off, staring into the distance, wishing I could drive off into the night just like she had.

Another car sat in front of Bishopcourt. Its driver leaned against it, smoking a cigarette.

Suddenly, my situation was overwhelming. Intolerable. Hiding here, waiting for death to find me. I glanced over my shoulder, well aware that Andre would have the hissy to end all hissies once he learned that I'd slipped away. And he'd know, thanks to our connection.

I decided I didn't care. Time for me was running out.

Plus, I had an idea where I wanted to go.

Chapter 24

JERICHO AQUINAS WAS a messenger.

That's what he called himself at least. He wouldn't elaborate on whom he was a messenger for, but I could guess. The scent of divinity rolled off of him. Like some of the other big players in this game, Jericho was more than just the withered old man he'd have me believe. He moved too fluidly, especially for a man with stooped shoulders and twisted hands.

And, judging by the slight crinkle of his nose, he could smell the damnation wafting off of me.

I watched him press a clothbound book into the shelves of his emporium. I read the spine: *The Extraordinarily Long Life of Comte de St. Germain, Vol. III (1706 – 1754).*

"Vampire?" I asked, nodding to the book.

"'Not all that glitters is gold.'"

Yay, another supernatural that spoke in riddles. Awesome.

"Aw, are you going Tolkien on me?" I asked, recognizing the quote.

Jericho peered at me though the thick lenses of his glasses. "I'm impressed you know the quote."

"Okay, now you're just trying to be offensive," I said, folding my arms and leaning my hip against the bookshelf.

A mischievous smile stretched across his face. "Aye, I am, aren't I? Apologies. And no, the Comte de St. Germain is not a vampire. What is it you've come to inquire about?"

Now that was the question. I hoped he could answer that for me, otherwise my little excursion through the town of Douglas to find this place would've all been for nothing.

"Nona sent me here."

He glanced at me sharply. "She did now? How is that wily fate?"

My throat worked. "Dead."

"Ah. I see," he nodded. Noticing my face, he patted my shoulder. "Now now, it does you no use to grieve over immortal beings. She'll be back soon enough. That's the way of things with fates."

I nodded, appreciating his words.

Jericho pulled a handkerchief out of his pocket and cleaned his glasses. "I'll be guessing that she wanted you to finally collect on your mother's deal."

My attention sharpened at his words. "My mother's deal?"

The thought that Celeste might've stood here and talked to Jericho had my heart twisting.

"Aye. It's not just fairies and devils that do deals."

"You mean *you* bargain as well?" I caught another whiff of divinity; the idea of something pure striking deals with humans seemed outlandish.

"I am a messenger. I do not have the power to make deals, but from time to time I fulfill deals on behalf of Her. Sometimes the Woman herself allows trades to be made—"

Whoa, whoa, whoa. "We are talking about God right now, and not like Satan's third cousin, twice removed that rules some other land I'd never heard of, right?" I asked.

God was a woman?

"We are."

I rubbed my temple, pulling my thoughts back on track. "But *She* doesn't make deals."

"Oh, she doesn't now?" Jericho said, mirth dancing in his eyes.

"No ... ?" It came out unsure.

"Isn't that what prayer is?" he asked.

"But that's a request, not a bargain," I argued.

"Ah—but the very act of praying is part of the deal. Faith and love have high currency in our world, and both go into prayer."

He hobbled down the aisle, pushing his cart of books and knickknacks, coming to a stop in front of a display of lamps and adding a lantern to it.

"Undying light," he said, nodding to the lantern as he set it on the table.

"So you mean to tell me praying actually works?" Why had I not gotten the memo sooner?

Jericho gave me a chastising look. "Of course it works," he said as he pushed the cart. "Doesn't mean every prayer is answered how the person intended. God does indeed move in mysterious ways."

He stopped again and pushed the cart into an alcove that housed several music boxes and perfumes encased in crystal decanters.

He dusted off his hands. "Follow me," he said, shuffling to the back of the building. I picked my way through the cluttered store, following him.

"So what are you saying?" I asked, picking up the conversation from where we left off. "That my mom prayed and God left the answer to her prayers here with you?"

Jericho made a noise at the back of his throat. "Your mother's case was a little more complicated than that." We walked up a narrow staircase. Here the dust was especially thick, and I waved my hand in front of me, coughing. My lungs heaved, unable to fully purge the cough.

"All the Hail Mary's in the world wouldn't save you. She knew that."

"Wait. Me?" I'd been assuming that whatever deal Celeste had made had to do with her.

"Yes, you. You'd been marked since before birth. There'd be no stopping the wheels of a fate this strong from turning. Even Nona knew that, which is why she sent your mother here in the first place."

"Nona sent her here?" I must've looked like I just found out Oliver had burned my wardrobe because Jericho quickly elaborated.

"Thick as thieves those two were. From what I hear, she and your mother were the best of friends. All I know was that Nona saw your mother's fate unravel along with yours, and she came to me seeking divine intervention."

"*What?*" This was all too much too quickly. Nona was once ... *young?* And she'd been friends with my mother?

That picture of my mother at Cecilia's house. The other girl had been her. Holy crap, my mother had been friends with a fate.

Jericho pulled a key ring out of his pocket and unlocked a door at the top of the stairs. He held the door open, and dazed, I stepped inside.

A wave of magic hit me, knocking the breath out of me, and I stumbled at the sensation.

Jericho chuckled. "It does that," he said, following behind me.

We'd entered some sort of storage room, only this one was full of magical—and likely very valuable—objects. A strange gemstone reflected hues of light I wasn't positive I'd ever seen before. The placard beneath it read, *Alchemist's Stone.* A series of goblets took up one of the walls, some with descriptions, some without.

Jericho walked over to the far wall and pulled down a domed glass case caked in dust. He placed it on a side table and grabbed a rag, wiping it down.

Beneath the dust, the glass case housed an iridescent feather. I stepped forward, eyes narrowed. On closer inspection I realized it wasn't simply a feather, but a quill.

"In return for a series of tasks, your mother and Nona

were given a celestial request quill to be bestowed upon you in a time of need."

"A celestial request quill?" I was so going to need a definition for that one.

"It's a pen that allows you to place an official request for the heavens to hear your case."

"My ... case?"

I glanced back at the quill and swallowed. I didn't have a good track record with quills. I tended to break them.

"The terms of its use are that the Celestial Plane—heaven—must hear your complaint and rectify it as they deem fit." He glanced down at it. "You can only use it once."

I looked at the quill. Had my mother and Nona meant for me to use it to write into God about my current situation?

I reached for it, but Jericho pulled the item out of my reach.

"You're not going to give it to me?" I eyed the case. I was not above grappling with an old, angelic being for the thing.

"Nona had her own conditions," Jericho said, "and there was one she was particularly adamant about."

My eyes flicked from the container to the man that held it. "What was it?"

"She said I was not to give it to you until after you married the devil."

Chapter 25

A<small>FTER</small> I <small>MARRIED</small> *the devil.*

The *devil.*

I shivered at the implications of that.

Jericho's hand rested lightly on my upper back as he walked me out. He held open the front door for me.

It hadn't struck me as strange that Cecilia never mentioned Jericho when I visited her. Not until now.

Because she hadn't meant for me to find him until after I'd met with Decima and after I watched her die. She'd wanted me to know that help wouldn't intervene in time to save my life.

But help might come later. After I died. It was the tiniest spark of hope in the darkness.

"Now you be safe, and come find me straight away when your situation changes," Jericho said, propping the door open with his body.

I let out a disturbed little laugh that ended in a whimper.

He clasped my hands in his dry, wrinkled ones. "For the record, you might smell damned, but I know an innocent soul when I see one."

"Thank you?"

He nodded, more to himself than to me, and left me there. I stared after the emporium, my mind a tangle of thoughts.

"I am seriously considering chaining you to our bed."

I yelped at the sound of Andre's voice.

He pushed off the wall he'd been leaning against and prowled towards me, the muscle in his jaw feathering. "That seems to be the only way to keep you out of danger these days."

"I had to come." Had he overheard my conversation with Jericho? Did he know?

"Here?" Andre gazed up at the weathered sign. In the late evening, on the abandoned street, the musty books and faded antiques seemed a little wilted behind their glass casing. "Whatever for?"

He hadn't overheard. I couldn't decide if I was relieved or anxious at that.

"Cecilia had given me another task."

His brows rose. "Why didn't you tell me?" If I didn't know better, I'd say that Andre sounded hurt.

"I needed to be alone."

"'Needed'?"

"Wanted," I corrected.

Andre nodded. "As you've done most things lately."

I took a step back. "What's that supposed to mean?"

He paced forward, refusing to put space between us. "Animals find quiet places to die alone. They sequester themselves away from the living."

And I was the dying animal in question.

"It might be a stretch to call you 'living.'"

He stared me down until I squirmed. I held my hands us. "Okay, okay, it's a distinction without a difference."

"You're not denying the rest of the statement."

I bit my upper lip, sucking it in. "What do you want me to say?" I whispered. "I can't pretend my situation away." I hated feeling like I was waiting death out.

Andre ran a hand through his hair. "You should've told me. All of this." He reached out and stroked my face. "My God, soulmate, I don't want you to shut me out. That's the last thing."

I glanced back at the window, feeling far, far older than seventeen. "I'm sorry." Not that I had any intention of giving up the rest of my secrets.

"I don't want your apologies, I want your faith. I'm losing you—and not even to the devil. I'm losing you to your own demons."

A traitorous tear snaked out of my eye. I was a big fucking mess.

His gaze latched onto the tear. "No," he said, his eyes flashing. "You made me a promise," his voice shook; I realized it was because he was scared. Absolutely petrified, "you wouldn't give up on me. You'd continue to fight."

"What do you think I'm doing here? I haven't broken

that promise."

Andre growled and ran a hand through his hair. "It infuriates me that you can be so reasonable about this. *Ay, dios mio*, I need to hurt someone."

"Andre?"

His stormy eyes met mine.

"I could really use a hug right now."

He exhaled, and then I was enveloped in his embrace, my body squished against his hard chest. I could feel his agitation drain away as he held me. I held tightly to him, like I might drift away if I let him go.

"I'm frightened," I admitted. Here in Andre's arms, I didn't have to pretend to be tough.

His words were barely a breath on the breeze. "So am I, love. So am I."

ONLY ONCE I was safely back inside Bishopcourt did Andre relax. As we moved through his estate, he kept me close—a hand at the small of my back, an arm slung around my waist, fingers threaded through mine.

Finally Andre simply picked me up, wrapped my legs around his waist, and carried me to his bedroom.

This position was one of the few times where I was able to stare down at him. "Sleepy?" I asked, watching those smoldering eyes of his.

He grinned up at me. "Are you ever *not* irreverent?" He was in a better mood.

I smirked back at him. "It's part of my charm." I was also feeling a bit perkier.

He kicked the door closed behind us, and all traces of humor were gone from his face.

"I need you," he said simply.

I'd like to say that lines like that didn't do me in. But I'd be lying if I said that it didn't work.

The last of the panic that had consumed him since he found me outside Jericho's Emporium only subsided once nothing separated us.

He moved against me, holding me close, his lips skimming my neck. He breathed me in, and I heard him shudder. He had to smell the death clinging to me.

Andre leaned his head against mine. "It's you and me, soulmate. Always." His fingers slid between mine, and I squeezed his hands, afraid he'd slip through mine if I didn't hold on firmly enough.

I fought down the lump in my throat. I wouldn't be sad. Not now.

We were together. We were meant to be. My fate and his didn't matter. I could be a world away from him, and I'd still love him. Nothing would change that. Not death. Not the devil. Nothing.

Our lips crashed together anew, and we finished what we started with all the franticness of two lovers who knew their time was coming to a close.

I LIFTED MY head from the pillow. "Where's my T-shirt?"

Andre raised an eyebrow. He looked like a cat that had lapped up all the cream.

I reached out and traced his lazy features, awed that I

could make anyone look that way. "You told me that I'd know when I'd 'done that and gotten the T-shirt.' So now I'm wondering where my shirt is."

Andre's brow furrowed for a moment as he stared at me. Then he threw his head back and let out a surprised laugh. When he caught his breath he said, "You mean to tell me a ring wasn't enough?"

"Not nearly. I'm planning on bleeding your bank account dry."

At that, Andre laughed again. "That will take some time—especially if you plan on draining my funds via T-shirts. But the lady will get what the lady wants."

After a pause he added, "I believe this is what you call being 'whipped.'"

I gave his shoulder a playful shove. "Punk."

Flashing a wicked smile, he rolled back on top of me, and kissed me thoroughly, his muscles bunching and releasing with the movement, and another hour was given up to complete and utter bliss.

Chapter 26

Two days left.

My eyes snapped open and stared at the ceiling. Not even two full days. Tomorrow evening he'd come for me. My hands twisted the sheets beneath me. I could taste my own fear at the back of my throat; I was practically choking on it.

What a way to wake up.

I drew in a deep breath. My chest tightened, and I began to cough. The action shook my entire body, and my heart fluttered arrhythmically before quickly righting itself.

That ... couldn't be good.

A hand rested on my exposed back. "Soulmate?"

Andre's naked body leaned over mine, and I realized we'd fallen asleep together this way. A blush should've spread across my face, ... but my alabaster skin stayed eerily pale.

"Are you okay, love?" Andre's voice was so gentle.

I nodded even as I continued to cough.

A vertical line bisected his brow. He threw the covers off, his form blurring. The door opened and slammed shut.

No more than five seconds later, he'd returned with a glass of water and a blood bag. He'd even managed to get a pair of pants on.

I sat up, taking the items from him as he handed them over. I took a sip of water, the liquid soothing the raw skin of my throat.

The blood bag would have to wait; I couldn't possibly drink it right now. Maybe later.

Two days.

Fear flooded my veins. Too soon. Far too soon. I wasn't ready to leave this man, this life.

Andre's nostrils flared. He knelt next to my bed and took my hand. With his other, he brushed my hair back. "You're fine, soulmate, and tonight will be fine."

I nodded. If I spoke, he'd know my fear hadn't stemmed from his assumptions.

But at the mention of this evening, I suppressed a groan. He and I were going to have to face off with his coven. They undoubtedly wanted to tear me to shreds now that they knew that, one, the devil had a massive hard-on for me, and two, I was supposedly going to lead to all their deaths.

Yay.

I could hardly freaking wait for tonight.

280

AN HOUR LATER, after choking down a sip or two of blood, showering, and getting changed, I left Andre's room ... and promptly ran into Vicca.

Not literally, thank you baby Jesus. I hear that bitchiness is contagious on contact, and I already had had plenty, thank-you-very-much.

Up until now, Andre had managed to keep all vamps away from Bishopcourt, most likely out of fear they'd kill me the moment he wandered away from me. However, tonight that all changed, my current situation case in point.

I ignored her. I might have to play nice with all vampires, but that didn't mean I had to go out of my way to make friendly with the woman who'd abducted me mere weeks ago.

Vicca, however, had other ideas. Her nostrils flared. For an instant, she looked startled. "You smell like *sickness*." She drew her head back. "Andre risks his coven's lives and his to protect a weak, dying girl? It's so unlikely I wouldn't believe it if I weren't standing in front of the proof."

Andre chose that moment to exit his room. "Soulmate, I thought we were going to walk together—?"

His eyes fell on the lovely Elder currently curling her lip at me.

"Vicca," he said, his tone cool, "what are you doing outside our room?" Andre came up to me, draping an arm around my waist.

I didn't miss his deliberate use of *our*, or the possessive way he pulled me into his side. Normally I wasn't a fan of these dominant maneuvers, but considering Vicca had been eyeing me like she might just off me and save everyone else the time and trouble, I'd take it. Gladly.

"Coming to get you," Vicca said. "Your coven awaits."

WE GATHERED IN the same room where I was first announced to the coven over four months ago. Like last time, we were the center of attention—though perhaps they were a little angrier now than they were before.

I sat next to Andre in a chair someone had drawn up for us on the room's stage. Though we were supposedly the target of the coven's wrath, the arrangement made me feel exalted; they'd either consciously or unwittingly enthroned us. Hell, knowing how much Andre's coven respected and feared him, it probably was a nod to our bond.

Not that they were happy about it.

"You hid this from us!" one man hissed from the crowd. Murmurs erupted and vampires nodded, their brows furrowed and their eyes angry.

Andre settled into his chair before he responded. "I hide much from you—from everyone. We have long known that not all truths should be voiced. This was one of them."

"She is your soulmate! This changes everything. You should be punished to the fullest extent of our law for what you did to Theodore on our behalf," this was said by one of the few vampires that actually looked his age—that's to say, *old*.

Andre was calm when he spoke. "Theodore was the aggressor. He attacked Gabrielle after we'd extended our protection to her—even after I'd made it clear *repeatedly* that she was not to be harmed. It was Gabrielle or Theodore. My soulmate, who was being attacked, or my oldest friend, her attacker. Perhaps you can understand both my sacrifice and my actions under the circumstances. Or perhaps you cannot—and that is why I am king, and you are not."

Ouch. Even I felt the contact burn from that one.

"A prophecy said she would lead to the extermination of all vampires—a prophecy you knew about. And not only did you not kill her, you saved her from someone that would," Vicca said, her voice rife with accusation. "You put your interests before ours."

Andre stood, staring the female vampire down. "Do you not understand the nature of soulmates? Our natures our entwined. She dies, I die." Some in the crowd hissed at Andre; others shifted restlessly.

Andre sat back down and spent several seconds getting comfortable. "That is not a threat. It is simply the way of soulmates. You've heard the tales—they are true. I've experienced it firsthand. One cannot live without the other. Had Theodore been successful, we would all be burning in the fires of hell at this very moment."

That silenced the crowd.

"Have you ever thought," Andre continued, "that perhaps Gabrielle's death would be what caused the extermination of vampires?"

You could hear a pin drop in the room. Several long seconds ticked by as people digested this. I could see the realization dawning in their eyes ... and the horror. These people were aware I was at the top of every supernatural hit list, and they could smell my ill health. They knew I'd kick the bucket soon, and if Andre spoke the truth, then his death could come on the wings of my own.

"This is ... a disturbing possibility we never considered," one of the Elders said. Around him, others murmured their agreement.

Andre inclined his head, acknowledging the vampire's admission. The room's rising anger deflated after that.

In the silence that followed, Andre spoke once more. "The devil wishes to abduct my mate." The words sighed out of him, so weary he sounded. "If he wills it, she'll be dragged to hell and forced to lay with him."

My grip tightened on the arm rests. Andre reached out, covering my hand with his.

A shudder worked its way through the crowd. Impressive that creatures who'd lost most of their humanity would still recoil at this. That definitely wasn't good.

Another vampire—*Something* Holloway—crept closer to the stage. He was the same man who interrogated me in Romania. "So, have you met him?" he asked, peering up at me.

There was absolute silence in the room as the coven waited for my answer.

I lifted my chin as I stared at them. "Yes."

I'd assumed that amongst all the secrets that had been published in the news, this would be among them. Maybe it was, maybe it wasn't, but the gasps in the crowd told me that either way, no one had believed it until this moment.

"Once?" Holloway gazed at me with curious eyes.

Andre's hand tightened on my own, before he withdrew it.

I shook my head. "Too many times to count."

The vampire steepled his fingers, and pressed the tips of them to his lips. An excited gleam had entered his eyes. "Tell us everything you know about the devil and these visits."

Again, an eerie silence descended over the room as they waited with baited breath.

Of course these men and women wanted to know. Just like me, the coven had been cursed to hell since the night they were turned. They'd probably spent centuries wondering what the devil was like, what their afterlife would be like.

A glance over at Andre told me that he wouldn't swoop in to save me from explaining myself.

I inhaled. "The devil has always been a presence in my life, as far back as my memory goes." Albeit, my memory was spotty before the age of seven.

"Even when you were a child?" Holloway sounded incredulous.

I nodded.

"When you were young, what did you think he was?"

I shrugged. "All children have night terrors. He was mine. I didn't realize until I was a little older that he wasn't just a night terror."

"And when you were older, what did you think of him then?"

Next to me, Andre rubbed a thumb over his lower lip, watching me with contemplative eyes. I'd never told him this, I realized.

My mouth opened, but I was at a loss for words. "I don't know. I called him 'The Man in the Suit' because I had nothing else to go on. He would appear and disappear like a ghost, but he ... wasn't one." I searched for words to explain what had always been inexplicable to me.

Holloway saved me from having to finish the thought. "How often did he show up?"

I had the room's rapt attention. Maybe it was the crowd's realization that my death—the very thing they'd been gunning for—might be what would lead to their own demise, or my unique insight into the lord of the Underworld, but they were staring at me with some strange mixture of wonder and awe.

"As a child, the devil used to visit me once every several months or so. When I got older, he showed up less. That all changed, however, once I arrived here."

"You mean to the Isle of Man?" Holloway had become the unofficial interviewer for the evening.

"Yes."

"In what way did it change?"

All those visits ... "He became bolder. He visited more frequently, came closer to me than he previously had, and he began speaking to me."

I didn't make eye contact with anyone in the crowd as I spoke. My gaze fixed on some distant point above them.

"Speaking to you?" Holloway repeated. "What did he have to say?"

I pressed my lips tightly together, clenching one of my fists as I remembered the last time he'd spoken to me, right before he ordered Cecilia killed.

"My soulmate does not wish to answer the question—"

"The devil had lots of things to say." My voice rose over Andre's. "Sometimes he simply said things to scare me—he likes doing that. Other times he'd threaten or bribe me, and at least once he warned me of danger." I didn't mention the creepy way he'd been *nice*—if you could call it that—to me lately. As it was, I'd come too close to suggesting just that.

It was the furthest thing from the truth.

"All those times that he visited you, what did he want?" Vicca cut in. Unlike her earlier hostility, I could see I'd gained something like respect in her eyes. Maybe *respect* was too generous a term. More like tolerance.

I glanced at Andre, whose brow was furrowed.

"Before I came to the Isle of Man, I had no idea I was a supernatural. I thought I was going insane." I got some snickers from that statement. Vampires and their screwed up senses of humor. "Now it seems as though he was keeping an eye on me. I think once I was Awoken, something changed. That's when he increased his presence in my life."

"So, since you came to the Isle of Man, the devil's approached you to chat?" Holloway asked.

"He's done a lot more than just chatted with me." I regretted the words almost immediately. Andre's jaw clenched and unclenched, and his hands tightened along the armrests. The crowd began to whisper, their voices rising.

"Are you telling us you've carried on a relationship with the devil while you've been with our king?"

Andre rubbed his face. "It's not quite that simple," he said. "It wasn't ... consensual."

Some of the audience hissed, and I sincerely hoped that was on my behalf.

The Elder that was questioning me cleared his throat. "We will adjourn and discuss all that we've learned in private. This meeting is over."

It only took them three hours to come to a decision.

I stood at a window in one of Andre's side rooms, staring at the night outside. My thoughts were dark.

I heard Andre rise from the wingback chair behind me. My hair stirred as he pressed a kiss to the side of my neck. One of his arms wrapped around my waist and the other slinked over my breasts. They really liked that.

Yo boobs, behave.

His hand laid flat over my heart. "It beats slower, soulmate."

"I know." I turned in his arms so that I faced him. "If I di—"

Andre pressed a finger to my lips. "No talk of death tonight."

A knock on the door sounded. A moment later it opened. "They've come to a verdict."

A verdict. Like this was some trial. The vampire led us back to the room we'd been publically interrogated in.

When we entered, the room stood. The vampire who led us here now directed us back to our seats.

Just as I was about to sit down, Andre caught my arm.

"Not yet."

I turned my confused stare from him to the crowd.

One of the Elders made his way through. I thought he would stop before us, but he came right up to me and took my hand. Then he did something even stranger: he knelt and kissed my knuckles.

"We welcome you, Gabrielle Fiori, daughter of the late Elder, Santiago Fiori, as our sire's soulmate."

Over his shoulder, I saw an entire room of vampires genuflect.

When the Elder stood, his face was grim. "We will protect you, come what may."

I nodded, blinking rapidly. I wasn't sure what I had expected, but it wasn't this. A weight lifted off my chest to see all these people supporting me. And okay, as far as fan bases go, mine were a bit more morally depraved than the norm. But I'd take it.

"We would request a public Joining to formally recognize you as our queen and host a celebration in honor of your union."

"Joining?" My eyes questioned Andre.

He glanced down at me, a troubled expression on his face. "The Joining will require some consideration on the part of my soulmate." Andre returned his attention to the Elder. "But we accept the celebration."

Chapter 27

"What is a Joining?" I stood, arms crossed in Andre's study with him and Oliver, who sauntered into Bishop-court ten minutes ago from who-knew-where.

Andre leaned against his desk, his gaze tracking my every move.

Behind him Oliver poked at a shrunken head Andre had on one of his shelves. The fairy let out a squeal when the head began to snap at him, its teeth clicking together.

"It's our version of a union, soulmate."

My eyes nearly popped out of my head at that. "As in *marriage?*"

Andre's mouth thinned, but he nodded.

Oliver snorted. "Sabertooth, you're boning the dude on a nightly basis. Best make an honest man out of him before you knock him up."

Andre and I both glared at Oliver.

"Keep talking, and I'll knock you *out*," I muttered.

"So violent," Oliver said. "Andre, you might want to rethink this whole Joining business—spousal abuse might happen with this one." He nudged his head towards me.

"Oh my God, *Oliver*."

"No Joining will occur in the near future," Andre stated.

"Oh." Oliver deflated.

If I was being honest with myself, I deflated a bit too. It wasn't that I wanted to get married—excuse me, *Joined*—anytime soon, but hearing Andre say those words so definitively just ... threw me off. I wanted to be the demanding, indecisive one, dammit!

As if he read my mind, Andre gave a longsuffering sigh. "Soulmate, I would love nothing more than to Join with you, but I will not ask you to take on anything you're not ready for. You already have my heart and my love."

Awww. My skin began to glow at his words.

Oliver looked between us. "Are you guys about to have hot, sweaty, monkey sex?"

We both ignored him.

"But there will still be a party?" I asked. A party that I probably wouldn't be around to enjoy.

My heart thumped weakly in my chest, and I shook my hands to get blood flowing through them. They were cold and clammy. Over the last couple days my circulation had gotten especially bad.

"That is what I agreed to, yes," Andre said.

"Had you even considered asking for my opinion before you agreed to that?" I asked.

"Oh," Oliver winced, "bad move, Andre boy. Boning will clearly be put on hold till this gets resolved. If the anti-Christ here ain't happy, ain't *nobody* happy."

"Who invited you in here anyway?" Andre demanded, turning on the fairy.

"She did." He immediately pointed to me.

I shook my head at Oliver and gave him a look that said, *You are so lucky I like you.*

"She may have invited you in," Andre said, "but I am ordering you out."

"Sheesh." Oliver slid off of Andre's desk. "I'm leaving I'm leaving."

We watched the door as it clicked shut. "It continues to astonish me that a creature like him could ever be friends with anyone," Andre said.

"Hey!" I said indignantly. "He's *my* friend."

"All the more proof that you harbor the heart of a saint."

Now he was just trying to butter me up.

Andre came over to me. He took my hands in his and he knelt. The image of him down on his knees shook me. His wide shoulders and the dangerous glint in his eyes said without words that he was a man more prone to violence than to love. But here he was, beseeching me with his body. "None of this matters so long as you are mine and I am yours. And I am still yours."

Seeing that kind of ferocity surrendering to love undid me. My throat worked. I squeezed his hands. "And I'm still yours."

Andre stood, a smile lighting his features.

I could run from the thought of marriage, but I couldn't run from our bond. We were already joined—and had been since the bond was Awoken in me.

Andre understood that, but he'd let me live amongst my pretty illusions until I came to terms with it as well.

He leaned in and kissed me, his hands still holding tightly to my own. I pinched my eyes shut.

Till death do us part.

"So when's this shindig, and what should Leanne and I wear to it?" Oliver asked when I found him hanging out in Andre's dining room.

Andre had wandered off to a series of private meetings with some of his coven members, leaving me to my own devices for the time being. And my own devices included hanging out with the little devil that perched on my shoulder—a.k.a., Oliver.

Oliver quickly slipped the phone he'd been on into his pocket, but not before I caught a flash of ...

Ew.

Dick pics.

"Hello?" Oliver snapped his fingers in front of my face. "Earth to Gabrielle. What's the dresscode?"

"You just assumed you were invited?"

He picked up the margarita sitting in front of him and slurped it down. He'd gotten Bishopcourt's chef to make him one, and by the smell of it, one with a little alcohol. Oliver would manage to swing that.

"Of course I'm invited," he said. "I'm your BBF, and you always invite your BBFs to parties, so, formal, I take it?"

I shrugged. "I have no clue."

He huffed. "You're supposed to know these things—it's your celebration after all."

"Well, I seriously doubt we're going to have a casual cookout, Oliver. Use your own judgment."

Oliver raised his eyebrows. "Whoa, someone needs to loosen up. Actually," he said, his eyes alighting, "both you and Andre could use a good roll in the hay—minus the hay, because ew, we're not beasts here."

Geez, did literally everything come down to sex with this one?

As I stared at him, I realized, *Why yes, yes it did.*

"There are a lot of things I need. I hate to break it to you Oliver, but sex is not exactly topping that list."

"Then your list is *wrong.*" He peered over the rim of his glass. "Also," he said, eyeing me, "I seriously doubt that."

"Whatever, Oliver." I drummed my fingers on the countertop. "By the way, where's Leanne?"

Oliver checked out his nails, right now painted Robin's Egg Blue. "She's busy—*with a man.*"

My brows shot up. "She has a hot date?" She hadn't mentioned anything the last time I saw her.

Oliver took a dainty sip of his margarita. "Eh," he lifted a shoulder, "it's a new development. She foresaw a chance encounter with a crush of hers. Not that she didn't want to be here. It was a tough call—spending the evening with a hot date over a depressing mess like you."

I gave him an arch look. "And yet you're here."

Oliver sniffed. "It was a tough call for her. An easy one for me."

Just when I thought Oliver was about as rude as they come, he went and said something like that.

"—Plus, I already got laid twice today. I had room to fit you into my schedule."

And there he went ruining it.

"Oli*ver*," I laughed. I pushed his shoulder with a little too much force.

"Aaaaiieeeek!" Oliver screeched as he toppled off his chair.

I cursed. "Oliver?"

Suddenly a hand holding a still-full margarita shot into view. "Saved the alchy! Oh—and I hate you." A moment later the rest of Oliver popped up.

"Sorry!"

"You wait—next time I'm choosing the beefy dude over your ass."

Trouble was, there'd be no next time.

ONCE OLIVER LEFT, I found Andre back in his study. He reclined in his chair, his feet kicked up on his desk, his phone cradled against his ear.

"...Chief Constable," he was saying when I entered, "I've been doing this for a long time. Far longer than you. You'd have to take this place apart brick-by-fucking-brick before you got your hands on her."

My gooseflesh puckered when I realized he was talking

about me to Chief Constable Morgan, my former boss.

Andre's eyes darted to me, his expression heating.

Andre swung his feet off the desk. "I can promise you two things," he said into the speaker. "One, you will never lay a finger on her. And two, if you think to try again, my wrath will make the devil's look like child's play." He dropped the phone onto the receiver without waiting for a response.

"Soulmate," he said, his voice gentling. He stood and came over to me. "I didn't mean for you to hear that."

I shook my head. "You've been coordinating my safety this whole time, haven't you? While I've been hanging out with Oliver."

He stopped in front of me, and his knuckles grazed my cheek. "I wanted you to be untroubled for a few hours. God knows you deserve it."

I closed my eyes and leaned into his touch. "Thank you."

"That does not deserve your gratitude."

I opened my eyes and gazed into Andre's beautiful face. That chiseled jaw that led to his soft, supple lips. That straight nose, that shock of dark hair. But above all, those deep, soulful eyes that could make his face look harsh or angelic.

I could draw him in my dreams, and I would. I'd carry his image with me, and I'd remember it when things got really bad.

"What are you thinking of?" Andre's eyes moved between mine.

I swallowed, pushing down the truth. "Why has no one

tried to attack this place?" I asked instead.

Andre frowned, and I had the distinct impression he knew my thoughts had lingered elsewhere. But he answered me anyway. "This place has centuries of complex enchantments. It should be impenetrable to foes."

He pinched his lower lip, his expression darkening. "But every stronghold has a weakness, and Bishopcourt is no exception. It won't last forever. We will have to leave—and soon."

"How soon?" If I could snatch back words, I would retrieve those ones. Here I was, making plans with Andre when I had no right to. Not anymore.

Andre lifted an eyebrow. "As soon as you'd like, soulmate, barring tonight or tomorrow—that's when my subjects want to host the celebration. But two days from now we could leave." His eyes glimmered with anticipation. Those wheels in his head turned at this very moment, scheming our escape.

"The celebration will be tomorrow?" Horror crept up my throat, trying to choke my windpipe. All that is holy, that was when I was slated to head to hell.

"Best to get it over with as quickly as possible. The coven's aware that we'll have to disappear again soon, and who knows the next chance we'll have to gather again."

I found my voice. "We can't do it tomorrow." I rushed the words out.

Andre peered at me, his eyes missing nothing. "Why not, soulmate?"

I opened and closed my mouth like a fish out of water. "Because people are after me!" Devil aside, a celebration in the midst of a manhunt was ridiculous.

"No one will be able to touch you here—unless you are planning another one of your grand escapes. I know you are fond of them when danger is nigh, soulmate."

I ignored the barb. Squeezing my scalp, I said, "Andre, we can't just do this ... I'm sick."

He stared down at my chest, his gaze far away. When his eyes finally found mine again, they were tormented. "Please. Let me pretend, soulmate. I can control everything else, but not that. Not that."

He looked so lost, and damn me, but I would do anything to wipe that expression from his face. I was going to agree to this, like the sucker I was. That meant getting dolled up, chatting with people, standing by Andre's side for an evening.

"Alright," I said, as though I really had a say in the whole thing, "let's have our celebration. Question: will my friends get eaten if I invite them?" I smiled as I said it.

His lips twitched. "Soulmate, I'm more concerned about my subjects falling victim to your friends—Oliver in particular." The sly devil winked, making me laugh.

"Ah, *Dios*, that laugh." Andre's eyes smoldered as he watched me, and my laugh dried up.

He leaned in, taking my mouth fiercely. His passion was like a damn breaking open. I could feel it pouring down on me. Had I been foolish enough to think that intimacy would curb our lust for each other?

It hadn't. It had merely raised the stakes.

I LEFT ANDRE when another call came in and my soulmate started making threats anew. There was nothing like hearing your soulmate promise to eviscerate someone to really curb the passion.

I headed down the hallway, pulling out my phone and texting Oliver and Leanne about the celebration.

Once I was done, I threaded my fingers over my head. Restlessness tore through me.

I made a beeline for the back of the mansion, where an expansive balcony overlooked Andre's backyard.

Reaching the back door, I stepped outside into the chilly night. I didn't stop moving until I'd reached the very edge, my hands palming the railing. The wind lifted my hair and twisted it in a thousand different directions. I embraced the chaos.

In the garden beneath me, the shadows moved. I startled at the movement, the peace I'd felt a moment ago now shattered.

The darkness seemed to ooze and roll, climbing the sides of the building, heading straight for me. I backed up, but I could not turn away.

I watched as the darkness gathered itself, condensing into a shadowy figure. Then I heard the laugh I had come to know, to dread.

The devil's form grew more substantial with each passing moment until, at some point, he had the appearance of a flesh and blood human.

I couldn't look away, even as I continued to back away from him; I could not summon my body to turn its back on something so dangerous.

"Oh no, no, no, Gabrielle. Do not think about leaving. I just arrived."

My upper lip involuntarily curled, as repulsion warred with cold, clammy terror.

The devil came to a stop in front of me and straightened the charcoal suit he wore.

He scrutinized me, taking in the subtle lines of sickness. "Not doing so good?" He shook his head, feigning sadness. A smile tugged the corners of his lips.

"You killed her."

He smirked, his strange eyes watching me with excitement. "Take it as a hard-learned lesson: I will kill each and every person you care about until you give me what I want."

Physically I might be sick, but I was not weak. My courage rose within me, causing my skin to flare with light. "My list of loved ones is short, Pluto. You'd better pick your battles because once they run out, you'll have nothing to blackmail me with."

"There she is. Ah, consort, you have fire to match my own."

"Go to hell."

Deliberately I turned my back on him.

"Not without you," I thought I heard him say.

My spine stiffened, but I didn't pause, even as his voice resonated behind me. "Gabrielle, the sands of your life are running out. Eat, drink, be merry—you have a day. Then you are mine."

Chapter 28

I WOKE WITH a gasp. Sweat beaded along my skin, chilling my already cold skin. It had dampened the sheets while I slept, like even the most unconscious parts of me feared what would happen ...

Tonight.

Bile rose at my encounter with the devil the night before. I put a hand to my face. I'd have to be near that for an eternity.

An eternity.

I couldn't keep down my rising sickness. I threw off my covers and ran across Andre's room and into to the bathroom, barely making it to the toilet in time. I leaned over the porcelain rim and vomited up blood and bile.

"Soulmate?"

A shirtless Andre stood in the doorway to the bathroom. His eyes darted from me to the toilet, then back.

I flushed down the evidence of my sickness and pushed myself up on shaky legs, but halfway there, they buckled.

Andre was next to me in an instant, wrapping me in his arms. He pressed my face into his chest, cradling it gently. And that was about when I lost it.

I began to cry heavy, gut-wrenching sobs. It was all falling apart. What was life for if it could be snatched away so quickly? Why was it so ghastly?

Andre held me, rocking us and rubbing my back while he whispered things in languages I didn't understand.

He still had no clue what deal I'd made with the devil. We'd both been so busy; it was just one of many things that got shelved for later. Not that it mattered. Even if I wasn't walking to my death later tonight, I'd still be doomed. The blood he'd given me only a week ago had been changing me at an accelerated rate, killing me in the process.

Andre trembled as he held me, and I took some strange comfort from the fact that he was just as scared as I was. At least we had camaraderie.

Andre leaned his head against mine. "You were right, as usual. I never should've agreed to this celebration."

I laughed—one of those thick, choked ones you let out after a good cry just so that you can hear the sound of happiness again. Because you need something to shake off the terrible sadness within you. "I think I could use a break from all this fighting and fleeing."

One of Andre's eyebrows arched. "I could help with that. You know, I have some really good ideas when it

302

comes to these things."

I bit back a reluctant grin. "Oh, I'm sure you do, and I'm eager to hear about them."

"Good." Pressing a firm kiss to my lips, Andre scooped me up and took me back to the bed.

SEVERAL HOURS LATER I pulled on the backless white gown laid out for me, my hands shaking as I did so. Someone had left it on the bed while I'd been in the shower. The material clung to me, exaggerating every pleasing line of my form.

That painting of Andre watched me the entire time. I swear tonight his eyes seemed sadder than usual.

There I went—*projecting*.

I could hear the sounds of conversation drifting in from the front of Bishopcourt, where guests gathered. Andre was already out there welcoming them; he'd insisted I take my time, and I was grateful for it. I had business to get in order before I made my appearance.

I slipped on the shoes and undergarments that went with the dress then headed into the bathroom.

When I caught a glimpse of my reflection, I paused. I looked unearthly—more so than usual. My features were exaggerated. My cheekbones were more pronounced, my alabaster skin exceptionally pale from lack of blood, my spooked eyes a bit wider than they'd been before. All of it shrouded by a mane of loose curls.

Death suits you. The voice that brushed against my ear wasn't my own.

I gritted my teeth. The devil was there, lingering just beyond my reach. Waiting. Waiting. Waiting ... until I was his.

And tonight I had to go to him. Tonight, I had to die.

I SNUCK INTO Andre's study, using his private line to place a call to the U.S. I fingered the Egyptian statue perched on his desk. The line rang and rang.

I squeezed my forehead when I remembered that my adoptive mother would still be at work. Perhaps it was better this way.

My heart was in my throat when her recorded voice came on the line, asking the caller to leave a message. It held none of the beguiling beauty that my biological mom's did, but it was so beloved. It was the same voice that had spoke soothingly to me when I was sick and scolded me when I was being a little punk.

Was this the last time I'd ever hear it? And was it twisted that I actually *wished* it might be? Because I hoped never to see a loved one in the place I was going.

The phone beeped, indicating that I was to begin my message.

"Mom—" I croaked. I cleared my voice and began again. "Hey Mom. Sorry I forgot to call you on New Year's"—I'd spent it dodging arrows and fleeing attackers—"I just wanted to tell you that I love you so much. I haven't told you that enough, and I miss you like crazy." A tear trickled out. "I hope your New Year's went well. I'll talk to you ... later. Bye."

I hung up the phone, breathing heavily. I wiped the tear off with the back of my hand. That message was totally going to freak her out. She'd be on the phone in an instant, calling me back, only to be sent directly to voicemail ... because that phone had been destroyed. It would only wig her out more. Rightfully so—she'd never speak to me again.

I ran my hands through my hair, pushing strands away from my forehead. *Don't go there.*

I needed to pull myself together. I still had one more person that I needed to leave a message with.

I blew out a breath and grabbed a sheet of paper from one of Andre's desk drawers and searched for a pen.

Instead my eyes landed on an ink well.

Damn.

"STUPID FUCKING QUILL," I cursed as another globe of ink obscured the "A" in Andre's name.

Already I was regretting this note.

Why Andre kept quills around when there was such a thing as computers, or even—hey—ballpoint pens was beyond me.

He wanted to channel his inner geezer, apparently.

And to think I needed to scribe an official plea using the angelic quill waiting for me back at Jericho's Emporium. I was done for.

Shut up, brain. No one asked you for your opinion.

I bit my lip and scribbled the rest of the note as fast as possible.

By the time I was done, I had ink on my fingertips and some lines of text had smeared onto my dress. Nailed it.

I appraised the letter. It was a train wreck. Smudged letters and giant globes of ink made the thing almost illegible. *Almost.* But not quite. I read over the words. This was all he'd get—a final, parting note.

On it I divulged everything I'd kept from him up until now. My deal with the devil, and the gift kept under lock and key that I was to collect only once I died. I even mentioned the possibility that my death might not be the end of me.

I bit my lip. Perhaps it was cruel to give him hope when I really had no idea what the future held.

It'd have to do because time was up.

I eyed the stick of red wax and the partially burnt candle resting next to the ink well.

Not even going to attempt it.

I HEADED BACK to our room and propped the note on the bed. I stared at it, biting the inside of my cheek until I drew blood.

Keep it together. I'd face down fate with my shoulders back; I wouldn't let anyone see me crack, especially not the devil.

My breaths came in short, soft bursts. I blinked as fatigue washed over me. Other than water, I hadn't eaten or drank anything in over a day.

I sat down on the edge of the bed for a second, catching my breath and collecting myself. Eventually I forced myself to stand.

Time to make an appearance.

I staggered down the hallway, my gown swishing around me. My breath still came in ragged pants.

Something felt ... wrong. My heartbeat palpitated strangely. I moved my hand to rub my chest.

Just as I touched the fabric of my gown, my heart altogether stopped.

Flat lining. I was flat lining.

I stumbled. Fell. I choked on my breath as my chest seized up.

No one was coming back here. This section of Bishopcourt was too private. Not even Andre would venture this way, not until our connection did something funky, and it hadn't—yet.

A burning pain spread through my body. My eyes fluttered and black spots clouded my vision.

I pounded my fist on my chest. Nothing. The spots that danced in front of me were spreading. I pounded again.

After a moment, my heart thumped once ... then twice. Slowly, the spots dissipated as my heartbeat fell back into rhythm.

I leaned against the wall and caught my breath. A body doesn't run properly with a sluggish heartbeat. Mine was no exception.

I stayed there, catching my breath, for another five minutes, and then, shakily, I rose to my feet.

I wiped the cold sweat off my brow and resumed walking haltingly towards the ballroom.

As soon as people caught sight of me, conversations escalated, eyes lingered. I'd been infamous, hated, and now I was intriguing. Andre de Leon's soulmate, the devil's consort. The anti-Christ.

Some of those nearest me flared their nostrils as I passed, and I could see their pitying glances in my periphery. The smell of sickness clung to me.

Across the room Andre caught my eye. I sucked in a breath at the sight of him.

It wasn't the first time I'd seen Andre in a tux, but his appearance always left me speechless. He cleaned up *nicely*.

He smiled at me, the action crinkling the laugh lines at the corners of his eyes and pressing in the skin of his cheeks. He had no idea I'd collapsed outside his room mere minutes ago.

A wicked gleam entered his eyes as his gaze moved over me, and I could practically feel him mentally undressing me across the room.

Keeping it classy, that one.

"Yoo-hoo! Penelope—er, crap, I mean Persephone—doomsday princess!"

My gaze drifted towards the speaker, but then Andre patted the shoulder of the man he was talking to and began to prowl my way. Totally not going to miss that walk. There are only so many times I could openly check out this man's stride, and this might be one of my last.

"She's ignoring me. Yo, Queen of the Damned!"

My attention turned back to the voice, which belonged to a certain fairy with ice blond hair and extra-sparkly skin. Next to him Leanne waved at me, grinning like an idiot. Judging by their appearances, the two of them had gotten their party on elsewhere and brought it here.

I laughed at the sight of them, the heavy cloud hanging over me temporarily lifting. I pushed through the throngs of people, nodding and giving guests cordial smiles, to get to my friends.

They both latched onto me. "I am higher than a *kite*," Oliver said.

"Proud friend moment," I said sarcastically.

"Blame her!" he pointed to Leanne. "She thought it would be fun to pregame your wedding."

When my eyes met Leanne's she giggled, but then her smile faltered.

Somehow she knew. Even though the seer's shroud was still in my system, she must've foreseen something—maybe someone else's future—and pieced it together. I'd bet money she drank to escape the vision, or to pretend it all away. And Oliver, being Oliver, hopped right onboard with 110 percent enthusiasm.

"Not a wedding, Oliver," I said, turning back to the fairy. Leanne's haunted eyes couldn't scare me any longer because I already knew.

"Pfft. As if you are not going to christen that bed of yours later tonight."

I ducked my head. "Oliver—ssssh."

Oliver pointed to me. "Ha! Haven't lost my touch." He buffed his nails on his suit. "I can still make you embarrassed like a little schoolgirl."

"Up until about a week ago I was a schoolgirl."

"Up until about a week ago you were also a vir-gin!" His

voice rose at the end of the statement, and nearby guests swiveled at the sound, raising their eyebrows when they saw me.

"Where *is* that slice of sex pie?" Oliver stood on tiptoes and peered over the crowd. "Oh, oh! I see him! Crap, he's walking away."

Hoofing it out of Oliver's vicinity most likely. Smart vampire.

"Mmm, hubba hubba," he said. "'Dat *ass*."

I put my forehead in my hand. Sober Oliver was a handful. Smashed Oliver was insane.

"Hey, I think he flipped me off." Oliver pouted.

"That's because he can hear you."

"I paid him a compliment."

Leanne snorted. "You were objectifying him," she said. "There's a difference."

"Ugh, I swear you gave up fun-ness along with petti-ness. Now when is this party going to start? I'm *bored*." Oliver glanced around, only stopping to do a double take when his eyes landed on a vampire standing close by.

"Whoa, is that blood?" he asked the vampire loudly, pressing in way too close to peer into the man's drink.

The vampire curled his upper lip and let out a slight hiss.

"Whoa," Oliver held his hands up, "no offense meant. That's, you know, ... chic ... in like an emo-hispter-gothy-creepy way ..."

Oliver continued to talk, and I used the moment to pull Leanne aside.

Our eyes met, and the lightness of Oliver's company

fell away.

"I know about tonight," I said softly, though my words weren't necessary.

Remorse shone in her eyes. "I foresaw the evening play out earlier," she admitted. Save for the devil himself, she was the only person who knew what would happen to me tonight. She'd be the only person I'd get a real goodbye with.

I hauled her in for a hug. We clasped each other tightly.

Pulling away, Leanne drew in a ragged breath. "For the record, I've never had a female best friend until I met you. And ... it's been really great."

I laughed even as I sniffled. "So great."

She took my hands and squeezed them. "Safe travels," she whispered, just as she had the night of Samhain.

I nodded and gave her a closed-lipped smile. "I'll give 'em hell."

ANDRE HEADED BACK to his room—*their* room—looking for that damn iPod. He'd uploaded it with all of Celeste's songs just so his mate could know the voice of the woman who loved her first.

He'd meant to give it to her earlier, but the damn thing had grown legs and disappeared, and it wasn't until last night that he'd found it sitting in its package in the library as though it hadn't been moved in the first place. Had the iPod been in any other room, Andre might've worried.

He'd headed out to greet the guests this evening without the device, and he nearly made a fool of himself only moments ago. Had the fairy not shown up, he would've swept Gabrielle up in his arms, then reached into his coat pocket to procure a gift that wasn't there.

He reached the door to their room and slipped inside. Instead of finding the iPod, he found a letter, carefully folded on the bed. He could smell her scent on it. A corner of his mouth quirked. She'd written him a note. Just when he was convinced she was a child of this century, she went and did something like this.

He could see his name scrawled along the front, partially obscured by a drop of ink. The sight made him grin.

He opened the letter up. The smile immediately left his face.

Andre,
If you are reading this, then I am dead. There are things you need to know, things that I've kept from you, but things that might now give you hope ...

Chapter 29

"A STRING QUARTET? A *string quartet?*" Oliver eyed the group of musicians gathered in the corner with obvious disdain. "You've got to be kidding me. And blood? Where's the Jäger and the strobe lights? The nearly-naked men and the drugs? This fairy wants to do body shots, then roll!"

"Oliver, this is a celebration, not a rager—" My heart shuddered then skipped a beat.

Damn. It was happening again.

I leaned a heavy arm on Oliver's shoulder.

"Sweets?" He sobered in an instant.

Next to him Leanne watched me, the whites of her eyes visible.

"Give me—a second."

The pain burning through my chest abated somewhat, and I straightened. I backed up, bumping into a nearby vampire.

Oliver reached out. "Gabrielle!" He never used my actual name, which meant he was legitimately worried.

"I'll be back—with your Jäger and half-clad men." The joke fell flat.

He dropped his hand. "Don't forget the drugs." His joke fell flat too.

I shoved my way through the crowd. My eyes scanned for the nearest escape. They landed on the door to the guest bathroom. Wasting no time, I made a beeline for it.

Once I slipped inside the restroom, I leaned against the wall, gasping out a sob as the pain rolled through me. My stomach spasmed. Organs were shutting down. The whole production was coming to a close. I drew in a shaky breath and pushed away from the door.

I whispered a prayer under my breath, a series of strange, broken words strung together that begged for any other fate save this one. But if deliverance was coming, it wouldn't be tonight.

I leaned over the counter and took several deep breaths. I couldn't seem to get enough air through my lungs.

I lifted my head and stared at my reflection. My haunted blue eyes glittered amongst pale skin, my lips a bright red slash against the creamy flesh. And surrounding it all was my dark, dark hair. I had my own shadowy halo, just like the devil.

Promised to two men. Was that all us sirens were? Beautiful, treacherous objects to be given or taken?

The tales were true. We ripped men's hearts out and shredded them without thinking. Even to those we loved.

314

Like Andre.

My mind drifted. Back at Bran Castle, Morta had mentioned something then. Something that I'd never forgotten and something that Jericho had reminded me of.

I would come back. I didn't know when and I didn't know how, but I'd be topside again. In fact, if what Morta had said was true, I'd become a creature that could traverse both earth and hell. Maybe all wasn't lost.

And maybe I was grasping at straws.

My hands slid off the cool marble countertop just as the door to the bathroom squeaked open.

Crap, I'd forgotten to lock it. I swiveled around, only to come face-to-face with Caleb.

"CALEB?" HOPE AND horror filled my voice. "What are you doing here?" I took in his tux, noting absently that he wore it well.

He didn't answer right away. I smelled his sweat and fear. His pulse hammered in his chest.

My gaze moved to his face. It was somewhat puffy, the skin around his eyes tinged red. He hardly looked better than me.

"Hey, are you okay?" Before I could think twice about it, I reached out for him.

Caleb stepped back. "Don't touch me. Please, Gabrielle, don't." His throat worked.

I let my hand fall and suppressed my hurt.

He scrubbed his face.

"It's okay. Whatever it is, it's okay," I said soothingly. And it was. When your fate was to die and reign hell alongside the devil, other things sort of became insignificant by comparison.

He shook his head. "It's not."

From down the hall, I felt my connection with Andre surge. And then he was moving rapidly towards me.

I swore. He'd found my note too soon. I was sure of it.

"Gabrielle!" he bellowed.

Yep. He definitely found the note.

While I stared off, listening to my soulmate stalk ever closer to me, I heard a click. My gaze snapped back to Caleb in time to see his hand move away from the door's lock. That was when I understood.

Caleb wasn't here to visit me, he was here to end me.

"SOULMATE!" ANDRE SHOUTED from somewhere in the distance. My gaze moved to the direction his voice was coming from. "I swear I *will* tie you to the bed this time, you hear me? You are not to sacrifice yourself for anyone!"

My eyes pinched shut, and I bit the inside of my cheek.

The sound of cool metal brushing against linen had my eyes snapping back open. Caleb held a gun, and he was pointing it right at my heart. His hands trembled violently. God his aim was going to be shit if he pulled that trigger.

"Don't do this," I pleaded, shaking my head. "We're friends. Partners."

"Gabrielle, I don't get a choice."

I gazed at him with sad eyes. My heart felt heavy with

the weight of so much conflict. So many things that my death would make wrong.

The bathroom door shook as Andre tried the handle only to find it locked. "Soulmate, I can feel you in there. Please let me in." His voice had lost much of his angry edge. Now it just held miles and miles of pain.

Caleb cursed.

"Who's in there with you?" Andre's voice rose. He tried the handle again, then pounded on the door. "Let me in, or I will break down the goddamn door!" *Anger revived.* Someone was channeling his inner big, bad wolf.

Caleb's eyes met mine, and his hands steadied. "I'm sorry—for everything."

And then he pulled the trigger.

I ALWAYS ASSUMED when you were shot in the heart, you died instantly.

I was wrong.

I could feel my blood seeping out of my body, trickling out the hole in my chest and seeping into my white dress.

My eyes widened and my lips moved. But I couldn't find the words to voice this betrayal. I didn't honestly think he'd do it. Not until that last second. My mistake.

"*Gabrielle!*" Andre roared.

Caleb dropped the gun like it burned him, his eyes wide. He reached for me, and I could see instant remorse. His features actually flickered, and for the merest moment, I stared back at myself. Then he disappeared, his clothes drifting to the ground.

The bathroom door burst open, and Andre stood at the threshold, looking like my avenging angel. His eyes fell on me.

"*Soulmate*," he choked out. In the next instant he held me. Beyond him I heard gasps as people crowded the room.

"Is she okay?" someone shouted behind him.

His eyes darted between me and the wound. He pressed a hand to my heart. In seconds it was covered with my blood.

A small noise escaped him.

His eyes moved back to me. "You're going to be okay." Andre's voice betrayed him.

I couldn't speak; the pain seemed to seize up my voice. This *was* it.

"I will save you again." Andre drew his hand away from my heart and brought his wrist up to his mouth.

His teeth pierced his flesh and the smell of Andre's blood mingled with mine. He lifted his bloody wrist to my lips. "Drink, soulmate."

Even as he spoke, my sight dimmed.

Ignoring his wrist, I reached out to stroke his face. "I love you." I tried to speak the words, but they came out as the barest whisper.

"Dammit, you stay with me, soulmate!" He pressed his wrist to my lips, his blood dripping into my mouth and down my throat. "It doesn't end like this!"

As his blood hit my system, my body seemed to flare up, trying to shake death from itself. And it was working.

I could feel the bullet wound slowly healing. I gasped in

a ragged breath, my back arching. My sight cleared enough to see Andre draw his hand away and reopen his wrist wound.

Caleb shot me. My friend and former partner shot me. The betrayal burned deep—though why should it? We stood on opposing ends of good and evil. Still, hot, bloody tears pooled in my eyes.

"Soulmate," Andre said, petting my hair, "you're not going to die." This time he sounded surer of himself.

In the background, voices were shouting. Someone was yelling about moving me. A moment later Andre cradled me in his arms, his wrist pressed against my mouth once more.

"You need to bite down, love."

I did so, weakly, taking in a few swallows of his blood before I released him. The taste of it still made me nauseous.

All around us guests watched as Andre carried me across the ballroom, heading for his private quarters.

We never made it.

Above us the chandelier shivered, its tiny crystals tinkling. No one else seemed to notice, not until the walls of Bishopcourt trembled and the floor shook.

Outside the estate, the wind intensified, howling as it battered against the walls. The pitch of it rose until it seemed to be screaming.

Andre's grip tightened. He figured out then what I already knew: the devil was coming for me, and he would not be denied.

With a sickening shriek, the windows blew in. Guests

screamed as glass pelted them.

The front doors banged open, and a violent wind tore through the ballroom, ripping me out of Andre's arms. It dragged me across the floor to the middle of the room.

I bit down hard on my cheek as the movement jostled my still-healing wound. The unearthly wind separated me not just from Andre, but from everyone.

The shadows of the night coalesced, dragged from the far corners of the room and the night beyond it. It twisted around me in a whirlwind as it came together. If I weren't entangled right in the middle of it, I would've said it looked beautiful. But I could feel the breath of evil licking up my skin, caressing me like a long-lost lover.

It fashioned itself into the shape of a man, and then from the darkness came features. Almond-shaped eyes, pale skin, hair swept back from a high brow, a self-satisfied smirk.

The devil always did like to make an entrance.

"I didn't crash a party now, did I?" he asked. He turned to me, raising an eyebrow. The show wasn't for them. It was for me.

"Time's up," he said quietly.

I braced myself on my forearms, staring up at him from where I lay on the floor. The wind still pressed against the crowd, keeping them at bay, and I could see Andre actively fighting against it. He wouldn't be able to pass through, just as I was sure I wouldn't be able to leave this maelstrom.

Not that I would try. The devil had already taken too much from me. I wouldn't risk Andre's life or anyone else's by turning my back on this deal.

The devil turned from me to the audience around us. "I hear there should've been a Joining tonight, and by the devil, there will be one."

THE WIND CONTINUED to twist around us, a tornado trapped in the ballroom, and the devil and I were at the eye of it. Guests covered their faces as the storm tore at their clothes and hair. Among them I caught sight of Leanne and Oliver.

"You can't have her!" Andre shouted. I could feel the static electricity snapping off of him. His hair lifted, a strange breeze blowing it in the wrong direction. His fangs had descended, and his lips curled back menacingly. The pupil's of his eyes stretched almost completely over his irises, making them look nearly black. Our connection throbbed, like it knew it was in danger of snapping.

The devil laughed. "Oh really? And what will you do about it? I made you; I can unmake you."

The devil snapped his fingers, the action quelling some of the electricity in the air. Some, but not all. Instead, the electricity changed form. Sparks jumped off of Andre and, holy crap, this was going to turn into Bishopcourt fiasco, part two.

Some of our guests had managed to escape out the front door or through the now broken windows, but most of them watched, captivated, as the devil wrought destruction down upon them.

I realized with a start that most of the vampires had never laid eyes on the devil. I'd gotten so used to his drop-ins, that the wonder of his presence was lost on me. But now vampires like Vicca stared at him, mouth agape—a strange mixture of fear and awe in their gazes. They'd never seen the thing responsible for their damnation.

Andre was the only other vampire in the room not shocked by the devil's presence. But boy he did look pissed. He strode towards the storm, pushing against the wall of wind.

The devil paid him no attention. "As I was saying," he glanced over the crowd, "tonight there will in fact be a Joining." Once more he turned to me, hand outstretched.

"I'm here tonight to claim Gabrielle Fiori as my consort, the Queen of Hell."

"Fight him, soulmate!" Andre shouted.

But all the fight had been drained from me. I was covered in blood, my dress torn where I'd been shot, my hair wild, and my wound still raw. I'd given the last days and hours of my life everything I had. I had nothing left of myself to give.

The room fell silent. Utterly silent—even the wind, which still twisted around us, had quieted, as though someone had turned down the volume. The only sounds were my sluggish heartbeats, pounding arrhythmically between my ears, and the whoosh of blood it moved through me.

Deep breath in. Slow breath out. As I stared down at the devil's hand, I calmed. My moment of truth was upon me. The destiny I'd been hurtling towards was finally here. No more innocent lives would be lost.

I reached out.

"Gabrielle, *no!*" I never again wanted to hear the note in Andre's voice. It was the sound of a creature in great pain, and I had caused it.

This ended tonight.

I grasped the devil's hand, and with a triumphant smile, he pulled me to my feet. He tugged me to face him, and his hand slid up my arm, twining around mine. "I, Rex Inferna, recognize you as my mate and doth bind you to me en infitum, Gabrielle Fiori, Regina Inferna."

I began shivering as the cold chill of fear seeped into me. On the other side of the twister Andre was creating his own storm with his rising emotions. The walls and floor shook as objects lifted themselves off the ground.

"And so it shall be, now and forever," the devil finished.

Andre let out a roar, and the chandelier shook violently. The house made a pained groan. It wouldn't last much longer under the strain of Andre's pain and anger.

The devil's hand locked around my wrist just as the whirlwind that spun around us suddenly ceased.

My eyes found Andre's wild ones.

"I love you," I said.

The shadows around the devil and me shifted and lengthened. I realized as they circled us that the darkness was made up of screaming souls. Andre strode through them, his hair whipping about his face and his jaw set, ready to fight the devil for me.

Seeing this, the devil turned his head so that his lips skimmed my temple. I shuddered as he pressed a kiss there. The shadows swarmed in on us, and I could feel myself—both body and soul—being ripped from the fabric of this world.

I reached out for Andre as the devil wrapped his arm around my waist.

"No!" Andre thundered. For one sheer moment, his fingers brushed my outstretched ones. Then both he and Bishopcourt disappeared, and the blackness consumed the devil and me.

One by one my senses disappeared. First sight, then smell and taste. I no longer choked on the sour tang of lost souls and ash, which made up the matrix I traveled in.

Touch—thankfully—went next. I could no longer feel the devil's grip on my body, nor his breath on my face. The last thing to go was my hearing, and I knew that only because the devil's final whispered words rang in my ears long after my other senses had fallen away—

"Finally, consort, you are *mine*."

Chapter 30

ANDRE DROPPED TO his knees as the shadows swallowed Gabrielle up.

"No." His voice broke over the word. Seven hundred years of his soulless existence, a few short months of something dangerously close to happiness, and all of it for naught.

The Lord giveth and the Lord taketh away. The Biblical reference rang like a dirge in his mind.

The devil had taken his soulmate. Just like all the tales said he would. A cry tore through Andre's throat.

He saw the moment the fire died from her eyes, the moment her soul was no longer *here* but *there*. But even the terror of that sight couldn't compare to the sickening way her life force severed itself from his heart. That invisible cord that he'd carried inside him like a flame for almost two decades, the one that had flared up the first time he laid eyes on Gabrielle in his club and had burst to life several days later when she'd Awoken. It had been snipped. He could practically hear Morta's cackle from somewhere *beyond*.

"*No*," he repeated. The word was a broken plea. It couldn't be. Not now, not after everything they had endured to be together. Not when he'd only just gotten a taste of what it would be like to be with her wholly and completely.

He pressed a hand hard against his heart as he hunched over himself, trying to stem the pain of the cord's absence. It was the same hand that had tried to stem Gabrielle's blood from seeping out of her only minutes ago, and now her blood smeared onto his clothes. He smelled like her. How *dare* she linger if she was gone.

Gone.

Around him, objects that still swirled around the room now crashed to the ground as his heart contracted. Distantly he heard people scream.

This time around there was no body to revive. But perhaps she could escape, like on Samhain.

His eyes closed and he shuddered. No one who entered the Underworld left. That had always been consistent throughout the myths. She'd been taken, and this time she wasn't coming back.

"No!" he bellowed, and Bishopcourt quaked with his agony.

At some point his coven dragged him away from the room.

Gone, gone, gone. She was once his. And now she was gone.

ACROSS THE WORLD, as the news came in, people cheered. All but a few. A monster's arms and legs were restrained, otherwise he would've already ended his life. His coven clustered around him, holding him as heaving sobs shook his monstrous frame and blood streamed down his cheeks. His wails only ceased when the first rays of dawn rose on the horizon.

Soulmates weren't meant to part.

In a dark room in Castle Rushen a shapeshifter shook, wiping the vomit off his chin. He hadn't stopped trembling since he'd pulled the trigger. She was dead—the girl who'd once been his friend, the girl he would've died for a month ago—and it was his fault. When he killed her, he killed some part of himself as well. Something integral. He retched again. In what world was this right? In what world was this just?

A seer closed her eyes and dreamed of great, leaping flames and hollow, endless pain. She screamed as it lacerated her skin over and over. With a gasp she woke, feverish from someone else's nightmare.

Next to her, a fairy lay in a pool of his shedded dust. Tears tracked down his cheeks as he thrashed in his sleep, twisting himself in the sheets of a dead woman.

In a musty emporium a stooped messenger cleaned off a glass case, which housed a priceless treasure. Its owner would be needing it soon.

And resting on a desk in the master bedroom of Bishopcourt, under the watchful gaze of a painted crusader, was a final line of hope written on an already forgotten letter:

I'll be coming back, Andre. Have faith. I love you, and I'll see you again soon.

Chapter 31

I woke with a gasp. The obsidian slab I lay upon chilled me to the bone. I sat up, and as I did so, dozens of spiders skittered off my body. I sucked in air to scream, when my outfit caught my attention.

The confection was nothing like I'd ever seen before. It moved like silk, but it was woven into web-like lace patterns. My eyes darted back to one of the rogue spiders fleeing from me.

Spider silk?

I felt a laugh rising to the surface, something hysterical that wouldn't stop once it started. I bit down on it when the unnatural chill of the place sank into my bones.

I slid off of the altar, barely registering its Satanic symbols as I padded barefoot across the hexagonal chamber. The walls were made of more obsidian, and torches glowed blue.

My breath misted in front of me as I left the room, the train of my dress dragging behind me. In the distance, I could hear shrieks and shouts. Moans and wails. My fangs descended at the sound and the hairs along my arms rose.

Something propelled me forward, even as terror coursed through me. Down dark, despondent hallways I traveled, the noise increasing with every step I took. Cold traveled up my bare feet as I padded along the glassy black floor.

I ended up at two night-dark doors, each propped open. On the other side of them was a staircase made of onyx, and beyond that ...

I grabbed the twisted wrought iron bannister and descended, my shaking hand sliding over the railing. The stairs opened to a balcony.

And there he waited.

He must've heard the slither of my silk dress, or maybe he felt my presence the same way I could now feel his, because he turned to face me.

I swallowed my gasp. The devil was the same, but he wasn't. He was taller, more filled out, and his face ...

I now understood why, to Christians, he was once known as the morning star, one of God's loveliest angels. Swathed in shadows, his full beauty stared back at me, hidden no more. Only now did I realize every physical facet this being held back from me. Held back until now.

The devil—*Hades*—reached a hand out for mine. Numbly I took it.

He brought my hand to his lips and kissed it. Then, he swiveled to face our empire.

The world below us was one of flame. Now that I was here, in this truly godforsaken land, I couldn't help the strange, new pull I felt towards him.

"Welcome to hell, my queen."

Keep a lookout for the sequel:

The Damned

Coming Fall 2015

Be sure to check out the first book in Laura Thalassa's
new adult post-apocalyptic series

The Queen of All that Dies

Out now!

Be sure to check out Laura Thalassa's new adult science fiction series

The Vanishing Girl

Out now!

Fans of Laura Thalassa's *Unearthly* series might also enjoy this brand new young adult series by Dan Rix.

Translucent

When a meteorite falls near her campsite in the San Rafael Wilderness, troubled teen Leona Hewitt ventures down into the crater looking for a souvenir. What she discovers changes her life.

Contained in the meteorite is a sticky, mucous-like fluid that bends light, cannot itself be seen, and seems to grow in the presence of living tissue. It's drawn to her.

But when a government team arrives in hazmat suits and cordons off the meteorite impact site, Leona questions her decision to take it home with her. For one thing, there are rumors of an extraterrestrial threat.

For another, it has been speaking to her.

It wants to be worn . . . stretched on like a second skin. It's seeking out her weaknesses, exploiting her deepest fear—that the only boy she's ever loved will unearth the vile secret in her past and see her as a monster. Now it promises salvation.

It can make her invisible.

BORN AND RAISED in Fresno, California, Laura Thalassa spent her childhood cooking up fantastic tales with her best friend. Lucky for her overactive imagination, she also happened to love writing. She now spends her days penning everything from paranormal romance to young adult novels. Laura Thalassa lives in Santa Barbara, California with her husband, author Dan Rix. When not writing, you can find her at www.laurathalassa.blogspot.com.

Made in the USA
Monee, IL
11 March 2023

29637205R00198